In The Devil's Abyss

Presently the old man drew back his hood. I only shuddered, because I was sure that the face was merely a devilish waxen mask. The flopping animals were now scratching restlessly at the lichens, and I saw that the old man was nearly as restless himself. When one of the things began to waddle and edge away he turned quickly to stop it, so that the suddenness of his motion dislodged the waxen mask from what should have been his head.

It was then that I flung myself into the oily underground river, flung myself into that putrescent juice of earth's inner horrors before the madness of my screams could bring down upon me all the charnel legions. . . .

Also by H. P. Lovecraft
Published by Ballantine Books:

AT THE MOUNTAINS OF MADNESS
and Other Tales of Terror

THE TOMB
and Other Tales

THE LURKING FEAR

THE DREAM QUEST OF UNKNOWN KADATH

THE CASE OF CHARLES DEXTER WARD

THE DOOM THAT CAME TO SARNATH

H. P. Lovecraft

A Del Rey Book

BALLANTINE BOOKS • NEW YORK

A Del Rey Book
Published by Ballantine Books

ISBN 0-345-30231-1

This edition published by arrangement with Arkham House

Manufactured in the United States of America

First Ballantine Books Edition: February 1971
Third Printing: March 1982

Cover art by Michael Whelan

I dedicate this collection
of his friend's stories, to

AUGUST DERLETH

without whose superb efforts as editor and publisher my library, and I, would be much poorer.

—LIN CARTER

CONTENTS

About The Doom That Came to Sarnath
and Howard Phillips Lovecraft:

FAREWELL TO THE DREAMLANDS

Howard Phillips Lovecraft was an unusual, and, in many ways, a unique individual. Born in Providence, Rhode Island, on August 20, 1890, he was a precocious, sensitive boy, and his early years were those of a semi-invalid, surrounded by doting female relatives. He grew to loathe the age into which an accident of fate had precipitated him (he would infinitely have preferred living in ancient Rome, colonial New England, or eighteenth century London), and as an adult he lived much like a recluse, with few friends (although many correspondents), and with little interest in women, although he was once married. But he produced a body of fiction and verse that finds its only equal in American literature in the macabre oeuvre of Poe.

Lovecraft was, as the cliché has it, a living bundle of contradictions. A rationalist, an absolute materialist, without a trace of superstition or a flicker of interest in religious matters, he based his entire life work on the supernatural, on evil and fallen gods and sinister magic and hierarchies of transmundane demonic intelligences. It is perhaps because of his complete atheism that he was able to make his malign and imaginary Great Old Ones so convincingly real to his readers. Uninvolved with supernaturalism himself, he could be coldly objective—and he calculated with exquisite finesse the means of rendering his hellish pantheon both credible and terrifying.

The so-called Cthulhu Mythos, while completely his own invention, was constructed along the guidelines established by earlier writers whom he greatly admired. From the Welsh writer, Arthur Machen (1863-1947), he borrowed, and improved upon, the notion of buttressing a fantastic tale with an illusion of authenticity by surrounding it with documentary, factual evidence. The notion was not exactly original with Machen: *Dracula* consists of excerpts from letters and diaries; Machen narrates some of his tales in this manner, and others by way of a montage of newspaper clippings, and in certain stories the central plot revolves on data from comparative mythology and folklore. Lovecraft adopted all of these devices and further strengthened the believability of his fiction with an internal structure of self-consistent mythic materials which form a continuous system of background data from story to story.

From the American novelist, Robert W. Chambers (1865-1933) he adapted a second notion. Several of Chambers' short weird stories employ as their central theme the devilish and seductive influence of a strange, corrupting book called *The King in Yellow*. Chambers describes it as a verse play of poisonous beauty, and quoted enigmatic fragments from it in some of the tales. The more gullible of his readers may have accepted, if only for the moment, the book's existence as a fact. Lovecraft used this idea in his stories, inventing a book of his own called the *Necronomicon,* quoted lavishly from its pages, and incorporated into his fiction a complex apparatus of names and dates of translators and editions, thus making a deliberate and surprisingly successful attempt to convince the reader that there actually was such a book. The degree with which Lovecraft succeeded in persuading his readers to accept this completely imaginary book as genuine is reflected in the amusing fact that antiquarian booksellers have actually advertised for copies.

But far beyond his borrowing of basic techniques from

Machen and Chambers, Lovecraft is more deeply indebted to the great Anglo-Irish fantasist, Lord Dunsany (1878-1957). Dunsany's earliest fiction, in collections like *The Gods of Pegāna* and *The Book of Wonder,* introduced a delicious innovation to the writing of fantasies. The baron created an imaginary pantheon of divinities, wrote their legends in a connected series of brief prose-poems, and then in later works used his "Pegāna mythos" as background detail for fantastic tales set in invented lands "at the Edge of the World." That is, not content to make up his own geography, Dunsany invented the *religion* to which his imaginary kingdoms paid worship. An extremely clever, even a brilliant, idea, and one which has been used by many writers after him. Lovecraft utilized this theme as the basis for his own Cthulhu Mythos.

As a young reader, Lovecraft was enthralled by Dunsany's superb fiction. Many of his earliest tales, actually written before his discovery of Dunsany, are Dunsanian in texture and color. In the stories he wrote after 1919, the year in which he first stumbled across the work of the great Irish fantasist, the Dunsanian flavor becomes predominant.

Last year I edited a volume of the most Dunsanian of these tales, a book called *The Dream-Quest of Unknown Kadath,* which included the little-known short novel of that title and five other stories. I would have liked to have included all of the fiction from Lovecraft's "Dunsanian period" in that single book, but the size of the volume would have been impractical. Hence, this second collection.

As I began researching early Lovecraft for the purpose of assembling this second volume, *The Doom that Came to Sarnath,* I began rediscovering some unusual items of Lovecraftiana that have not previously been published in any of the several paperback collections of his work. I decided to include these curiosities in this book, for, even if they do not strictly belong to his Dunsanian period, they are transitional between the early Dreamlands stories and the later masterpieces of supernatural horror for which he is best known.

Those readers who know only the Cthulhu stories, know only a single side of Lovecraft. Besides these weird tales and the Dunsanian fantasies, he also dabbled very briefly in science fiction (see "In the Walls of Eryx"), tried his hand at straight, traditional horror stories (see "The Tomb"), and for a large part of his career supported himself by revising other people's fiction and by straight ghostwriting (see "Imprisoned with the Pharaohs"). He also wrote a large amount of verse (see "Nathicana"), and a number of prose poems doubtless inspired by Dunsany's ventures into this form in *The Gods of Pegāna* (see "Ex Oblivione," "Memory," etc.). If you are one of those rare readers with a scholarly bent, and would like to know the precise sequence and progression of these tales, you may refer to a chronological list at the back of this volume (page 207).

Although the readers of *Weird Tales* clamored for his work, Lovecraft achieved no real success or general recognition until long after his death in 1937. Save for the readers of three or four American pulp magazines, he was unknown to the larger world of literature.

Today, thirty-four years later, he is universally acknowledged to be the greatest American master of the macabre since Poe, and one of the finest writers in the genre which this century has seen. His works are enormously in vogue among French intellectuals; the controversial British author Colin Wilson built a major work (*The Strength to Dream*) around a study of Lovecraft and his writings; at least four motion pictures have been adapted (very loosely) from his stories; dramatizations of some of his best tales have been broadcast on the radio; the actor Roddy McDowell has made an album of readings from his tales; and a popular rock group has adopted his name. Virtually every word he ever wrote, including the revisions, poems, and letters, has been preserved in the dignity of hardcover books, and there has been hardly a single anthology of weird fiction published during the last twenty-five years that did not include at least one Lovecraft story.

To a very great extent, Lovecraft's posthumous success and recognition is the work of a single man, one of the younger of his literary disciples and correspondents, August W. Derleth. After the death of their friend, Mr. Derleth and another Lovecraft correspondent, Donald Wandrei, conceived the excellent notion of establishing a publishing house with the express purpose of reprinting H. P. Lovecraft's best work in book form. This firm, Arkham House, not only succeeded in preserving Lovecraft's work but also put into hardcover the best work of most of the writers of the *Weird Tales* era—Clark Ashton Smith, Robert E. Howard, Seabury Quinn, E. Hoffman Price, Frank Belknap Long, and others—to say nothing of more recent writers such as Fritz Leiber, Ray Bradbury, Robert Bloch, and L. Sprague de Camp. Going far beyond the purpose for which it was originally founded, Arkham House has performed an invaluable service for American connoisseurs of macabre literature by bringing into print, in their only American editions rare and important works by such English writers as Lord Dunsany, Arthur Machen, William Hope Hodgson, Lady Cynthia Asquith, Algernon Blackwood, M. P. Shiel, A. E. Coppard, and others.

At the close of the Second World War, a number of small publishers specializing in science fiction, fantasy or weird fiction were established in this country, and hundreds of rare pulp magazine short story series and novels were brought into book form. This brought about a stir of interest in the world of general publishing, and caused a boom of interest in imaginative literature which still has not subsided. But, whether due to poor business methods, inadequate financing, or sheer bad luck, every one of these small publishing houses has since gone out of business. Only Arkham House, the pioneer of them all, survived.

Today, thirty-two years after the publication of the first of its one hundred and nine books, brochures, pamphlets, and magazine issues, Arkham House is still very much in business; and throughout all these years the unusually high quality of Arkham House's printing, paper, binding, typography, and jacket illustration, have not declined. Arkham House books go rather quickly out of print and soon become prized collector's items. If you would like more information, I suggest you write for a current booklist to: Arkham House, Sauk City, Wisconsin 53583.

Few writers are as lucky as H. P. Lovecraft in finding a disciple to carry on their work and crusade for their recognition as tirelessly and with as much enthusiasm as August Derleth has done. The current fame Lovecraft enjoys is due entirely to Mr. Derleth, and for that reason I take the liberty of dedicating this collection of his friend's work to him. Lovecraft himself, I am certain, would have heartily approved.

—LIN CARTER
Editorial Consultant:
The Ballantine Adult Fantasy Series

Hollis, Long Island, New York

THE DOOM THAT CAME TO SARNATH

Why should I fret in microcosmic bonds
  That chafe the spirit, and the mind repress,
When through the clouds gleam beckoning beyonds
  Whose shining vistas mock man's littleness?

—H. P. Lovecraft, "Phaeton" (1918)

These first three stories show Lovecraft in his Dunsanian mood. The most Dunsanian of them, "Sarnath" itself, was written in 1919, the year in which Lovecraft first stumbled across a book by the glorious Irish fantasist. Early in November of that same year, Dunsany was in Boston on one of his rare American speaking-tours, and Lovecraft attended the reading and saw Dunsany at close hand; although he was too diffident to walk up and speak to the great Irish writer after the reading, he was enormously impressed. These two events—first reading Dunsany and then hearing him speak—made a tremendous impression on Lovecraft. For months thereafter, his letters reverberate with the impact of his Dunsanian discovery. A typical passage follows, from a letter to Reinhardt Kleiner dated December 3, 1919:

> As you infer, "The White Ship"[1] is in part influenced by my new Dunsanian studies. There are many highly effective points in Dunsany's style, and any writer of imaginative prose will be the better for having read him . . . Today I go down to obtain the very latest Dunsany book—just published—*Unhappy Far-Off Things*, which I saw advertised in the November *Atlantic* . . . you surely must read Dunsany—in places his work is pure poetry despite the prose medium.

[1]reprinted in *The Dream-Quest of Unknown Kadath*, (New York: Ballantine Books, May 1970).

THE OTHER GODS

Atop the tallest of earth's peaks dwell the gods of earth, and suffer no man to tell that he hath looked upon them. Lesser peaks they once inhabited; but ever the men from the plains would scale the slopes of rock and snow, driving the gods to higher and higher mountains till now only the last remains. When they left their older peaks they took with them all signs of themselves, save once, it is said, when they left a carven image on the face of the mountain which they called Ngranek.

But now they have betaken themselves to unknown Kadath in the cold waste where no man treads, and are grown stern, having no higher peak whereto to flee at the coming of men. They are grown stern, and where once they suffered men to displace them, they now forbid men to come; or coming, to depart. It is well for men that they know not of Kadath in the cold waste; else they would seek injudiciously to scale it.

Sometimes when earth's gods are homesick they visit in the still night the peaks where once they dwelt, and weep softly as they try to play in the olden way on remembered slopes. Men have felt the tears of the gods on white-capped Thurai, though they have thought it rain; and have heard the sighs of the gods in the plaintive dawn-winds of Lerion. In cloud-ships the gods are wont to travel, and wise cotters have legends that keep them from certain high peaks at night when it is cloudy, for the gods are not lenient as of old.

In Ulthar, which lies beyond the river Skai, once dwelt an old man avid to behold the gods of earth; a man deeply learned in the seven cryptical books of earth, and familiar with the *Pnakotic Manuscripts* of distant and frozen Lomar. His name was Barzai the Wise, and the villagers tell of how he went up a mountain on the night of the strange eclipse.

Barzai knew so much of the gods that he could tell of their comings and goings, and guessed so many of their secrets that he was deemed half a god himself. It was he who wisely advised the burgesses of Ulthar when they passed their remarkable law against the slaying of cats, and who first told the young priest Atal where it is that black cats go at midnight on St. John's Eve. Barzai was learned in the lore of the earth's gods, and had gained a desire to look upon their faces. He believed that his great secret knowledge of gods could shield him from their wrath, so resolved to go up to the summit of high and rocky Hatheg-Kla on a night when he knew the gods would be there.

Hatheg-Kla is far in the stony desert beyond Hatheg, for which it is named, and rises like a rock statue in a silent temple. Around its peak the mists play always mournfully, for mists are the memories of the gods, and the gods loved Hatheg-Kla when they dwelt upon it in the old days. Often the gods of earth visit Hatheg-Kla in their ships of cloud, casting pale vapors over the slopes as they dance reminiscently on the summit under a clear moon. The villagers of Hatheg say it is ill to climb the Hatheg-Kla at any time, and deadly to climb it by night when pale vapors hide the summit and the moon; but Barzai heeded them not when he came from neighboring Ulthar with the young priest Atal, who was his disciple. Atal was only the son of an innkeeper, and was sometimes afraid; but Barzai's father had been a landgrave who dwelt in an ancient castle, so he had no common superstition in his blood, and only laughed at the fearful cotters.

Barzai and Atal went out of Hatheg into the stony desert despite the prayers of peasants, and talked of earth's gods by their campfires at night. Many days they traveled, and from afar saw lofty Hatheg-Kla with his aureole of mournful mist. On the thirteenth day they reached the mountain's lonely base, and Atal spoke of his fears. But Barzai was old and learned and had no fears, so led the way boldly up the slope that no man had scaled since the time of Sansu, who is written of with fright in the moldy *Pnakotic Manuscripts.*

The way was rocky, and made perilous by chasms, cliffs, and falling stones. Later it grew cold and snowy; and Barzai and Atal often slipped and fell as they hewed and plodded upward with staves and axes. Finally the air grew thin, and the sky changed color, and the climbers found it hard to breathe; but still they toiled up and up, marveling at the strangeness of the scene and thrilling at the thought of what would happen on the summit when the moon was out and the pale vapors spread around. For three days they climbed higher and higher toward the roof of the world; then they camped to wait for the clouding of the moon.

For four nights no clouds came, and the moon shone down cold through the thin mournful mist around the silent pinnacle. Then on the fifth night, which was the night of the full moon, Barzai saw some dense clouds far to the north, and stayed up with Atal to watch them draw near. Thick and majestic they sailed, slowly and deliberately onward; ranging themselves round the peak high above the watchers, and hiding the moon and the summit from view. For a long hour the watchers gazed, whilst the vapors swirled and the screen of clouds grew thicker and more restless. Barzai was wise in the lore of earth's gods, and listened hard for certain sounds, but Atal felt the chill of the vapors and the awe of the night, and feared much. And when Barzai began to climb higher and beckon eagerly, it was long before Atal would follow.

So thick were the vapors that the way was hard, and though Atal followed at last, he could scarce see the gray shape of Barzai on the dim slope above in the clouded moonlight. Barzai forged very far ahead, and seemed despite his age to climb more easily than Atal; fearing not the steepness that began to grow too great for any save a strong and dauntless man, nor pausing at wide black chasms that Atal could scarce leap. And so they went up wildly over rocks and gulfs, slipping and stumbling, and sometimes awed at the vastness and horrible silence of bleak ice pinnacles and mute granite steeps.

Very suddenly Barzai went out of Atal's sight, scaling a hideous cliff that seemed to bulge outward and block the path for any climber not inspired of earth's gods. Atal was far below, and planning what he should do when he reached the place, when curiously he noticed that the light had grown strong, as if the cloudless peak and moonlit meetingplace of the gods were very near. And as he scrambled on toward the bulging cliff and litten sky he felt fears more shocking then any he had known before. Then through the high mists he heard the voice of Barzai shouting wildly in delight:

"I have heard the gods. I have heard earth's gods singing in revelry on Hatheg-Kla! The voices of earth's gods are known to Barzai the Prophet! The mists are thin and the moon is bright, and I shall see the gods dancing wildly on Hatheg-Kla that they loved in youth. The wisdom of Barzai hath made him greater than earth's gods, and against his will their spells and barriers are as naught; Barzai will behold the gods, the proud gods, the secret gods, the gods of earth who spurn the sight of man!"

Atal could not hear the voices Barzai heard, but he was now close to the bulging cliff and scanning it for footholds. Then he heard Barzai's voice grow shriller and louder:

"The mist is very thin, and the moon casts shadows on the slope; the voices of earth's gods are high and wild, and they fear the coming of Barzai the Wise, who is greater than they. . . . The moon's light flickers, as earth's gods dance against it; I shall see the dancing forms of the gods that leap and howl in the moonlight. . . . The light is dimmer and the gods are afraid. . . ."

Whilst Barzai was shouting these things Atal felt a

spectral change in all the air, as if the laws of earth were bowing to greater laws; for though the way was steeper than ever, the upward path was now grown fearsomely easy, and the bulging cliff proved scarce an obstacle when he reached it and slid perilously up its convex face. The light of the moon had strangely failed, and as Atal plunged upward through the mists he heard Barzai the Wise shrieking in the shadows:

"The moon is dark, and the gods dance in the night; there is terror in the sky, for upon the moon hath sunk an eclipse foretold in no books of men or of earth's gods. . . . There is unknown magic on Hatheg-Kla, for the screams of the frightened gods have turned to laughter, and the slopes of ice shoot up endlessly into the black heavens whither I am plunging. . . . Hei! Hei! At last! In the dim light I behold the gods of earth!"

And now Atal, slipping dizzily up over inconceivable steeps, heard in the dark a loathsome laughing, mixed with such a cry as no man else ever heard save in the Phlegethon of unrelatable nightmares; a cry wherein reverberated the horror and anguish of a haunted lifetime packed into one atrocious moment:

"The other gods! The other gods! The gods of the outer hells that guard the feeble gods of earth! . . . Look away. . . . Go back. . . . Do not see! Do not see! The vengeance of the infinite abysses. . . . That cursed, that damnable pit. . . . Merciful gods of earth, I am falling into the sky!"

And as Atal shut his eyes and stopped his ears and tried to jump downward against the frightful pull from unknown heights, there resounded on Hatheg-Kla that terrible peal of thunder which awaked the good cotters of the plains and the honest burgesses of Hatheg, Nir and Ulthar, and caused them to behold through the clouds that strange eclipse of the moon that no book ever predicted. And when the moon came out at last Atal was safe on the lower snows of the mountain without sight of earth's gods, or of the other gods.

Now it is told in the moldy *Pnakotic Manuscripts* that Sansu found naught but wordless ice and rock when he did climb Hatheg-Kla in the youth of the world. Yet when the men of Ulthar and Nir and Hatheg crushed their fears and scaled that haunted steep by day in search of Barzai the Wise, they found graven in the naked stone of the summit a curious and cyclopean symbol fifty cubits wide, as if the rock had been riven by some titanic chisel. And the symbol was like to one that learned men have discerned in those frightful parts of the *Pnakotic Manuscripts* which were too ancient to be read. This they found.

Barzai the Wise they never found, nor could the holy priest Atal ever be persuaded to pray for his soul's repose. Moreover, to this day the people of Ulthar and Nir and Hatheg fear eclipses, and pray by night when pale vapors hide the mountain-top and the moon. And above the mists on Hatheg-Kla, earth's gods sometimes dance reminiscently; for they know they are safe, and love to come from unknown Kadath in ships of cloud and play in the olden way, as they did when earth was new and men not given to the climbing of inaccessible places.

THE TREE

On a verdant slope of Mount Maenalus, in Arcadia, there stands an olive grove about the ruins of a villa. Close by is a tomb, once beautiful with the sublimest sculptures, but now fallen into as great decay as the house. At one end of that tomb, its curious roots displacing the time-stained blocks of Pentelic marble, grows an unnaturally large olive tree of oddly repellent shape; so like to some grotesque man, or death-distorted body of a man, that the country folk fear to pass it at night when the moon shines faintly through the crooked boughs. Mount Maenalus is a chosen haunt of dreaded Pan, whose queer companions are many, and simple swains believe that the tree must have some hideous kinship to these weird Panisci; but an old bee-keeper who lives in the neighboring cottage told me a different story.

Many years ago, when the hillside villa was new and resplendent, there dwelt within it the two sculptors Kalos and Musides. From Lydia to Neapolis the beauty of their work was praised, and none dared say that the one excelled the other in skill. The Hermes of Kalos stood in a marble shrine in Corinth, and the Pallas of Musides surmounted a pillar in Athens near the Parthenon. All men paid homage to Kalos and Musides, and marvelled that no shadow of artistic jealousy cooled the warmth of their brotherly friendship.

But though Kalos and Musides dwelt in unbroken harmony, their natures were not alike. Whilst Musides revelled by night amidst the urban gaieties of Tegea, Kalos would remain at home; stealing away from the sight of his slaves into the cool recesses of the olive grove. There he would meditate upon the visions that filled his mind, and there devise the forms of beauty which later became immortal in breathing marble. Idle folk, indeed, said that Kalos conversed with the spirits of the grove, and that his statues were but images of the fauns and dryads he met there—for he patterned his work after no living model.

So famous were Kalos and Musides, that none wondered when the Tyrant of Syracuse sent to them deputies to speak of the costly statue of Tyche which he had planned for his city. Of great size and cunning workmanship must the statue be, for it was to form a wonder of nations and a goal of travellers. Exalted beyond thought would be he whose work should gain acceptance, and for this honor Kalos and Musides were invited to compete. Their brotherly love was well known, and the crafty Tyrant surmised that each, instead of concealing his work from the other, would offer aid and advice; this charity producing two images of unheard of beauty, the lovelier of which would eclipse even the dreams of poets.

With joy the sculptors hailed the Tyrant's offer, so that in the days that followed their slaves heard the ceaseless blows of chisels. Not from each other did Kalos and Musides conceal their work, but the sight was for them alone. Saving theirs, no eyes beheld the two divine figures released by skilful blows from the rough blocks that had imprisoned them since the world began.

At night, as of yore, Musides sought the banquet halls of Tegea whilst Kalos wandered alone in the olive grove. But as time passed, men observed a want of gaiety in the once sparkling Musides. It was strange, they said amongst themselves, that depression should thus seize one with so great a chance to win art's loftiest reward. Many months passed, yet in the sour face of Musides came nothing of the sharp expectancy which the situation should arouse.

Then one day Musides spoke of the illness of Kalos, after which none marvelled again at his sadness, since the sculptors' attachment was known to be deep and sacred. Subsequently many went to visit Kalos, and indeed noticed the pallor of his face; but there was about him a happy serenity which made his glance more magical than the glance of Musides—who was clearly distracted with anxiety and who pushed aside all the slaves in his eagerness to feed and wait upon his friend with his own hands. Hidden behind heavy curtains stood the two unfinished figures of Tyche, little touched of late by the sick man and his faithful attendant.

As Kalos grew inexplicably weaker and weaker despite the ministrations of puzzled physicians and of his assiduous friend, he desired to be carried often to the grove which he so loved. There he would ask to be left alone, as if wishing to speak with unseen things. Musides ever granted his requests, though his eyes filled with visible tears at the thought that Kalos should care more for the fauns and the dryads than for him. At last the end drew near, and Kalos discoursed of things beyond this life. Musides, weeping, promised him a sepulchre more lovely than the tomb of Mausolus; but Kalos bade him speak no more of marble glories. Only one wish now haunted the mind of the dying man; that twigs from certain olive trees in the grove be buried by his resting place—close to his head. And one night, sitting alone in the darkness of the olive grove, Kalos died.

Beautiful beyond words was the marble sepulchre which stricken Musides carved for his beloved friend. None but Kalos himself could have fashioned such bas-reliefs, wherein were displayed all the splendours of Elysium. Nor did Musides fail to bury close to Kalos' head the olive twigs from the grove.

As the first violence of Musides' grief gave place to resignation, he labored with diligence upon his figure of Tyche. All honour was now his, since the Tyrant of Syracuse would have the work of none save him or Kalos. His task proved a vent for his emotion and he toiled more steadily each day, shunning the gaieties he once had relished. Meanwhile his evenings were spent beside the tomb of his friend, where a young olive tree had sprung up near the sleeper's head. So swift was the growth of this tree, and so strange was its form, that all who beheld it exclaimed in surprise; and Musides seemed at once fascinated and repelled.

Three years after the death of Kalos, Musides despatched a messenger to the Tyrant, and it was whispered in the agora at Tegea that the mighty statue was finished. By this time the tree by the tomb had attained amazing proportions, exceeding all other trees of its kind, and sending out a singularly heavy branch above the apartment in which Musides labored. As many visitors came to view the prodigious tree, as to admire the art of the sculptor, so that Musides was seldom alone. But he did not mind his multitude of guests; indeed, he seemed to dread being alone now that his absorbing work was done. The bleak mountain wind, sighing through the olive grove and the tomb-tree, had an uncanny way of forming vaguely articulate sounds.

The sky was dark on the evening that the Tyrant's emissaries came to Tegea. It was definitely known that they had come to bear away the great image of Tyche and bring eternal honour to Musides, so their reception by the proxenoi was of great warmth. As the night wore on a violent storm of wind broke over the crest of Maenalus, and the men from far Syracuse were glad that they rested snugly in the town. They talked of their illustrious Tyrant, and of the splendour of his capital and exulted in the glory of the statue which Musides had wrought for him. And then the men of Tegea spoke of the goodness of Musides, and of his heavy grief for his friend; and how not even the coming laurels of art could console him in the absence of Kalos, who might have worn those laurels instead. Of the tree which grew by the tomb, near the head of Kalos, they also spoke. The wind shrieked more horribly, and both the Syracusans and the Arcadians prayed to Aiolos.

In the sunshine of the morning the proxenoi led the Tyrant's messengers up the slope to the abode of the sculptor, but the night wind had done strange things. Slaves' cries ascended from a scene of desolation, and no more amidst the olive grove rose the gleaming colonnades of that vast hall wherein Musides had dreamed and toiled. Lone and shaken mourned the humble courts and the lower walls, for upon the sumptuous greater peristyle had fallen squarely the heavy overhanging bough of the strange new tree, reducing the stately poem in marble with odd completeness to a mound of unsightly ruins. Strangers and Tegeans stood aghast, looking from the wreckage to the great, sinister tree whose aspect was so weirdly human and whose roots reached so queerly into the sculptured sepulchre of Kalos. And their fear and dismay increased when they searched the fallen apartment, for of the gentle Musides, and of the marvellously fashioned image of Tyche, no trace could be discovered. Amidst such stupendous ruin only chaos dwelt, and the representatives of two cities left disappointed; Syracusans that they had no statue to bear home, Tegeans that they had no artist to crown. However, the Syracusans obtained after a while a very splendid statue in Athens, and the Tegeans consoled themselves by erecting in the agora a marble temple commemorating the gifts, virtues, and brotherly piety of Musides.

But the olive grove still stands, as does the tree growing out of the tomb of Kalos, and the old bee-keeper told me that sometimes the boughs whisper to one another in the night wind, saying over and over again. "Oida! Oida! —I know! I know!"

THE DOOM THAT CAME TO SARNATH

There is in the land of Mnar a vast still lake that is fed by no stream, and out of which no stream flows. Ten thousand years ago there stood by its shore the mighty city of Sarnath, but Sarnath stands there no more.

It is told that in the immemorial years when the world was young, before ever the men of Sarnath came to the land of Mnar, another city stood beside the lake; the gray stone city of Ib, which was old as the lake itself, and peopled with beings not pleasing to behold. Very odd and ugly were these beings, as indeed are most beings of a world yet inchoate and rudely fashioned. It is written on the brick cylinders of Kadatheron that the beings of Ib were in hue as green as the lake and the mists that rise above it; that they had bulging eyes, pouting, flabby lips, and curious ears, and were without voice. It is also written that they descended one night from the moon in a mist; they and the vast still lake and gray stone city Ib. However this may be, it is certain that they worshipped a sea-green stone idol chiseled in the likeness of Bokrug, the great water-lizard; before which they danced horribly when the moon was gibbous. And it is written in the papyrus of Ilarnek, that they one day discovered fire, and thereafter kindled flames on many ceremonial occasions. But not much is written of these beings, because they lived in very ancient times, and man is young, and knows but little of the very ancient living things.

After many eons men came to the land of Mnar, dark shepherd folk with their fleecy flocks, who built Thraa, Ilarnek, and Kadatheron on the winding river Ai. And certain tribes, more hardy than the rest, pushed on to the border of the lake and built Sarnath at a spot where precious metals were found in the earth.

Not far from the gray city of Ib did the wandering tribes lay the first stones of Sarnath, and at the beings of Ib they marveled greatly. But with their marveling was mixed hate, for they thought it not meet that beings of such aspect should walk about the world of men at dusk. Nor did they like the strange sculptures upon the gray monoliths of Ib, for those sculptures lingered so late in the world, even until the coming men, none can tell; unless it was because the land of Mnar is very still, and remote from most other lands, both of waking and of dream.

As the men of Sarnath beheld more of the beings of Ib their hate grew, and it was not less because they found the beings weak, and soft as jelly to the touch of stones and arrows. So one day the young warriors, the slingers and the spearmen and the bowmen, marched against Ib and slew all the inhabitants thereof, pushing the queer bodies into the lake with long spears, because they did not wish to touch them. And because they did not like the gray sculptured monoliths of Ib they cast these also into the lake; wondering from the greatness of the labor how ever the stones were brought from afar, as they must have been, since there is naught like them in the land of Mnar or in the lands adjacent.

Thus of the very ancient city of Ib was nothing spared, save the seagreen stone idol chiseled in the likeness of Bokrug, the water-lizard. This the young warriors took back with them as a symbol of conquest over the old gods and beings of Ib, and as a sign of leadership in Mnar. But on the night after it was set up in the temple, a terrible thing must have happened, for weird lights were seen over the lake, and in the morning the people found the idol gone and the high-priest Taran-Ish lying dead, as from some fear unspeakable. And before he died, Taran-Ish had scrawled upon the altar of chrysolite with coarse shaky strokes the sign of DOOM.

After Taran-Ish there were many high-priests in Sarnath but never was the sea-green stone idol found. And many centuries came and went, wherein Sarnath prospered exceedingly, so that only priests and old women remembered what Taran-Ish had scrawled upon the altar of chrysolite. Betwixt Sarnath and the city of Ilarnek arose a caravan route, and the precious metals from the earth were exchanged for other metals and rare cloths and jewels and books and tools for artificers and all things of luxury that are known to the people who dwell along the winding river Ai and beyond. So Sarnath waxed mighty and learned and beautiful, and sent forth conquering armies to subdue the neighboring cities; and in time there sate upon a throne in Sarnath the kings of all the land of Mnar and of many lands adjacent.

The wonder of the world and the pride of all mankind was Sarnath the magnificent. Of polished desert-quarried marble were its walls, in height three hundred cubits and in breadth seventy-five, so that chariots might pass each other as men drove them along the top. For full five hundred stadia did they run, being open only on the side toward the lake where a green stone sea-wall kept back the waves that rose oddly once a year at the festival of the destroying of Ib. In Sarnath were fifty streets from the lake to the gates of the caravans, and fifty more intersecting them. With onyx were they paved, save those whereon the horses and camels and elephants trod, which were paved with granite. And the gates of Sarnath were as many as the landward ends of the streets, each of bronze, and flanked by the figures of lions and elephants carven from some stone no longer known among men. The houses of Sarnath were of glazed brick and chalcedony, each having its walled garden and crystal lakelet. With strange art were they builded, for no other city had houses like them; and travelers from Thraa and Ilarnek and Kadatheron marveled at the shining domes wherewith they were surmounted.

But more marvelous still were the palaces and the temples, and the gardens made by Zokkar the olden king. There were many palaces, the last of which were mightier than any in Thraa or Ilarnek or Kadatheron. So high were they that one within might sometimes fancy himself beneath only the sky; yet when lighted with torches dipt in the oil of Dother their walls showed vast paintings of kings and armies, of a splendor at once inspiring and stupefying to the beholder. Many were the pillars of the palaces, all of tinted marble, and carven into designs of surpassing beauty. And in most of the palaces the floors were mosaics of beryl and lapis lazuli and sardonyx and carbuncle and other choice materials, so disposed that the beholder might fancy himself walking over beds of the rarest flowers. And there were likewise fountains, which cast scented waters about in pleasing jets arranged with cunning art. Outshining all others was the palace of the kings of Mnar and of the lands adjacent. On a pair of golden crouching lions rested the throne, many steps above the gleaming floor. And it was wrought of one piece of ivory, though no man lives who knows whence so vast a piece could have come. In that palace there were also many galleries, and many amphitheaters where lions and men and elephants battled at the pleasure of the kings. Sometimes the amphitheaters were flooded with water conveyed from the lake in mighty aqueducts, and then were enacted stirring sea-fights, or combats betwixt swimmers and deadly marine things.

Lofty and amazing were the seventeen tower-like temples of Sarnath, fashioned of a bright multi-colored stone not known elsewhere. A full thousand cubits high stood the greatest among them, wherein the highpriests dwelt with a magnificence scarce less than that of the kings. On the ground were halls as vast and splendid as those of the palaces; where gathered throngs in worship of Zo-Kalar and Tamash and Lobon, the chief gods of Sarnath, whose incense-enveloped shrines were as the thrones of monarchs. Not like the eikons of other gods were those of

Zo-Kalar and Tamash and Lobon. For so close to life were they that one might swear the graceful bearded gods themselves sate on the ivory thrones. And up unending steps of zircon was the tower-chamber, wherefrom the high-priests looked out over the city and the plains and the lake by day; and at the cryptic moon and significant stars and planets, and their reflections in the lake, at night. Here was done the very secret and ancient rite in detestation of Bokrug, the water-lizard, and here rested the altar of chrysolite which bore the Doom-scrawl of Taran-Ish.

Wonderful likewise were the gardens made by Zokkar the olden king. In the center of Sarnath they lay, covering a great space and encircled by a high wall. And they were surmounted by a mighty dome of glass, through which shone the sun and moon and planets when it was clear, and from which were hung fulgent images of the sun and moon and stars and planets when it was not clear. In summer the gardens were cooled with fresh odorous breezes skilfully wafted by fans, and in winter they were heated with concealed fires, so that in those gardens it was always spring. There ran little streams over bright pebbles, dividing meads of green and gardens of many hues, and spanned by a multitude of bridges. Many were the waterfalls in their courses, and many were the lilied lakelets into which they expanded. Over the streams and lakelets rode white swans, whilst the music of rare birds chimed in with the melody of the waters. In ordered terraces rose the green banks, adorned here and there with bowers of vines and sweet blossoms, and seats and benches of marble and porphyry. And there were many small shrines and temples where one might rest or pray to small gods.

Each year there was celebrated in Sarnath the feast of the destroying of Ib, at which time wine, song, dancing and merriment of every kind abounded. Great honors were then paid to the shades of those who had annihilated the odd ancient beings, and the memory of those beings and of their elder gods was derided by dancers and lutanists crowned with roses from the gardens of Zokkar.

And the kings would look out over the lake and curse the bones of the dead that lay beneath it.

At first the high-priests liked not these festivals, for there had descended amongst them queer tales of how the sea-green eikon had vanished, and how Taran-Ish had died from fear and left a warning. And they said that from their high tower they sometimes saw lights beneath the waters of the lake. But as many years passed without calamity even the priests laughed and cursed and joined in the orgies of the feasters. Indeed, had they not themselves, in their high tower, often performed the very ancient and secret rite in detestation of Bokrug, the water-lizard? And a thousand years of riches and delight passed over Sarnath, wonder of the world.

Gorgeous beyond thought was the feast of the thousandth year of the destroying of Ib. For a decade had it been talked of in the land of Mnar, and as it drew nigh there came to Sarnath on horses and camels and elephants men from Thraa, Ilarnek, and Kadatheron, and all the cities of Mnar and the lands beyond. Before the marble walls on the appointed night were pitched the pavilions of princes and the tents of travelers. Within his banquet-hall reclined Nargis-Hei, the king, drunken with ancient wine from the vaults of conquered Pnoth, and surrounded by feasting nobles and hurrying slaves. There were eaten many strange delicacies at that feast; peacocks from the distant hills of Implan, heels of camels from the Bnazic desert, nuts and spices from Sydathrian groves, and pearls from wave-washed Mtal dissolved in the vinegar of Thraa. Of sauces there were an untold number, prepared by the subtlest cooks in all Mnar, and suited to the palate of every feaster. But most prized of all the viands were the great fishes from the lake, each of vast size, and served upon golden platters set with rubies and diamonds.

Whilst the king and his nobles feasted within the palace, and viewed the crowning dish as it awaited them on golden platters, others feasted elsewhere. In the tower of the great temple the priests held revels, and in pavilions without the walls the princes of neighboring lands made merry. And it was the high-priest Gnai-Kah who first saw the shadows that descended from the gibbous moon into the lake, and the damnable green mists that arose from the lake to meet the moon and to shroud in a sinister haze the towers and the domes of fated Sarnath. Thereafter those in the towers and without the walls beheld strange lights on the water, and saw that the gray rock Akurion, which was wont to rear high above it near the shore, was almost submerged. And fear grew vaguely yet swiftly, so that the princes of Ilarnek and of far Rokol took down and folded their tents and pavilions and departed, though they scarce knew the reason for their departing.

Then, close to the hour of midnight, all the bronze gates of Sarnath burst open and emptied forth a frenzied throng that blackened the plain, so that all the visiting princes and travelers fled away in fright. For on the faces of this throng was writ a madness born of horror unendurable, and on their tongues were words so terrible that no hearer paused for proof. Men whose eyes were wild with fear shrieked aloud of the sight within the king's banquet-hall, where through the windows were seen no longer the forms of Nargis-Hei and his nobles and slaves, but a horde of indescribable green voiceless things with bulging eyes, pouting, flabby lips, and curious ears; things which danced horribly, bearing in their paws golden platters set with rubies and diamonds and containing uncouth flames. And the princes and travelers, as they fled from the doomed city of Sarnath on horses and camels and elephants, looked again upon the mist-begetting lake and saw the gray rock Akurion was quite submerged. Through all the land of Mnar and the land adjacent spread the tales of those who had fled from Sarnath, and caravans sought that accursed city and its precious metals no more. It was long ere any travelers went thither, and even then only the brave and adventurous young men of yellow hair and blue eyes, who are no kin to the men of Mnar. These men indeed went to the lake to view Sarnath; but though they found the vast still lake itself, and the gray rock Akurion which rears high above it near the shore, they beheld not the wonder of the world and pride of all mankind. Where once had risen walls of three hundred cubits and towers yet higher, now stretched only the marshy shore, and where once had dwelt fifty million of men now crawled the detestable water-lizard. Not even the mines of precious metal remained. DOOM had come to Sarnath.

But half buried in the rushes was spied a curious green idol; an exceedingly ancient idol chiseled in the likeness of Bokrug, the great water-lizard. That idol, enshrined in the high temple at Ilarnek, was subsequently worshipped beneath the gibbous moon throughout the land of Mnar.

The next few tales illustrate Lovecraft's early attempts at writing more-or-less in the formal tradition of macabre fiction. "The Tomb," with its memorable and dramatic first line and verse, reminds me very much of Poe. Lovecraft was surely influenced by Poe, and much of his consciously archaic prose style undoubtedly derived from Poe. In a letter dated February 2, 1916, he remarks on this influence:

> I used to write detective stories very often, the works of A. Conan Doyle being my model so far as plot was concerned. But Poe was my God of Fiction. I used to love the horrible and the grotesque—much more than I do now—and can recall tales of murderers, spirits, reincarnations, metempsychoses, and every shudder-producing device known to literature!

Lovecraft was to return to his early love, the macabre, more frequently and seriously in the 1920's, to produce works like "The Outsider" (1921), "The Lurking Fear" (1922), and "The Shunned House" (1924), until this phase of his work became predominant, submerged and absorbed the early fictions, and, with the writing of "The Call of Cthulhu" in 1926, launched him into his greatest period, that of the Cthulhu Mythos.

THE TOMB

In relating the circumstances which have led to my confinement within this refuge for the demented, I am aware that my present position will create a natural doubt of the authenticity of my narrative. It is an unfortunate fact that the bulk of humanity is too limited in its mental vision to weigh with patience and intelligence those isolated phenomena, seen and felt only by a psychologically sensitive few, which lie outside its common experience. Men of broader intellect know that there is no sharp distinction betwixt the real and the unreal; that all things appear as they do only by virtue of the delicate individual physical and mental media through which we are made conscious of them; but the prosaic materialism of the majority condemns as madness the flashes of supersight which penetrate the common veil of obvious empiricism.

My name is Jervas Dudley, and from earliest childhood I have been a dreamer and a visionary. Wealthy beyond the necessity of a commercial life, and temperamentally unfitted for the formal studies and social recreation of my acquaintances, I have dwelt ever in realms apart from the visible world; spending my youth and adolescence in ancient and little known books, and in roaming the fields and groves of the region near my ancestral home. I do not think that what I read in these books or saw in these fields and groves was exactly what other boys read and saw there; but of this I must say little, since detailed speech would but confirm those cruel slanders upon my intellect which I sometimes overhear from the whispers of the stealthy attendants around me. It is sufficient for me to relate events without analyzing causes.

I have said that I dwelt apart from the visible world, but I have not said that I dwelt alone. This no human creature may do; for lacking the fellowship of the living, he inevitably draws upon the companionship of things that are not, or are no longer, living. Close by my home there lies a singular wooded hollow, in whose twilight deeps I spent most of my time; reading, thinking, and dreaming! Down its moss-covered slopes my first steps of infancy were taken, and around its grotesquely gnarled oak trees my first fancies of boyhood were woven. Well did I come to know the presiding dryads of those trees, and often have I watched their wild dances in the struggling beams of a waning moon—but of these things I must not now speak. I will tell only of the lone tomb in the darkest of the hillside thickets; the deserted tomb of the Hydes, an old and exalted family whose last direct descendant had been laid within its black recesses many decades before my birth.

The vault to which I refer is of ancient granite, weathered and discolored by the mists and dampness of generations. Excavated back into the hillside, the structure is visible only at the entrance. The door, a ponderous and forbidding slab of stone, hangs upon rusted iron hinges, and is fastened ajar in a queerly sinister way by means of heavy iron chains and padlocks, according to a gruesome fashion of half a century ago. The abode of the race whose scions are here inurned had once crowned the declivity which holds the tomb, but had long since fallen victim to the flames which sprang up from a stroke of lightning. Of the midnight storm which destroyed this gloomy mansion, the older inhabitants of the region sometimes speak in hushed and uneasy voices; alluding to what they call "divine wrath" in a manner that in later years vaguely increased the always strong fascination which I had felt for the forest-darkened sepulcher. One man only had perished in the fire. When the last of the Hydes was buried in this place of shade and stillness, the sad urnful of ashes had come from a distant land, to which the family had repaired when the mansion burned down. No one remains to lay flowers before the granite portal, and few care to brave the depressing shadows which seem to linger strangely about the water-worn stones.

I shall never forget the afternoon when first I stumbled upon the half-hidden house of death. It was in mid-summer, when the alchemy of nature transmutes the sylvan landscape to one vivid and almost homogeneous mass of green; when the senses are well-nigh intoxicated with the surging seas of moist verdure and the subtly indefinable odors of the soil and the vegetation. In such surroundings the mind loses its perspective; time and space become trivial and unreal, and echoes of a forgotten prehistoric past beat insistently upon the enthralled consciousness.

All day I had been wandering through the mystic groves of the hollow; thinking thoughts I need not discuss, and conversing with things I need not name. In years a child of ten, I had seen and heard many wonders unknown to the throng; and was oddly aged in certain respects. When, upon forcing my way between two savage clumps of briars, I suddenly encountered the entrance of the vault, I had no knowledge of what I had discovered. The dark blocks of granite, the door so curiously ajar, and the funeral carvings above the arch, aroused in me no associations of mournful or terrible character. Of graves and tombs I knew and imagined much, but had on account of my peculiar temperament been kept from all personal contact with churchyards and cemeteries. The strange stone house on the woodland slope was to me only a source of interest and speculation; and its cold, damp interior, into which I vainly peered through the aperture so tantalizingly left, contained for me no hint of death or decay. But in that instant of curiosity was born the madly unreasoning desire which has brought me to this hell of confinement. Spurred on by a voice which must have come from the hideous soul of the forest, I resolved to enter the beckoning gloom in spite of the ponderous chains which barred my passage. In the waning light of day I alternately rattled the rusty impediments with a view to throwing wide the stone door, and essayed to squeeze my slight form through the space already provided; but neither plan met with success. At first curious, I was now frantic; and when in the thickening twilight I returned to my home, I had sworn to the hundred gods of the grove that *at any cost* I would some day force an entrance to the black, chilly depths that seemed calling out to me. The physician with the iron-grey beard who comes each day to my room, once told a visitor that this decision marked the beginning of a pitiful monomania; but I will leave final judgment to my readers when they shall have learnt all.

The months following my discovery were spent in futile attempts to force the complicated padlock of the slightly open vault, and in carefully guarded inquiries regarding the nature and history of the structure. With the traditionally receptive ears of the small boy, I learned much; though an habitual secretiveness caused me to tell no one of my information or my resolve. It is perhaps worth mentioning that I was not at all surprised or terrified on learning of the nature of the vault. My rather original ideas regarding life and death had caused me to associate the cold clay with the breathing body in a vague fashion; and I felt that the great and sinister family of the burned-down mansion was in some way represented within the stone space I sought to explore. Mumbled tales of the weird rites and godless revels of bygone years in the ancient hall gave to me a new and potent interest in the tomb, before whose door I would sit for hours at a time each day. Once I thrust a candle within the nearly closed entrance, but could see nothing save a flight of damp stone steps leading downward. The odor of the place repelled yet bewitched me. I felt I had known it before, in a past remote beyond all recollection; beyond even my tenancy of the body I now possesss

The year after I first beheld the tomb, I stumbled upon a worm-eaten translation of Plutarch's *Lives* in the book-filled attic of my home. Reading the life of Theseus, I was much impressed by that passage telling of the great stone beneath which the boyish hero was to find his tokens of destiny whenever he should become old enough to lift its enormous weight. The legend had the effect of dispelling my keenest impatience to enter the vault, for it made me feel that the time was not yet ripe. Later, I told myself, I should grow to a strength and ingenuity which might enable me to unfasten the heavily chained door with ease; but until then I would do better by comforming to what seemed the will of Fate.

Accordingly my watches by the dank portal became less persistent, and much of my time was spent in other though equally strange pursuits. I would sometimes rise very quietly in the night, stealing out to walk in those churchyards and places of burial from which I had been kept by my parents. What I did there I may not say, for I am not now sure of the reality of certain things; but I know that on the day after such a nocturnal ramble I would often astonish those about me with my knowledge of topics almost forgotten for many generations. It was after a night like this that I shocked the community with a queer conceit about the burial of the rich and celebrated Squire Brewster, a maker of local history who was interred in 1711, and whose slate headstone, bearing a graven skull and crossbones, was slowly crumbling to powder. In a moment of childish imagination I vowed not only that the undertaker, Goodman Simpson, had stolen the silver-buckled shoes, silken hose, and satin small-clothes of the deceased before burial; but that the Squire himself, not fully inanimate, had turned twice in his mound-covered coffin on the day after interment.

But the idea of entering the tomb never left my thoughts; being indeed stimulated by the unexpected genealogical discovery that my own maternal ancestry possessed at least a slight link with the supposedly extinct family of the Hydes. Last of my paternal race, I was likewise the last of this older and more mysterious line. I began to feel that the tomb was *mine,* and to look forward with hot eagerness to the time when I might pass within that stone door and down those slimy stone steps in the dark. I now formed the habit of listening very intently at the slightly open portal, choosing my favorite hours of midnight stillness for the odd vigil. By the time I came of age, I had made a small clearing in the thicket before the mold-stained façade of the hillside, allowing the surrounding vegetation to encircle and overhang the space like the walls and roof of a sylvan bower. This bower was my temple, the fastened door my shrine, and here I would lie outstretched on the mossy ground, thinking strange thoughts and dreaming strange dreams.

The night of the first revelation was a sultry one. I must have fallen asleep from fatigue, for it was with a distinct sense of awakening that I heard the voices. Of these tones and accents I hesitate to speak; of their quality I will not speak; but I may say that they presented certain uncanny differences in vocabulary, pronunciation, and mode of utterance. Every shade of New England dialect, from the uncouth syllables of the Puritan colonists to the precise rhetoric of fifty years ago, seemed represented in that shadowy colloquy, though it was only later that I noticed the fact. At the time, indeed, my attention was distracted from this matter by another phenomenon; a phenomenon so fleeting that I could not take oath upon its reality. I barely fancied that as I awoke, a *light* had been hurriedly extinguished within the sunken sepulcher. I do not think I was either astounded or panic-stricken, but I know that I was greatly and permanently *changed* that night. Upon returning home I went with much directness to a rotting chest in the attic, wherein I found the key which next day unlocked with ease the barrier I had so long stormed in vain.

It was in the soft glow of late afternoon that I first entered the vault on the abandoned slope. A spell was upon me, and my heart leaped with an exultation I can but ill describe. As I closed the door behind me and descended the dripping steps by the light of my lone candle, I seemed to know the way; and though the candle sputtered with the stifling reek of the place, I felt singularly at home in the musty, charnel-house air. Looking about me, I beheld many marble slabs bearing coffins, or the remains of coffins. Some of these were sealed and intact, but others had nearly vanished, leaving the silver handles and plates isolated amidst certain curious heaps of whitish dust. Upon one plate I read the name of Sir Geoffrey Hyde, who had come from Sussex in 1640 and died here a few years later. In a conspicuous alcove was one fairly well preserved and untenanted casket, adorned with a single name which brought me both a smile and a shudder. An odd impulse caused me to climb upon the broad slab, extinguish my candle, and lie down within the vacant box.

In the gray light of dawn I staggered from the vault and locked the chain of the door behind me. I was no longer a young man, though but twenty-one winters had chilled my bodily frame. Early-rising villagers who observed my homeward progress looked at me strangely, and marveled at the signs of ribald revelry which they saw in one whose life was known to be sober and solitary. I did not appear before my parents till after a long and refreshing sleep.

Henceforward I haunted the tomb each night; seeing, hearing, and doing things I must never recall. My speech, always susceptible to environmental influences, was the first thing to succumb to the change; and my suddenly acquired archaism of diction was soon remarked upon. Later a queer boldness and recklessness came into my demeanor, till I unconsciously grew to possess the bearing of a man of the world despite my lifelong seclusion. My formerly silent tongue waxed voluble with the easy grace of a Chesterfield or the godless cynicism of a Rochester. I displayed a peculiar erudition utterly unlike the fantastic, monkish lore over which I had pored in youth; and covered the fly-leaves of my books with facile impromptu epigrams which brought up suggestions of Gay, Prior, and the sprightliest of the Augustan wits and rimesters. One morning at breakfast I came close to disaster by declaiming in palpably liquorish accents an effusion of Eighteenth Century bacchanalian mirth, a bit of Georgian playfulness never recorded in a book, which ran something like this:

Come hither, my lads, with your tankards of ale,
And drink to the present before it shall fail;
Pile each on your platter a mountain of beef,
For 'tis eating and drinking that bring us relief:
So fill up your glass,
For life will soon pass;
When you're dead ye'll ne'er drink to your king or your lass!

Anacreon had a red nose, so they say;
But what's a red nose if ye're happy and gay?
Gad split me! I'd rather be red whilst I'm here,
Than white as a lily—and dead half a year!
So Betty, my miss,
Come give me kiss;
In hell there's no innkeeper's daughter like this!

Young Harry, propp'd up just as straight as he's able,
Will soon lose his wig and slip under the table,
But fill up your goblets and pass 'em around—
Better under the table than under the ground!
So revel and chaff
As ye thirstily quaff:
Under six feet of dirt 'tis less easy to laugh!

The fiend strike me blue! I'm scarce able to walk,
And damn me if I can stand upright or talk!
Here, landlord, bid Betty to summon a chair;
I'll try home for a while, for my wife is not there!
So lend me a hand;
I'm not able to stand,
But I'm gay whilst I linger on top of the land!

About this time I conceived my present fear of fire and thunderstorms. Previously indifferent to such things, I had now an unspeakable horror of them; and would retire to the innermost recesses of the house whenever the heavens threatened an electrical display. A favorite haunt of mine during the day was the ruined cellar of the mansion that had burned down, and in fancy I would picture the structure as it had been in its prime. On one occasion I startled a villager by leading him confidently to a shallow sub-cellar, of whose existence I seemed to know in spite of the fact that it had been unseen and forgotten for many generations.

At last came that which I had long feared. My parents, alarmed at the altered manner and appearance of their only son, commenced to exert over my movements a kindly espionage which threatened to result in disaster. I had told no one of my visits to the tomb, having guarded my secret purpose with religious zeal since childhood; but now I was forced to exercise care in threading the mazes of the wooded hollow, that I might throw off a possible pursuer. My key to the vault I kept suspended from a cord about my neck, its presence known only to me. I never carried out of the sepulcher any of the things I came upon whilst within its walls.

One morning as I emerged from the damp tomb and fastened the chain of the portal with none too steady hand, I beheld in an adjacent thicket the dreaded face of a watcher. Surely the end was near; for my bower was discovered, and the objective of my nocturnal journeys revealed. The man did not accost me, so I hastened home in an effort to overhear what he might report to my careworn father. Were my sojourns beyond the chained door about to be proclaimed to the world? Imagine my delighted astonishment on hearing the spy inform my parent in a cautious whisper *that I had spent the night in the bower outside the tomb;* my sleep-filmed eyes fixed upon the crevice where the padlocked portal stood ajar! By what miracle had the watcher been thus deluded? I was now convinced that a supernatural agency protected me. Made bold by this heaven-sent circumstance, I began to resume perfect openness in going to the vault; confident that no one could witness my entrance. For a week I tasted to the full joys of that charnel conviviality which I must not describe, when the *thing* happened, and I was borne away to this accursed abode of sorrow and monotony.

I should not have ventured out that night; for the taint of thunder was in the clouds, and a hellish phosphorescence rose from the rank swamp at the bottom of the hollow. The call of the dead, too, was different. Instead of the hillside tomb, it was the charred cellar on the crest of the slope whose presiding demon beckoned to me with unseen fingers. As I emerged from an intervening grove upon the plain before the ruin, I beheld in the misty moonlight a thing I had always vaguely expected. The mansion, gone for a century, once more reared its stately height to the raptured vision; every window ablaze with the splendor of many candles. Up the long drive rolled the coaches of the Boston gentry, whilst on foot came a numerous assemblage of powdered exquisites from the neighboring mansions. With this throng I mingled, though I knew I belonged with the hosts rather than with the guests. Inside the hall were music, laughter, and wine on every hand. Several faces I recognized; though I should have known them better had they been shriveled or eaten away by death and decomposition. Amidst a wild and reckless throng I was the wildest and most abandoned. Gay blasphemy poured in torrents from my lips, and in shocking sallies I heeded no law of God, man, or nature.

Suddenly a peal of thunder, resonant even above the din of the swinish revelry, clave the very roof and laid a hush of fear upon the boisterous company. Red tongues of flame and searing gusts of heat engulfed the house; and the roysterers, struck with terror at the descent of a calamity which seemed to transcend the bounds of unguided nature, fled shrieking into the night. I alone remained, riveted to my seat by a groveling fear which I had never felt before. And then a second horror took possession of my soul. Burnt alive to ashes, my body dispersed by the four winds, *I might never lie in the tomb of the Hydes!* Was not my coffin prepared for me? Had I not a right to rest till eternity amongst the descendants of Sir Geoffrey Hyde? Aye! I would claim my heritage of death, even though my soul go seeking through the ages for another corporeal tenement to represent it on that vacant slab in the alcove of the vault. *Jervas Hyde* should never share the sad fate of Palinurus!

As the phantom of the burning house faded, I found

myself screaming and struggling madly in the arms of two men, one of whom was the spy who had followed me to the tomb. Rain was pouring down in torrents, and upon the southern horizon were flashes of lightning that had so lately passed over our heads. My father, his face lined with sorrow, stood by as I shouted my demands to be laid within the tomb, frequently admonishing my captors to treat me as gently as they could. A blackened circle on the floor of the ruined cellar told of a violent stroke from the heavens; and from this spot a group of curious villagers with lanterns were prying a small box of antique workmanship, which the thunderbolt had brought to light.

Ceasing my futile and now objectless writhing, I watched the spectators as they viewed the treasure-trove, and was permitted to share in their discoveries. The box, whose fastenings were broken by the stroke which had unearthed it, contained many papers and objects of value, but I had eyes for one thing alone. It was the porcelain miniature of a young man in a smartly curled bag-wig, and bore the initials "J. H." The face was such that as I gazed, I might well have been studying my mirror.

On the following day I was brought to this room with the barred windows, but I have been kept informed of certain things through an aged and simple-minded servitor, for whom I bore a fondness in infancy, and who, like me, loves the churchyard. What I have dared relate of my experiences within the vault has brought me only pitying smiles. My father, who visits me frequently, declares that at no time did I pass the chained portal, and swears that the rusted padlock had not been touched for fifty years when he examined it. He even says that all the village knew of my journeys to the tomb, and that I was often watched as I slept in the bower outside the grim façade, my half-open eyes fixed on the crevice that leads to the interior. Against these assertions I have no tangible proof to offer, since my key to the padlock was lost in the struggle on that night of horrors. The strange things of the past which I have learned during those nocturnal meetings with the dead he dismisses as the fruits of my lifelong and omnivorous browsing amongst the ancient volumes of the family library. Had it not been for my old servant Hiram, I should have by this time become quite convinced of my madness.

But Hiram, loyal to the last, has held faith in me, and has done that which impels me to make public at least part of my story. A week ago he burst open the lock which chains the door of the tomb perpetually ajar,and descended with a lantern into the murky depths. On a slab in an alcove he found an old but empty coffin whose tarnished plate bears the single word: *Jervas*. In that coffin and in that vault they have promised me I shall be buried.

POLARIS

Into the North Window of my chamber glows the Pole Star with uncanny light. All through the long hellish hours of blackness it shines there. And in the autumn of the year, when the winds from the north curse and whine, and the red-leaved trees of the swamp mutter things to one another in the small hours of the morning under the horned waning moon, I sit by the casement and watch that star. Down from the heights reels the glittering Cassiopeia as the hours wear on, while Charles' Wain lumbers up from behind the vapour-soaked swamp trees that sway in the night wind. Just before dawn Arcturus winks ruddily from above the cemetery on the low hillock, and Coma Berenices shimmers weirdly afar off in the mysterious east; but still the Pole Star leers down from the same place in the black vault, winking hideously like an insane watching eye which strives to convey some strange message, yet recalls nothing save that it once had a message to convey. Sometimes, when it is cloudy, I can sleep.

Well do I remember the night of the great Aurora, when over the swamp played the shocking coruscations of the daemon light. After the beam came clouds, and then I slept.

And it was under a horned waning moon that I saw the city for the first time. Still and somnolent did it lie, on a strange plateau in a hollow betwixt strange peaks. Of ghastly marble were its walls and its towers, its columns, domes, and pavements. In the marble streets were marble pillars, the upper parts of which were carven into the images of grave bearded men. The air was warm and stirred not. And overhead, scarce ten degrees from the zenith, glowed that watching Pole Star. Long did I gaze on the city, but the day came not. When the red Aldebaran, which blinked low in the sky but never set, had crawled a quarter of the way around the horizon, I saw light and motion in the houses and the streets. Forms strangely robed, but at once noble and familiar, walked abroad and under the horned waning moon men talked wisdom in a tongue which I understood, though it was unlike any language I had ever known. And when the red Aldebaran had crawled more than half-way around the horizon, there were again darkness and silence.

When I awaked, I was not as I had been. Upon my memory was graven the vision of the city, and within my soul had arisen another and vaguer recollection, of whose nature I was not then certain. Thereafter, on the cloudy nights when I could sleep, I saw the city often; sometimes under the hot, yellow rays of a sun which did not set, but which wheeled low around the horizon. And on the clear nights the Pole Star leered as never before.

Gradually I came to wonder what might be my place in that city on the strange plateau betwixt strange peaks. At first content to view the scene as an all-observant uncorporeal presence, I now desired to define my relation to it, and to speak my mind amongst the grave men who conversed each day in the public squares. I said to myself, "This is no dream, for by what means can I prove the greater reality of that other life in the house of stone and brick south of the sinister swamp and the cemetery on the low hillock, where the Pole Star peeps into my north window each night?"

One night as I listened to the discourse in the large square containing many statues, I felt a change; and perceived that I had at last a bodily form. Nor was I a stranger in the streets of Olathoe, which lies on the plateau of Sarkia, betwixt the peaks Noton and Kadiphonek. It was my friend Alos who spoke, and his speech was one that pleased my soul, for it was the speech of a true man and patriot. That night had the news come of Daikos' fall, and of the advance of the Inutos; squat, hellish yellow fiends who five years ago had appeared out of the unknown west to ravage the confines of our kingdom, and to besiege many of our towns. Having taken the fortified places at the foot of the mountains, their way now lay open to the plateau, unless every citizen could resist with the strength of ten men. For the squat creatures were mighty in the arts of war, and knew not the scruples of honour which held back our tall, grey-eyed men of Lomar from ruthless conquest.

Alos, my friend, was commander of all the forces on the plateau, and in him lay the last hope of our country. On this occasion he spoke of the perils to be faced and exhorted the men of Olathoe, bravest of the Lomarians, to sustain the traditions of their ancestors, who when forced to move southward from Zobna before the advance of the great ice sheet (even as our descendants must some day flee from the land of Lomar) valiantly and victoriously swept aside the hairy, long-armed, cannibal Gnophkehs that stood in their way. To me Alos denied a warrior's part, for I was feeble and given to strange faintings when subjected to stress and hardships. But my eyes were the keenest in the city, despite the long hours I gave each day to the study of the Pnakotic manuscripts and the wisdom of the Zobnarian Fathers; so my friend, desiring not to doom me to inaction, rewarded me with that duty which was second to nothing in importance. To the watchtower of Thapnen he sent me, there to serve as the eyes of our army. Should the Inutos attempt to gain the citadel by the narrow pass behind the peak Noton and thereby surprise the garrison, I was to give the signal of fire which would warn the waiting soldiers and save the town from immediate disaster.

Alone I mounted the tower, for every man of stout body was needed in the passes below. My brain was sore dazed with excitement and fatigue, for I had not slept in many days; yet was my purpose firm, for I loved my native land of Lomar, and the marble city Olathoe that lies betwixt the peaks of Noton and Kadiphonek.

But as I stood in the tower's topmost chamber, I beheld the horned waning moon, red and sinister, quivering through the vapours that hovered over the distant valley of Banof. And through an opening in the roof glittered the pale Pole Star, fluttering as if alive, and leering like a fiend and tempter. Methought its spirit whispered evil counsel, soothing me to traitorous somnolence with a damable rhythmical promise which it repeated over and over:

Slumber, watcher, till the spheres,
Six and twenty thousand years
Have revolv'd, and I return
To the spot where now I burn.
Other stars anon shall rise
To the axis of the skies;
Stars that soothe and stars that bless
With a sweet forgetfulness:
Only when my round is o'er
Shall the past disturb thy door.

Vainly did I struggle with my drowsiness, seeking to connect these strange words with some lore of the skies which I had learnt from the Pnakotic manuscripts. My head, heavy and reeling, drooped to my breast, and when next I looked up it was in a dream, with the Pole Star grinning at me through a window from over the horrible swaying trees of a dream swamp. And I am still dreaming.

In my shame and despair I sometimes scream frantically, begging the dream-creatures around me to waken me ere the Inutos steal up the pass behind the peak Noton and take the citadel by surprise; but these creatures are daemons, for they laugh at me and tell me I am not dreaming. They mock me whilst I sleep, and whilst the squat yellow foe may be creeping silently upon us. I have failed in my duty and betrayed the marble city of Olathoe;

I have proven false to Alos, my friend and commander. But still these shadows of my dreams deride me. They say there is no land of Lomar, save in my nocturnal imaginings; that in these realms where the Pole Star shines high, and red Aldebaran crawls low around the horizon, there has been naught save ice and snow for thousands of years, and never a man save squat, yellow creatures, blighted by the cold, whom they call "Esquimaux."

And as I writhe in my guilty agony, frantic to save the city whose peril every moment grows, and vainly striving to shake off this unnatural dream of a house of stone and brick south of a sinister swamp and a cemetery on a low hillock, the Pole Star, evil and monstrous, leers down from the black vault, winking hideously like an insane watching eye which strives to convey some message, yet recalls nothing save that it once had a message to convey.

BEYOND THE WALL OF SLEEP

I have often wondered if the majority of mankind ever pause to reflect upon the occasionally titanic significance of dreams, and of the obscure world to which they belong. Whilst the greater number of our nocturnal visions are perhaps no more than faint and fantastic reflections of our waking experiences—Freud to the contrary with his puerile symbolism—there are still a certain remainder whose immundane and ethereal character permit of no ordinary interpretation, and whose vaguely exciting and disquieting effect suggests possible minute glimpses into a sphere of mental existence no less important than physical life, yet separated from that life by an all but impassable barrier. From my experience I cannot doubt but that man, when lost to terrestrial consciousness, is indeed sojourning in another and uncorporeal life of far different nature from the life we know, and of which only the slightest and most indistinct memories linger after waking. From those blurred and fragmentary memories we may infer much, yet prove little. We may guess that in dreams life, matter, and vitality, as the earth knows such things, are not necessarily constant; and that time and space do not exist as our waking selves comprehend them. Sometimes I believe that this less material life is our truer life, and that our vain presence on the terraqueous globe is itself the secondary or merely virtual phenomenon.

It was from a youthful revery filled with speculations of this sort that I arose one afternoon in the winter of 1900-01, when to the state psychopathic institution in which I served as an intern was brought the man whose case has ever since haunted me so unceasingly. His name, as given on the records, was Joe Slater, or Slaader, and his appearance was that of the typical denizen of the Catskill Mountain region; one of those strange, repellent scions of a primitive Colonial peasant stock whose isolation for nearly three centuries in the hilly fastnesses of a little-traveled countryside has caused them to sink to a kind of barbaric degeneracy, rather than advance with their more fortunately placed brethren of the thickly settled districts. Among these odd folk, who correspond exactly to the decadent element of "white trash" in the South, law and morals are non-existent; and their general mental status is probably below that of any other section of native American people.

Joe Slater, who came to the institution in the vigilant custody of four state policemen, and who was described as a highly dangerous character, certainly presented no evidence of his perilous disposition when I first behold him. Though well above the middle stature, and of somewhat brawny frame, he was given an absurd appearance of harmless stupidity by the pale, sleepy blueness of his small watery eyes, the scantiness of his neglected and never-shaven growth of yellow beard, and the listless drooping of his heavy nether lip. His age was unknown, since among his kind neither family records nor permanent family ties exist; but from the baldness of his head in front, and from the decayed condition of his teeth, the head surgeon wrote him down as a man of about forty.

From the medical and court documents we learned all that could be gathered of his case: this man, a vagabond, hunter and trapper, had always been strange in the eyes of his primitive associates. He had habitually slept at night beyond the ordinary time, and upon waking would often talk of unknown things in a manner so bizarre as to inspire fear even in the hearts of an unimaginative populace. Not that his form of language was at all unusual, for he never spoke save in the debased patois of his environment; but the tone and tenor of his utterances were of such mysterious wildness, that none might listen without apprehension. He himself was generally as terrified and baffled as his auditors, and within an hour after awakening would forget all that he had said, or at least all that had caused him to say what he did; relapsing into a bovine, half-amiable normality like that of the other hilldwellers.

As Slater grew older, it appeared, his matutinal aberrations had gradually increased in frequency and violence; till about a month before his arrival at the institution had occurred the shocking tragedy which caused his arrest by the authorities. One day near noon, after a profound sleep begun in a whiskey debauch at about five of the previous afternoon, the man had roused himself most suddenly, with ululations so horrible and unearthly that they brought several neighbors to his cabin —a filthy sty where he dwelt with a family as indescribable as himself. Rushing out into the snow, he had flung his arms aloft and commenced a series of leaps directly upward in the air; the while shouting his determination to reach some "big, big cabin with brightness in the roof and walls and floor and the loud queer music far away." As two men of moderate size sought to restrain him, he had struggled with maniacal force and fury, screaming of his desire and need to find and kill a certain "thing that shines and shakes and laughs." At length, after temporarily felling one of his detainers with a sudden blow, he had flung himself upon the other in a demoniac ecstasy of blood-thirstiness, shrieking fiendishly that he would "jump high in the air and burn his way through anything that stopped him."

Family and neighbors had now fled in a panic, and when the more courageous of them returned, Slater was gone, leaving behind an unrecognizable pulp-like thing that had been a living man but an hour before. None of the mountaineers had dared to pursue him, and it is likely that they would have welcomed his death from the cold; but when several mornings later they heard his screams from a distant ravine they realized that he had somehow managed to survive, and that his removal in one way or another would be necessary. Then had followed an armed searching-party, whose purpose (whatever it may have been originally) became that of a sheriff's posse after one of the seldom popular state troopers had by accident observed, then questioned, and finally joined the seekers.

On the third day Slater was found unconscious in the hollow of a tree, and taken to the nearest jail, where alienists from Albany examined him as soon as his senses returned. To them he told a simple story. He had, he said, gone to sleep one afternoon about sundown after drinking much liquor. He had awakened to find himself standing bloody-handed in the snow before his cabin, the mangled corpse of his neighbor Peter Slader at his feet. Horrified, he had taken to the woods in a vague effort to escape from the scene of what must have been his crime. Beyond these things he seemed to know nothing, nor could the expert questioning of his interrogators bring out a single additional fact.

That night Slater slept quietly, and the next morning he awakened with no singular feature save a a certain alteration of expression. Doctor Barnard, who had been watching the patient, thought he noticed in the pale blue eyes a certain gleam of peculiar quality, and in the flaccid lips an all but imperceptible tightening, as if of intelligent determination. But when questioned, Slater relapsed into the habitual vacancy of the mountaineer, and only reiterated what he had said on the preceding day.

On the third morning occurred the first of the man's mental attacks. After some show of uneasiness in sleep, he burst forth into a frenzy so powerful that the combined efforts of four men were needed to bind him in a straightjacket. The alienists listened with keen attention to his words, since their curiosity had been aroused to a high pitch by the suggestive yet mostly conflicting and incoherent stories of his family and neighbors. Slater raved for upward of fifteen minutes, babbling in his backwoods dialect of green edifices of light, oceans of space, strange music, and shadowy mountains and valleys. But most of all did he dwell upon some mysterious blazing entity that shook and laughed and mocked at him. This vast, vague personality seemed to have done him a terrible wrong, and to kill it in triumphant revenge was his paramount desire. In order to reach it, he said, he would soar through abysses of emptiness, *burning* every obstacle that stood in his way. Thus ran his discourse, until with the greatest suddenness he ceased. The fire of madness died from his eyes, and in dull wonder he looked at his questioners and asked why he was bound. Dr. Barnard unbuckled the leather harness and did not restore it till night, when he succeeded in persuading Slater to don it of his own volition, for his own good. The man had now admitted that he sometimes talked queerly, though he knew not why.

Within a week two more attacks appeared, but from them the doctors learned little. On the *source* of Slater's visions they speculated at length, for since he could neither read nor write, and had apparently never heard a legend or fairy-tale, his gorgeous imagery was quite inexplicable. That it could not come from any known myth or romance was made especially clear by the fact that the unfortunate lunatic expressed himself only in his own simple manner. He raved of things he did not understand and could not interpret; things which he claimed to have experienced, but which he could not have learned through any normal or connected narration. The alienists soon agreed that abnormal dreams were the foundation of the trouble; dreams whose vividness could for a time completely dominate the waking mind of this basically inferior man. With due formality Slater was tried for murder, acquitted on the ground of insanity, and committed to the institution wherein I held so humble a post.

I have said that I am a constant speculator concerning dream-life, and from this you may judge of the eagerness with which I applied myself to the study of the new patient as soon as I had fully ascertained the facts of his case. He seemed to sense a certain friendliness in me, born no doubt of the interest I could not conceal, and the gentle manner in which I questioned him. Not that he ever recognized me during his attacks, when I hung breathlessly upon his chaotic but cosmic word-pictures; but he knew me in his quiet hours, when he would sit by his barred window weaving baskets of straw and willow, and perhaps pining for the mountain freedom he could never again enjoy. His family never called to see him; probably it had found another temporary head, after the manner of decadent mountain folk.

By degrees I commenced to feel an overwhelming wonder at the mad and fantastic conceptions of Joe Slater. The man himself was pitiably inferior in mentality and language alike; but his glowing, titanic visions, though described in a barbarous disjointed jargon, were assuredly things which only a superior or even exceptional brain could conceive. How, I often asked myself, could the stolid imagination of a Catskill degenerate conjure up sights whose very possession argued a lurking spark of genius? How could any backwoods dullard have gained so much as an idea of those glittering realms of supernal radiance and space about which Slater ranted in his furious delirium? More and more I inclined to the belief that in the pitiful personality who cringed before me lay the disordered nucleus of something beyond my comprehension; something infinitely beyond the comprehension of my more experienced but less imaginative medical and scientific colleagues.

And yet I could extract nothing definite from the man. The sum of all my investigation was, that in a kind of semi-corporeal dream-life Slater wandered or floated through resplendent and prodigious valleys, meadows, gardens, cities, and palaces of light, in a region unbounded and unknown to man; that there he was no peasant or degenerate, but a creature of importance and vivid life, moving proudly and dominantly, and checked only by a certain deadly enemy, who seemed to be a being of visible yet ethereal structure, and who did not appear to be of human shape, since Slater never referred to it as a *man,* or as aught save a *thing.* This *thing* had done Slater some hideous but unnamed wrong, which the maniac (if maniac he were) yearned to avenge.

From the manner in which Slater alluded to their dealings, I judged that he and the luminous *thing* had met on equal terms; that in his dream existence the man was himself a luminous *thing* of the same race as his enemy. This impression was sustained by his frequent references to *flying through space* and *burning* all that impeded his progress. Yet these conceptions were formulated in rustic words wholly inadequate to convey them, a circumstance which drove me to the conclusion that if a dream world indeed existed, oral language was not its medium for the transmission of thought. Could it be that the dream soul inhabiting this inferior body was desperately struggling to speak things which the simple and halting tongue of dullness could not utter? Could it be that I was face to face with intellectual emanations which would explain the mystery if I could but learn to discover and read them? I did not tell the older physicians of these things, for middle age is skeptical, cynical, and disinclined to accept new ideas. Besides, the head of the institution had but lately warned me in his paternal way that I was overworking; that my mind needed a rest.

It had long been my belief that human thought consists basically of atomic or molecular motion, convertible into ether waves or radiant energy like heat, light and electricity. This belief had early led me to contemplate the possibility of telepathy or mental communication by means of suitable apparatus, and I had in my college days prepared a set of transmitting and receiving instruments somewhat similar to the cumbrous devices employed in wireless telegraphy at that crude, pre-radio period. These I had tested with a fellow-student, but achieving no result, had soon packed them away with other scientific odds and ends for possible future use.

Now, in my intense desire to probe into the dream-life of Joe Slater, I sought these instruments again, and spent several days in repairing them for action. When they were complete once more I missed no opportunity for their trial. At each outburst of Slater's violence, I would fit the transmitter to his forehead and the receiver to my own, constantly making delicate adjustments for various hypothetical wave-lengths of intellectual energy. I had but little notion of how the thought-impressions would, if successfully conveyed, arouse an intelligent response in my brain, but I felt certain that I could detect and interpret them. Accordingly I continued my experiments, though informing no one of their nature.

It was on the twenty-first of February, 1901, that the thing occurred. As I look back across the years I realize how unreal it seems, and sometimes wonder if old Doctor Fenton was not right when he charged it all to my excited imagination. I recall that he listened with great kindness and patience when I told him, but afterward gave me a nerve-powder and arranged for the half-year's vacation on which I departed the next week.

That fateful night I was wildly agitated and perturbed, for despite the excellent care he had received, Joe Slater was unmistakably dying. Perhaps it was his mountain freedom that he missed, or perhaps the turmoil in his brain had grown too acute for his rather sluggish physique; but at all events the flame of vitality flickered low in the decadent body. He was drowsy near the end, and as darkness fell he dropped off into a troubled sleep.

I did not strap on the straightjacket as was customary when he slept, since I saw that he was too feeble to be dangerous, even if he woke in mental disorder once more before passing away. But I did place upon his head and mine the two ends of my cosmic "radio," hoping against hope for a first and last message from the dream world in the brief time remaining. In the cell with us was one nurse, a mediocre fellow who did not understand the purpose of the apparatus, or think to inquire into my course. As the hours wore on I saw his head droop awkwardly in sleep, but I did not disturb him. I myself, lulled by the rhythmical breathing of the healthy and the dying man, must have nodded a little later.

The sound of weird lyric melody was what aroused me. Chords, vibrations, and harmonic ecstasies echoed passionately on every hand, while on my ravished sight burst the stupendous spectacle of ultimate beauty. Walls, columns, and architraves of living fire blazed effulgently around the spot where I seemed to float in air, extending upward to an infinitely high vaulted dome of indescribable splendor. Blending with this display of palatial magnificence, or rather, supplanting it at times in kaleidoscopic rotation, were glimpses of wide plains and graceful valleys, high mountains and inviting grottoes, covered with every lovely attribute of scenery which my delighted eyes could conceive of, yet formed wholly of some glowing, ethereal plastic entity, which in consistency partook as much of spirit as of matter. As I gazed, I perceived that my own brain held the key to these enchanting metamorphoses; for each vista which appeared to me was the one my changing mind most wished to behold. Amidst this elysian realm I dwelt not as a stranger, for each sight and sound was familiar to me; just as it had been for uncounted eons of eternity before, and would be for like eternities to come.

Then the resplendent aura of my brother of light drew near and held colloquy with me, soul to soul, with silent and perfect interchange of thought. The hour was one of approaching triumph, for was not my fellow-being escaping at last from a degrading periodic bondage; escaping forever, and preparing to follow the accursed oppressor even unto the uttermost fields of ether, that upon it might be wrought a flaming cosmic vengeance which would shake the spheres? We floated thus for a little time, when I perceived a slight blurring and fading of the objects around us, as though some force were recalling me to earth—where I least wished to go. The form near me seemed to feel a change also, for it gradually brought its discourse toward a conclusion, and itself prepared to quit the scene, fading from my sight at a rate somewhat less rapid than that of the other objects. A few more thoughts were exchanged, and I knew that the luminous one and I were being recalled to bondage, though for my brother of light it would be the last time. The sorry planet shell being well-nigh spent, in less than an hour my fellow would be free to pursue the oppressor along the Milky Way and past the hither stars to the very confines of infinity.

A well-defined shock separates my final impression of the fading scene of light from my sudden and somewhat shamefaced awakening and straightening up in my chair as I saw the dying figure on the couch move hesitantly. Joe Slater was indeed awaking, though probably for the last time. As I looked more closely, I saw that in the sallow cheeks shone spots of color which had never before been present. The lips, too, seemed unusual, being tightly compressed, as if by the force of a stronger character than had been Slater's. The whole face finally began to grow tense, and the head turned restlessly with closed eyes.

I did not rouse the sleeping nurse, but readjusted the slightly disarranged headband of my telepathic "radio," intent to catch any parting message the dreamer might have to deliver. All at once the head turned sharply in my direction and the eyes fell open, causing me to stare in blank amazement at what I beheld. The man who had been Joe Slater, the Catskill decadent, was gazing at me with a pair of luminous, expanding eyes whose blue seemed subtly to have deepened. Neither mania nor degeneracy was visible in that gaze, and I felt beyond a doubt that I was viewing a face behind which lay an active mind of high order.

At this juncture my brain became aware of a steady external influence operating upon it. I closed my eyes to concentrate my thoughts more profoundly and was rewarded by the positive knowledge that *my long-sought mental message had come at last*. Each transmitted idea formed rapidly in my mind, and though no actual language was employed, my habitual association of conception and expression was so great that I seemed to be receiving the message in ordinary English.

"Joe Slater is dead," came the soul-petrifying voice of an agency from beyond the wall of sleep. My opened eyes sought the couch of pain in curious horror, but the blue eyes were still calmly gazing, and the countenance was still intelligently animated. "He is better dead, for he

was unfit to bear the active intellect of cosmic entity. His gross body could not undergo the needed adjustments between ethereal life and planet life. He was too much an animal, too little a man; yet it is through his deficiency that you have come to discover me, for the cosmic and planet souls rightly should never meet. He has been in my torment and diurnal prison for forty-two of your terrestrial years.

"I am an entity like that which you yourself become in the freedom of dreamless sleep. I am your brother of light, and have floated with you in the effulgent valleys. It is not permitted me to tell your waking earth-self of your real self, but we are all roamers of vast spaces and travelers in many ages. Next year I may be dwelling in the Egypt which you call ancient, or in the cruel empire of Tsan Chan which is to come three thousand years hence. You and I have drifted to the worlds that reel about the red Arcturus, and dwelt in the bodies of the insect-philosophers that crawl proudly over the fourth moon of Jupiter. How little does the earth self know life and its extent! How little, indeed, ought it to know for its own tranquility!

"Of the oppressor I cannot speak. You on earth have unwittingly felt its distant presence—you who without knowing idly gave the blinking beacon the name of *Algol, the Demon-Star*. It is to meet and conquer the oppressor that I have vainly striven for eons, held back by bodily encumbrances. Tonight I go as a Nemesis bearing just and blazingly cataclysmic vengeance. *Watch me in the sky close by the Demon-Star.*

"I cannot speak longer, for the body of Joe Slater grows cold and rigid, and the coarse brains are ceasing to vibrate as I wish. You have been my only friend on this planet—the only soul to sense and seek for me within the repellent form which lies on this couch. We shall meet again—perhaps in the shining mists of Orion's Sword, perhaps on a bleak plateau in prehistoric Asia, perhaps in unremembered dreams tonight, perhaps in some other form an eon hence, when the solar system shall have been swept away."

At this point the thought-waves abruptly ceased, the pale eyes of the dreamer—or can I say dead man?—commenced to glaze fishily. In a half-stupor I crossed over to the couch and felt of his wrist, but found it cold, stiff, and pulseless. The sallow cheeks paled again, and the thick lips fell open, disclosing the repulsively rotten fangs of the degenerate Joe Slater. I shivered, pulled a blanket over the hideous face, and awakened the nurse. Then I left the cell and went silently to my room. I had an instant and unaccountable craving for a sleep whose dreams I should not remember.

The climax? What plain tale of science can boast of such a rhetorical effect? I have merely set down certain things appealing to me as facts, allowing you to construe them as you will. As I have already admitted, my superior, old Doctor Fenton, denies the reality of everything I have related. He vows that I was broken down with nervous strain, and badly in need of a long vacation on full pay which he so generously gave me. He assures me on his professional honor that Joe Slater was but a low-grade paranoiac, whose fantastic notions must have come from the crude hereditary folk-tales which circulated in even the most decadent of communities. All this he tells me—yet I cannot forget what I saw in the sky on the night after Slater died. Lest you think me a biased witness, another pen must add this final testimony, which may perhaps supply the climax you expect. I will quote the following account of the star *Nova Persei* verbatim from the pages of that eminent astronomical authority, Professor Garrett P. Serviss:

"On February 22, 1901, a marvelous new star was discovered by Doctor Anderson of Edinburgh, *not very far from Algol.* No star had been visible at that point before. Within twenty-four hours the stranger had become so bright that it outshone Capella. In a week or two it had visibly faded, and in the course of a few months it was hardly discernible with the naked eye."

Lovecraft's early weird fiction, which we have just sampled, is rather traditional in style. In the preceding three tables it is hard to see any prefiguring of the imaginative brilliance of the Cthulhu Mythos stories which was to follow in the closing years of the 1920's and to continue to manifest itself thenceforward until the end of his career.

It is not so much that "The Tomb," "Polaris," and "Beyond the Wall of Sleep" are poor stories. They are simply . . . uninspired.

Here follows something a bit different, his prose poems, or sketches, or vignettes—whatever you may wish to call them. The prose poem was popular with the more decadent French poets of the last century. In Lovecraft's day, his contemporary, colleague and correspondent, Clark Ashton Smith, also did excellent work in this form (see Smith's *Poems in Prose*, Arkham House, 1964).

MEMORY

In the valley of Nis the accursed waning moon shines thinly, tearing a path for its light with feeble horns through the lethal foliage of a great upas-tree. And within the depths of the valley, where the light reaches not, move forms not meant to be beheld. Rank is the herbage on each slope, where evil vines and creeping plants crawl amidst the stones of ruined palaces, twining tightly about broken columns and strange monoliths, and heaving up marble pavements laid by forgotten hands. And in trees that grow gigantic in crumbling courtyards leap little apes, while in and out of deep treasure-vaults writhe poison serpents and scaly things without a name.

Vast are the stones which sleep beneath coverlets of dank moss, and mighty were the walls from which they fell. For all time did their builders erect them, and in sooth they yet serve nobly, for beneath them the grey toad makes his habitation.

At the very bottom of the valley lies the river Than, whose waters are slimy and filled with weeds. From hidden springs it rises, and to subterranean grottoes it flows, so that the Daemon of the Valley knows not why its waters are red, nor whither they are bound.

The Genie that haunts the moonbeams spake to the Daemon of the Valley, saying, "I am old, and forget much. Tell me the deeds and aspect and name of them who built these things of Stone." And the Daemon replied, "I am Memory, and am wise in lore of the past, but I too am old. These beings were like the waters of the river Than, not to be understood. Their deeds I recall not, for they were but of the moment. Their aspect I recall dimly, it was like to that of the little apes in the trees. Their name I recall clearly, for it rhymed with that of the river. These beings of yesterday were called Man."

So the Genie flew back to the thin horned moon, and the Daemon looked intently at a little ape in a tree that grew in a crumbling courtyard.

WHAT THE MOON BRINGS

I hate the moon—I am afraid of it—for when it shines on certain scenes familiar and loved it sometimes makes them unfamiliar and hideous.

It was in the spectral summer when the moon shone down on the old garden where I wandered; the spectral summer of narcotic flowers and humid seas of foliage that bring wild and many-coloured dreams. And as I walked by the shallow crystal stream I saw unwonted ripples tipped with yellow light, as if those placid waters were drawn on in resistless currents to strange oceans that are not in the world. Silent and sparkling, bright and baleful, those moon-cursed waters hurried I knew not whither; whilst from the embowered banks white lotos-blossoms fluttered one by one in the opiate night-wind and dropped despairingly into the stream, swirling away horribly under the arched, carven bridge, and staring back with the sinister resignation of calm, dead faces.

And as I ran along the shore, crushing sleeping flowers with heedless feet and maddened ever by the fear of unknown things and the lure of the dead faces, I saw that the garden had no end under that moon; for where by day the walls were, there stretched now only new vistas of trees and paths, flowers and shrubs, stone idols and pagodas, and bendings of the yellow-litten stream past grassy banks and under grotesque bridges of marble. And the lips of the dead lotos-faces whispered sadly, and bade me follow, nor did I cease my steps till the stream became a river, and joined amidst marshes of swaying reeds and beaches of gleaming sand the shore of a vast and nameless sea.

Upon that sea the hateful moon shone, and over its unvocal waves weird perfumes breeded. And as I saw therein the lotos-faces vanish, I longed for nets that I might capture them and learn from them the secrets which the moon had brought upon the night. But when that moon went over to the west and the still tide ebbed from the sullen shore, I saw in that light old spires that the waves almost uncovered, and white columns gay with festoons of green seaweed. And knowing that to this sunken place all the dead had come, I trembled and did not wish again to speak with the lotos-faces.

Yet when I saw afar out in the sea a black condor descend from the sky to seek rest on a vast reef, I would fain have questioned him, and asked him of those whom I had known when they were alive. This I would have asked him had he not been so far away, but he was very far, and could not be seen at all when he drew nigh that gigantic reef.

So I watched the tide go out under that sinking moon, and saw gleaming the spires, the towers, and the roofs of that dead, dripping city. And as I watched, my nostrils tried to close against the perfume-conquering stench of the world's dead; for truly, in this unplaced and forgotten spot had all the flesh of the churchyards gathered for puffy sea-worms to gnaw and glut upon.

Over these horrors the evil moon now hung very low, but the puffy worms of the sea need no moon to feed by. And as I watched the ripples that told of the writhing of worms beneath, I felt a new chill from afar out whither the condor had flown, as if my flesh had caught a horror before my eyes had seen it.

Nor had my flesh trembled without cause, for when I raised my eyes I saw that the waters had ebbed very low, shewing much of the vast reef whose rim I had seen before. And when I saw that the reef was but the black basalt crown of a shocking eikon whose monstrous forehead now shown in the dim moonlight and whose vile hooves must paw the hellish ooze miles below, I shrieked and shrieked lest the hidden face rise above the waters, and lest the hidden eyes look at me after the slinking away of that leering and treacherous yellow moon.

And to escape this relentless thing I plunged gladly and unhesitantly into the stinking shallows where amidst weedy walls and sunken streets fat sea-worms feast upon the world's dead.

NYARLATHOTEP

Nyarlathotep . . . the crawling chaos . . . I am the last . . . I will tell the audient void . . .

I do not recall distinctly when it began, but it was months ago. The general tension was horrible. To a season of political and social upheaval was added a strange and brooding apprehension of hideous physical danger; a danger widespread and all-embracing, such a danger as may be imagined only in the most terrible phantasms of the night. I recall that the people went about with pale and worried faces, and whispered warnings and prophecies which no one dared consciously repeat or acknowledge to himself that he had heard. A sense of monstrous guilt was upon the land, and out of the abysses between the stars swept chill currents that made men shiver in dark and lonely places. There was a demoniac alteration in the sequence of the seasons—the autumn heat lingered fearsomely, and everyone felt that the world and perhaps the universe had passed from the control of known gods or forces to that of gods or forces which were unknown.

And it was then that Nyarlathotep came out of Egypt. Who he was, none could tell, but he was of the old native blood and looked like a Pharaoh. The fellahin knelt when they saw him, yet could not say why. He said he had risen up out of the blackness of twenty-seven centuries, and that he had heard messages from places not on this planet.

Into the lands of civilisation came Nyarlathotep, swarthy, slender, and sinister, always buying strange instruments of glass and metal and combining them into instruments yet stranger. He spoke much of the sciences—of electricity and psychology and gave exhibitions of power which sent his spectators away speechless, yet which swelled his fame to exceeding magnitude. Men advised one another to see Nyarlathotep, and shuddered. And where Nyarlathotep went, rest vanished, for the small hours were rent with the screams of nightmare. Never before had the screams of nightmare been such a public problem; now the wise men almost wished they could forbid sleep in the small hours, that the shrieks of cities might less horribly disturb the pale, pitying moon as it glimmered on green waters gliding under bridges, and old steeples crumbling against a sickly sky.

I remember when Nyarlathotep came to my city—the great, the old, the terrible city of unnumbered crimes. My friend had told me of him, and of the impelling fascination and allurement of his revelations, and I burned with eagerness to explore his uttermost mysteries. My friend said they were horrible and impressive beyond my most fevered imaginings; that what was thrown on a screen in the darkened room prophesied things none but Nyarlathotep dared prophesy, and in the sputter of his sparks there was taken from men that which had never been taken before yet which shewed only in the eyes. And I heard it hinted abroad that those who knew Nyarlathotep looked on sights which others saw not.

It was in the hot autumn that I went through the night with the restless crowds to see Nyarlathotep; through the stifling night and up the endless stairs into the choking room. And shadowed on a screen, I saw hooded forms amidst ruins, and yellow evil faces peering from behind fallen monuments. And I saw the world battling against blackness; against the waves of destruction from ultimate space; whirling, churning, struggling around the dimming, cooling sun. Then the sparks played amazingly around the heads of the spectators, and hair stood up on end whilst shadows more grotesque than I can tell came out and squatted on the heads. And when I, who was colder and more scientific than the rest, mumbled a trembling protest about "imposture" and "static electricity," Nyarlathotep drove us all out, down the dizzy stairs into the damp, hot, deserted midnight streets. I screamed aloud that I was *not* afraid; that I never could be afraid; and others screamed with me for solace. We swore to one another that the city *was* exactly the same, and still alive; and when the electric lights began to fade we cursed the company over and over again, and laughed at the queer faces we made.

I believe we felt something coming down from the greenish moon, for when we began to depend on its light we drifted into curious involuntary marching formations and seemed to know our destinations though we dared not think of them. Once we looked at the pavement and found the blocks loose and displaced by grass, with scarce a line of rusted metal to shew where the tramways had run. And again we saw a tram-car, lone, windowless, dilapidated, and almost on its side. When we gazed around the horizon, we could not find the third tower by the river, and noticed that the shilhouette of the second tower was ragged at the top. Then we split up into narrow columns, each of which seemed drawn in a different direction. One disappeared in a narrow alley to the left, leaving only the echo of a shocking moan. Another filed down a weed-choked subway entrance, howling with a laughter that was mad. My own column was sucked toward the open country, and presently I felt a chill which was not of the hot autumn; for as we stalked out on the dark moor, we beheld around us the hellish moon-glitter of evil snows. Trackless, inexplicable snows, swept asunder in one direction only, where lay a gulf all the blacker for its glittering walls. The column seemed very thin indeed as it plodded dreamily into the gulf. I lingered behind, for the black rift in the green-litten snow was frightful, and I thought I had heard the reverberations of a disquieting wail as my companions vanished; but my power to linger was slight. As if beckoned by those who had gone before, I half-floated between the titanic snowdrifts, quivering and afraid, into the sightless vortex of the unimaginable.

Screamingly sentient, dumbly delirious, only the gods that were can tell. A sickened, sensitive shadow writhing in hands that are not hands, and whirled blindly past ghastly midnights of rotting creation, corpses of dead worlds with sores that were cities, charnel winds that brush the pallid stars and make them flicker low. Beyond the worlds vague ghosts of monstrous things; half-seen columns of unsanctified temples that rest on nameless rocks beneath space and reach up to dizzy vacua above the spheres of light and darkness. And through this revolting graveyard of the universe the muffled, maddening beating of drums, and thin, monotonous whine of blasphemous flutes from inconceivable, unlighted chambers beyond Time; the detestable pounding and piping whereunto dance slowly, awkwardly, and absurdly the gigantic, tenebrous ultimate gods—the blind, voiceless, mindless gargoyles whose soul is Nyarlathotep.

EX OBLIVIONE

When the last days were upon me, and the ugly trifles of existence began to drive me to madness like the small drops of water that torturers let fall ceaselessly upon one spot of their victim's body, I loved the irradiate refuge of sleep. In my dreams I found a little of the beauty I had vainly sought in life, and wandered through old gardens and enchanted woods.

Once when the wind was soft and scented I heard the south calling, and sailed endlessly and languorously under strange stars.

Once when the gentle rain fell I glided in a barge down a sunless stream under the earth till I reached another world of purple twilight, iridescent arbours, and undying roses.

And once I walked through a golden valley that led to shadowy groves and ruins, and ended in a mighty wall green with antique vines, and pierced by a little gate of bronze.

Many times I walked through that valley, and longer and longer would I pause in the spectral half-light where the giant trees squirmed and twisted grotesquely, and the grey ground stretched damply from trunk to trunk, sometimes disclosing the mould-stained stones of buried temples. And always the goal of my fancies was the mighty vine-grown wall with the little gate of bronze therein.

After a while, as the days of waking became less and less bearable from their greyness and sameness, I would often drift in opiate peace through the valley and the shadowy groves, and wonder how I might seize them for my eternal dwelling-place, so that I need no more crawl back to a dull world stript of interest and new colours. And as I looked upon the little gate in the mighty wall, I felt that beyond it lay a dream-country from which, once it was entered, there would be no return.

So each night in sleep I strove to find the hidden latch of the gate in the ivied antique wall, though it was exceedingly well hidden. And I would tell myself that the realm beyond the wall was not more lasting merely, but more lovely and radiant as well.

Then one night in the dream-city of Zakarion I found a yellowed papyrus filled with the thoughts of dream-sages who dwelt of old in that city, and who were too wise ever to be born in the waking world. Therein were written many things concerning the world of dream, and among them was lore of a golden valley and a sacred grove with temples, and a high wall pierced by a little bronze gate. When I saw this lore, I knew that it touched on the scenes I had haunted, and I therefore read long in the yellowed papyrus.

Some of the dream-sages wrote gorgeously of the wonders beyond the irrepassable gate, but others told of horror and disappointment. I knew not which to believe, yet longed more and more to cross for ever into the unknown land; for doubt and secrecy are the lure of lures, and no new horror can be more terrible than the daily torture of the commonplace. So when I learned of the drug which would unlock the gate and drive me through, I resolved to take it when next I awaked.

Last night I swallowed the drug and floated dreamily into the golden valley and the shadowy groves; and when I came this time to the antique wall, I saw that the small gate of bronze was ajar. From beyond came a glow that weirdly lit the giant twisted trees and the tops of the buried temples, and I drifted on songfully, expectant of the glories of the land from whence I should never return.

But as the gate swung wider and the sorcery of the drug and dream pushed me through, I knew that all sights and glories were at an end; for in that new realm was neither land nor sea, but only the white void of unpeopled and illimitable space. So, happier than I had ever dared hope to be, I dissolved again into that native infinity of crystal oblivion from which the daemon Life had called me for one brief and desolate hour.

The next story, "The Cats of Ulthar," had an amusing genesis. In a long, chatty letter to his friend, Reinhardt Kleiner, dated May 21, 1920, Lovecraft described the germinal roots of the tale:

> I had a visitor the other night, who gave me an idea for a good story. He was a furry, four-footed young visitor, with a black coat, white gloves and boots, and white around the tip of his nose and the tip of his tail. He sat in a chair near me, purring most inspiringly, when I permitted my fancy to consider his ancient race and heritage. I am intensely fond of his species, as I have doubtless told you more than once; and as I looked upon him my thoughts ran thus: . . . The cat is the soul of antique Aegyptus, and bearer of tales from forgotten empires in Moroë [*sic.*; Lovecraft means "Meroë"] and Ophir. He is the kin of the jungle's lords, and heir to the secrets of hoary and sinister Africa. The Sphinx is his cousin, and he speaks her language; but he is more ancient than the Sphinx, and remembers that which she hath forgotten . . . As I mused, a plot took form in my mind. A simple, yet a ghastly plot. And the plot will some day reach the amateur publick in the form of a tale to be entitled "The Cats of Ulthar" . . . I am only beginning my delvings into the world of literary fantasy.

THE CATS OF ULTHAR

It is said that in Ulthar, which lies beyond the river Skai, no man may kill a cat; and this I can verily believe as I gaze upon him who sitteth purring before the fire. For the cat is cryptic, and close to strange things which men cannot see. He is the soul of antique Aegyptus, and bearer of tales from forgotten cities in Meroë and Ophir. He is the kin of the jungle's lords, and heir to the secrets of hoary and sinister Africa. The Sphinx is his cousin, and he speaks her language; but he is more ancient than the Sphinx, and remembers that which she hath forgotten.

In Ulthar, before ever the burgesses forbade the killing of cats, there dwelt an old cotter and his wife who delighted to trap and slay the cats of their neighbors. Why they did this I know not; save that many hate the voice of the cat in the night, and take it ill that cats should run stealthily about yards and gardens at twilight. But whatever the reason, this old man and woman took pleasure in trapping and slaying every cat which came near to their hovel; and from some of the sounds heard after dark, many villagers fancied that the manner of slaying was exceedingly peculiar. But the villagers did not discuss such things with the old man and his wife; because of the habitual expression on the withered faces of the two, and because their cottage was so small and so darkly hidden under spreading oaks at the back of a neglected yard. In truth, much as the owners of cats hated these odd folk, they feared them more; and instead of berating them as brutal assassins, merely took care that no cherished pet or mouser should stray toward the remote hovel under the dark trees. When through some unavoidable oversight a cat was missed, and sounds heard after dark, the loser would lament impotently; or console himself by thanking Fate that it was not one of his children who had thus vanished. For the people of Ulthar were simple, and knew not whence it is all cats first came.

One day a caravan of strange wanderers from the South entered the narrow cobbled streets of Ulthar. Dark wanderers they were, and unlike the other roving folk who passed through the village twice every year. In the market-place they told fortunes for silver, and bought gay beads from the merchants. What was the land of these wanderers none could tell; but it was seen that they were given to strange prayers, and that they had painted on the sides of their wagons strange figures with human bodies and the heads of cats, hawks, rams and lions. And the leader of the caravan wore a headdress with two horns and a curious disk betwixt the horns.

There was in this singular caravan a little boy with no father or mother, but only a tiny black kitten to cherish. The plague had not been kind to him, yet had left him this small furry thing to mitigate his sorrow; and when one is very young, one can find great relief in the lively antics of a black kitten. So the boy whom the dark people called Menes smiled more often than he wept as he sat playing with his graceful kitten on the steps of an oddly painted wagon.

On the third morning of the wanderers' stay in Ulthar, Menes could not find his kitten; and as he sobbed aloud in the market-place certain villagers told him of the old man and his wife, and of sounds heard in the night. And when he heard these things his sobbing gave place to meditation, and finally to prayer. He stretched out his arms toward the sun and prayed in a tongue no villager could understand; though indeed the villagers did not try very hard to understand, since their attention was mostly taken up by the sky and the odd shapes the clouds were assuming. It was very peculiar, but as the little boy uttered his petition there seemed to form overhead the shadowy, nebulous figures of exotic things; of hybrid creatures crowned with horn-flanked disks. Nature is full of such illusions to impress the imaginative.

That night the wanderers left Ulthar, and were never seen again. And the householders were troubled when they noticed that in all the village there was not a cat to be found. From each hearth the familiar cat had vanished; cats large and small, black, grey, striped, yellow and white. Old Kranon, the burgomaster, swore that the dark folk had taken the cats away in revenge for the killing of Menes' kitten; and cursed the caravan and the little boy. But Nith, the lean notary, declared that the old cotter and his wife were more likely persons to suspect; for their hatred of cats was notorious and increasingly bold. Still, no one durst complain to the sinister couple; even when little Atal, the innkeeper's son, vowed that he had at twilight seen all the cats of Ulthar in that accursed yard under the trees, pacing very slowly and solemnly in a circle around the cottage, two abreast, as if in performance of some unheard-of rite of beasts. The villagers did not know how much to believe from so small a boy; and though they feared that the evil pair had charmed the cats to their death, they preferred not to chide the old cotter till they met him outside his dark and repellent yard.

So Ulthar went to sleep in vain anger; and when the people awakened at dawn—behold! every cat was back at his accustomed hearth! Large and small, black, grey, striped, yellow and white, none was missing. Very sleek and fat did the cats appear, and sonorous with purring content. The citizens talked with one another of the affair, and marveled not a little. Old Kranon again insisted that it was the dark folk who had taken them, since cats did not return alive from the cottage of the ancient man and his wife. But all agreed on one thing: that the refusal of all the cats to eat their portions of meat or drink their saucers of milk was exceedingly curious. And for two whole days the sleek, lazy cats of Ulthar would touch no food, but only doze by the fire or in the sun.

It was fully a week before the villagers noticed that no lights were appearing at dusk in the windows of the cottage under the trees. Then the lean Nith remarked that no one had seen the old man or his wife since the night the cats were away. In another week the burgomaster decided to overcome his fears and call at the strangely silent dwelling as a matter of duty, though in so doing he was careful to take with him Shang the blacksmith and Thul the cutter of stone as witnesses. And when they had broken down the frail door they found only this: two cleanly picked human skeletons on the earthen floor, and a number of singular beetles crawling in the shadowy corners.

There was subsequently much talk among the burgesses of Ulthar. Zath, the coroner, disputed at length with Nith, the lean notary; and Kranon and Shang and Thul were overwhelmed with questions. Even little Atal, the innkeeper's son, was closely questioned and given a sweetmeat as reward. They talked of the old cotter and his wife, of the caravan of dark wanderers, of small Menes and his black kitten, of the prayer of Menes and of the sky during that prayer, of the doings of the cats on the night the caravan left, and of what was later found in the cottage under the dark trees in the repellent yard.

And in the end the burgesses passed that remarkable law which is told of by traders in Hatheg and discussed by travelers in Nir; namely, that in Ulthar no man may kill a cat.

Lovecraft was very interested from his earliest youth in Greek mythology and literature. This element in his range of interests is seen in "The Tree," which appeared earlier in this book, "Hypnos," the tale which follows, and the poem "Nathicana" after it.

As for Hypnos himself, he is (or was) a very minor, although genuine, deity in the Greek pantheon, and does not belong among H.P.L.'s invented gods like Nyarlathotep, Azathoth, or Cthulhu, whom Lovecraft, lumped together in a single pantheon and called "the Old Ones." I suppose it is known only to specialists, but Greek mythology includes a very great number of minor godlings and godlets, besides the more famous Olympians: divinities such as Moros, Momus, Oizus, Eris, Pontus, Tyche, Metis, Eos, and others.* At any rate, the *Larousse Encyclopedia of Mythology* states that Hypnos (Sleep) and his brother Thanatos (Death) were the sons of the goddess of Night. Hypnos himself fathered Morpheus (Dreams), and Homer tells how at the request of Hera, Queen of Heaven, he took the form of a night bird and sent Zeus to sleep on Mount Ida. These allegorical divinities, incidentally, were not each the subject of worship, with his own temple and priests: some of them were merely names in the various genealogies of the Gods, such as the above, which is from the *Theogony* of Hesiod.

*Moros is Doom, Momus is "Gaiety," Oizus is "Misery," Eris is "Strife," Pontos is "Sea," Tyche is "Fortune," Metis is "Wisdom," and Eos is "Dawn." I suppose many of these little gods became absorbed in later, more important divinities; Pontos in Poseidon, for example, or Metis in Athene.

HYPNOS

> Apropos of sleep, that sinister adventure of all our nights, we may say that men go to bed daily with an audacity that would be incomprehensible if we did not know that it is the result of ignorance of the danger.
>
> —BAUDELAIRE

May the merciful gods, if indeed there be such, guard those hours when no power of the will, or drug that the cunning of man devises, can keep me from the chasm of sleep. Death is merciful, for there is no return therefrom, but with him who has come back out of the nethermost chambers of night, haggard and knowing, peace rests nevermore. Fool that I was to plunge with such unsanctioned phrensy into mysteries no man was meant to penetrate; fool or god that he was—my only friend, who led me and went before me, and who in the end passed into terrors which may yet be mine!

We met, I recall, in a railway station, where he was the center of a crowd of the vulgarly curious. He was unconscious, having fallen in a kind of convulsion which imparted to his slight black-clad body a strange rigidity. I think he was then approaching forty years of age, for there were deep lines in the face, wan and hollow-cheeked, but oval and actually beautiful; and touches of gray in the thick, waving hair and small full beard which had once been of the deepest raven black. His brow was white as the marble of Pentelicus, and of a height and breadth almost god-like.

I said to myself, with all the ardor of a sculptor, that this man was a faun's statue out of antique Hellas, dug from a temple's ruins and brought somehow to life in our stifling age only to feel the chill and pressure of devastating years. And when he opened his immense, sunken, and wildly luminous black eyes I knew he would be thenceforth my only friend—the only friend of one who had never possessed a friend before—for I saw that such eyes must have looked fully upon the grandeur and the terror of realms beyond normal consciousness and reality; realms which I had cherished in fancy, but vainly sought. So as I drove the crowd away I told him he must come home with me and be my teacher and leader in unfathomed mysteries, and he assented without speaking a word. Afterward I found that his voice was music—the music of deep viols and of crystalline spheres. We talked often in the night, and in the day, when I chiseled busts of him and carved miniature heads in ivory to immortalize his different expressions.

Of our studies it is impossible to speak, since they held so slight a connection with anything of the world as living men conceive it. They were of that vaster and more appalling universe of dim entity and consciousness which lies deeper than matter, time, and space, and whose existence we suspect only in certain forms of sleep—those rare dreams beyond dreams which come never to common men, and but once or twice in the lifetime of imaginative men. The cosmos of our waking knowledge, born from such an universe as a bubble is born from the pipe of a jester, touches it only as such a bubble may touch its sardonic source when sucked back by the jester's whim. Men of learning suspect it little and ignore it mostly. Wise men have interpreted dreams, and the gods have laughed. One man with Oriental eyes has said that all time and space are relative, and men have laughed. But even that man with Oriental eyes has done no more than suspect. I had wished and tried to do more than suspect, and my friend had tried and partly succeeded. Then we both tried together, and with exotic drugs courted terrible and forbidden dreams in the tower studio chamber of the old manor-house in hoary Kent.

Among the agonies of these after days is that chief of torments—inarticulateness. What I learned and saw in those hours of impious exploration can never be told—for want of symbols or suggestions in any language. I say this because from first to last our discoveries partook only of the nature of sensations; sensations correlated with no impression which the nervous system of normal humanity is capable of receiving. They were sensations, yet within them lay unbelievable elements of time and space—things which at bottom possess no distinct and definite existence. Human utterance can best convey the general character of our experiences by calling them plungings or soarings; for in every period of revelation some part of our minds broke boldly away from all that is real and present, rushing aerially along shocking, unlighted, and fear-haunted abysses, and occasionally tearing through certain well-marked and typical obstacles describable only as viscous, uncouth clouds of vapors.

In these black and bodiless flights we were sometimes alone and sometimes together. When we were together, my friend was always far ahead; I could comprehend his presence despite the absence of form by a species of pictorial memory whereby his face appeared to me, golden from a strange light and frightful with its weird beauty, its anomalously youthful cheeks, its burning eyes, its Olympian brow, and its shadowing hair and growth of beard.

Of the progress of time we kept no record, for time had become to us the merest illusion. I know only that there must have been something very singular involved, since we came at length to marvel why we did not grow old. Our discourse was unholy, and always hideously ambitious—no god or daemon could have aspired to discoveries and conquest like those which we planned in whispers. I shiver as I speak of them, and dare not be explicit; though I will say that my friend once wrote on paper a wish which he dared not utter with his tongue, and which made me burn the paper and look affrightedly out of the window at the spangled night sky. I will hint—only hint—that he had designs which involved the rulership of the visible universe and more; designs whereby the earth and the stars would move at his command, and the destinies of all living things be his. I affirm—I swear—that I had no share in these extreme aspirations. Anything my friend may have said or written to the contrary must be erroneous, for I am no man of strength to risk the unmentionable spheres by which alone one might achieve success.

There was a night when winds from unknown spaces whirled us irresistibly into limitless vacua beyond all thought and entity. Perceptions of the most maddeningly untransmissible sort thronged upon us; perceptions of infinity which at the time convulsed us with joy, yet which are now partly lost to my memory and partly incapable of presentation to others. Viscous obstacles were clawed through in rapid succession, and at length I felt that we had been borne to realms of greater remoteness than any we had previously known.

My friend was vastly in advance as we plunged into this awesome ocean of virgin aether, and I could see the sinister exultation on his floating, luminous, too-youthful memory-face. Suddenly that face became dim and quickly disappeared, and in a brief space I found myself projected against an obstacle which I could not penetrate. It was like the others, yet incalculably denser; a sticky clammy mass, if such terms can be applied to analogous qualities in a non-material sphere.

I had, I felt, been halted by a barrier which my friend and leader had successfully passed. Struggling anew, I came to the end of the drug-dream and opened my physical eyes to the tower studio in whose opposite corner reclined the pallid and still unconscious form of my fellow dreamer, weirdly haggard and wildly beautiful as the moon shed gold-green light on his marble features.

Then, after a short interval, the form in the corner stirred; and may pitying heaven keep from my sight and sound another thing like that which took place before me. I cannot tell you how he shrieked, or what vistas of unvisitable hells gleamed for a second in black eyes crazed with fright. I can only say that I fainted, and did not stir till he himself recovered and shook me in his phrensy for someone to keep away the horror and desolation.

That was the end of our voluntary searchings in the caverns of dream. Awed, shaken, and portentous, my friend who had been beyond the barrier warned me that we must never venture within those realms again. What he had seen, he dared not tell me; but he said from his wisdom that we must sleep as little as possible, even if drugs were necessary to keep us awake. That he was right, I soon learned from the unutterable fear which engulfed me whenever consciousness lapsed.

After each short and inevitable sleep I seemed older, whilst my friend aged with a rapidity almost shocking. It is hideous to see wrinkles form and hair whiten almost before one's eyes. Our mode of life was now totally altered. Heretofore a recluse so far as I know—his true name and origin never having passed his lips—my friend now became frantic in his fear of solitude. At night he would not be alone, nor would the company of a few persons calm him. His sole relief was obtained in revelry of the most general and boisterous sort; so that few assemblies of the young and gay were unknown to us.

Our appearance and age seemed to excite in most cases a ridicule which I keenly resented, but which my friend considered a lesser evil than solitude. Especially was he afraid to be out of doors alone when the stars were shining, and if forced to this condition he would often glance furtively at the sky as if hunted by some monstrous thing therein. He did not always glance at the same place in the sky—it seemed to be a different place at different times. On spring evenings it would be low in the northeast. In the summer it would be nearly overhead. In the autumn it would be in the northwest. In winter it would be in the east, but mostly if in the small hours of morning.

Midwinter evenings seemed least dreadful to him. Only after two years did I connect this fear with anything in particular; but then I began to see that he must be looking at a special spot on the celestial vault whose position at different times corresponded to the direction of his glance —a spot roughly marked by the constellation Corona Borealis.

We now had a studio in London, never separating, but never discussing the days when we had sought to plumb the mysteries of the unreal world. We were aged and weak from our drugs, dissipations, and nervous overstrain, and the thinning hair and beard of my friend had become snow-white. Our freedom from long sleep was surprising, for seldom did we succumb more than an hour or two at a time to the shadow which had now grown so frightful a menace.

Then came one January of fog and rain, when money ran low and drugs were hard to buy. My statues and ivory heads were all sold, and I had no means to purchase new materials, or energy to fashion them even had I possessed them. We suffered terribly, and on a certain night my friend sank into a deep-breathing sleep from which I could not awaken him. I can recall the scene now—the desolate, pitch-black garret studio under the eaves with the rain beating down; the ticking of our lone clock; the fancied ticking of our watches as they rested on the dressing-table; the creaking of some swaying shutter in a remote part of the house; certain distant city noises muffled by fog and space; and, worst of all, the deep, steady, sinister breathing of my friend on the couch—a rhythmical breathing which seemed to measure moments of supernal fear and agony for his spirit as it wandered in spheres forbidden, unimagined, and hideously remote.

The tension of my vigil became oppressive, and a wild train of trivial impressions and associations thronged through my almost unhinged mind. I heard a clock strike somewhere—not ours, for that was not a striking clock—and my morbid fancy found in this a new starting-point for idle wanderings. Clocks—time—space—infinity—and then my fancy reverted to the locale as I reflected that even now, beyond the roof and the fog and the rain and the atmosphere, Corona Borealis was rising in the northeast. Corona Borealis, which my friend had appeared to dread, and whose scintillant semicircle of stars must even now be glowing unseen through the measureless abysses of aether. All at once my feverishly sensitive ears seemed to detect a new and wholly distinct component in the soft medley of drug-magnified sounds—a low and damnably insistent whine from very far away; droning, clamoring, mocking, calling, *from the northeast.*

But it was not that distant whine which robbed me of my faculties and set upon my soul such a seal of fright as may never in life be removed; not that which drew the shrieks and excited the convulsions which caused lodgers and police to break down the door. It was not what I heard, but what I saw; for in that dark, locked, shuttered, and curtained room there appeared from the black northeast corner a shaft of horrible red-gold light—a shaft which bore with it no glow to disperse the darkness, but which streamed only upon the recumbent head of the troubled sleeper, bringing out in hideous duplication the luminous and strangely youthful memory-face as I had known it in dreams of abysmal space and unshackled time, when my friend had pushed behind the barrier to those secret, innermost and forbidden caverns of nightmare.

And as I looked, I beheld the head rise, the black, liquid, and deep-sunken eyes open in terror, and the thin, shadowed lips part as if for a scream too frightful to be uttered. There dwelt in that ghastly and flexible face, as it shone bodiless, luminous, and rejuvenated in the blackness, more of stark, teeming, brain-shattering fear than all the rest of heaven and earth has ever revealed to me.

No word was spoken amidst the distant sound that grew nearer and nearer, but as I followed the memory-face's mad stare along that cursed shaft of light to its source, the source whence also the whining came, I, too, saw for an instant what it saw, and fell with ringing ears in that fit of shrieking epilepsy which brought the lodgers and the police. Never could I tell, try as I might, what it actually was that I saw; nor could the still face tell, for although it must have seen more than I did, it will never speak again. But always I shall guard against the mocking and insatiate Hypnos, lord of sleep, against the night sky, and against the mad ambitions of knowledge and philosophy.

Just what happened is unknown, for not only was my own mind unseated by the strange and hideous thing, but others were tainted with a forgetfulness which can mean nothing if not madness. They have said, I know not for what reason, that I never had a friend; but that art, philosophy, and insanity had filled all my tragic life. The lodgers and police on that night soothed me, and the doctor administered something to quiet me, nor did anyone see what a nightmare event had taken place. My stricken friend moved them to no pity, but what they found on the couch in the studio made them give me a praise which sickened me, and now a fame which I spurn in despair as I sit for hours, bald, gray-bearded, shriveled, palsied, drug-crazed, and broken, adoring and praying to the object they found.

For they deny that I sold the last of my statuary, and point with ecstasy at the thing which the shining shaft of light left cold, petrified, and unvocal. It is all that remains of my friend; the friend who led me on to madness and wreckage; a godlike head of such marble as only old Hellas could yield, young with the youth that is outside time, and with beauteous bearded face, curved, smiling lips, Olympian brow, and dense locks waving and poppy-crowned. They say that that haunting memory-face is modeled from my own, as it was at twenty-five; but upon the marble base is carven a single name in the letters of Attica—HYPNOS.

Lovecraft thought of himself as a poet and he wrote endless reams of the stuff. A considerable quantity of his verse was written in imitation of the "occasional" verse of his beloved eighteenth century; his models were long-winded versifiers like Alexander Pope, Robert Southey, *et al.*, and this portion of his verse is pretty awful. He also produced some macabre verse, such as his sonnet sequence, *Fungi from Yuggoth*, or the narrative poem *Psychopompos*, which is a werewolf legend set in medieval France. This part of his work is not bad at all; the sonnets in particular are quite striking and effective.

Ballantine Books plans to issue some of Lovecraft's verse soon, so I was forced to travel rather far afield to find a sample of his poetry for inclusion here that would not duplicate the contents of the prospective verse collection. The following poem, a verse narrative ninety-nine lines long, was obviously written in imitation of such poems of Edgar Allan Poe as "Ulalume." It merits reprinting here, if only because of its extreme rarity.

"Nathicana" first appeared in an amateur magazine, *The Vagrant*, in 1927; it was published under one of Lovecraft's pen names, "Albert Frederick Willie." For some reason Arkham House did not include it in Lovecraft's *Collected Poems*, which they had published in 1963; since it first appeared in *The Vagrant* it has been reprinted only once, and that appearance was in 1955, in a mimeographed compilation called *The Lovecraft Collector's Library*, published in North Tonawanda, N. Y., in a limited printing of seventy-five copies.

NATHICANA

It was in the pale garden of Zais;
The mist-shrouded gardens of Zais,
Where blossoms the white nephalot,
The redolent herald of midnight.
There slumber the still lakes of crystal,
And streamlets that flow without murm'ring;
Smooth streamlets from caverns of Kathos
Where broodth the calm spirits of twilight.
And over the lakes and the streamlets
Are bridges of pure alabaster,
White bridges all cunningly carven
With figures of fairies and daemons.
Here glimmer strange suns and strange planets,
And strange is the crescent Banapis
That sets 'yond the ivy-grown ramparts
Where thicken the dusk of the evening.
Here fall the white vapours of Yabon;
The thought-blotting vapours of Yabon;
And here in the swirl of the vapours
I saw the divine Nathicana;
The garlanded, white Nathicana;
The slender, black-hair'd Nathicana;
The sloe-eyed, red-lipped Nathicana;
The silver-voiced, sweet Nathicana;
The pale-rob'd, belov'd Nathicana.

And ever was she my beloved,
From ages when time was unfashioned;
From days when the stars were not fashioned
Nor anything fashion'd but Yabon.
And here dwelt we ever and ever,
The innocent children of Zais,
At peace in the paths and the arbours,
White-crowned with the blest nephalote.
How oft would we float in the twilight
O'er flow'r-cover'd pastures and hillsides
All white with the lowly astalthon;
The lowly yet lovely astalthon,
And dream in a world made of dreaming
The dreams that are fairer than Aidenn;
Bright dreams that are truer than reason!
So dreamed and so lov'd we thro' ages,
Till came the cursed season of Dzannin;
The daemon-damn'd season of Dzannin;
When red shone the suns and the planets,
And red gleamed the crescent Banapis,
And red fell the vapours of Yabon.
Then redden'd the blossoms and streamlets
And lakes that lay under the bridges,
And even the calm alabaster
Glowed pink with uncanny reflections
Till all the carv'd fairies and daemons
Leer'd redly from backgrounds of shadow.
Now redden'd my vision, and madly
I strove to peer thro' the dense curtain
And glimpsed the divine Nathicana;
The pure, ever-pale Nathicana;
The lov'd, the unchang'd Nathicana.
But vortex on vortex of madness
Beclouded my labouring vision;
My damnable, reddening vision
That built a new world for my seeing;
A new world of redness and darkness,
A horrible coma called living.
So now in this coma call'd living
I view the bright phantoms of beauty;

The false, hollow phantoms of beauty
That cloak all the evils of Dzannin.
I view them with infinite longing,
So like do they seem to my lov'd one:
Yet foul from their eyes shines their evil;
Their cruel and pitiless evil,
More evil than Thaphron or Latgoz,
Twice ill for its gorgeous concealment.
And only in slumbers of midnight
Appears the lost maid Nathicana,
The pallid, the pure Nathicana
Who fades at the glance of the dreamer.
Again and again do I seek her;
I woo with deep draughts of Plathotis,
Deep draughts brew'd in wine of Astarte
And strengthen'd with tears of long weeping.
I yearn for the gardens of Zais;
The lovely, lost gardens of Zais
Where blossoms the white nephalot,
The redolent herald of midnight.
The last potent draught am I brewing;
A draught that the daemons delight in;
A draught that will banish the redness;
The horrible coma call'd living.
Soon, soon, if I fail not in brewing,
The redness and madness will vanish,
And deep in the worm-peopl'd darkness
Will rot the base chains that have bound me.
Once more shall the gardens of Zais
Dawn white on my long-tortur'd vision,
And there midst the vapours of Yabon
Will stand the divine Nathicana;
The deathless, restor'd Nathicana
Whose like is not met with in living

Lovecraft's "traditional" weird fiction gradually transmogrified itself into his Cthulhu tales, the precise transition occurring with the writing of "The Call of Cthulhu" in 1926. In the three macabre tales which follow, you can observe the Cthulhuoid elements gathering in his stories until they begin to predominate. ("From Beyond," incidentally, was written on November 18, 1920—one week after he wrote "Celephais," which is one of the most Dunsanian of all his dream-fantasies).

FROM BEYOND

Horrible beyond conception was the change which had taken place in my best friend, Crawford Tillinghast. I had not seen him since that day, two months and a half before, when he told me toward what goal his physical and metaphysical researches were leading; when he had answered my awed and almost frightened remonstrances by driving me from his laboratory and his house in a burst of fanatical rage, I had known that he now remained mostly shut in the attic laboratory with that accursed electrical machine, eating little and excluding even the servants, but I had not thought that a brief period of ten weeks could so alter and disfigure any human creature. It is not pleasant to see a stout man suddenly grown thin, and it is even worse when the baggy skin becomes yellowed or greyed, the eyes sunken, circled, and uncannily glowing, the forehead veined and corrugated, and the hands tremulous and twitching. And if added to this there be a repellent unkemptness, a wild disorder of dress, a bushiness of dark hair white at the roots, and an unchecked growth of white beard on a face once clean-shaven, the cumulative effect is quite shocking. But such was the aspect of Crawford Tillinghast on the night his half coherent message brought me to his door after my weeks of exile; such was the spectre that trembled as it admitted me, candle in hand, and glanced furtively over its shoulder as if fearful of unseen things in the ancient, lonely house set back from Benevolent Street.

That Crawford Tillinghast should ever have studied science and philosophy was a mistake. These things should be left to the frigid and impersonal investigator for they offer two equally tragic alternatives to the man of feeling and action; despair, if he fail in his quest, and terrors unutterable and unimaginable if he succeed. Tillinghast had once been the prey of failure, solitary and melancholy; but now I knew, with nauseating fears of my own, that he was the prey of success. I had indeed warned him ten weeks before, when he burst forth with his tale of what he felt himself about to discover. He had been flushed and excited then, talking in a high and unnatural, though always pedantic, voice.

"What do we know," he had said, "of the world and the universe about us? Our means of receiving impressions are absurdly few, and our notions of surrounding objects infinitely narrow. We see things only as we are constructed to see them, and can gain no idea of their absolute nature. With five feeble senses we pretend to comprehend the boundlessly complex cosmos, yet other beings with a wider, stronger, or different range of senses might not only see very differently the things we see, but might see and study whole worlds of matter, energy, and life which lie close at hand yet can never be detected with the senses we have. I have always believed that such strange, inaccessible worlds exist at our very elbows, *and now I believe I have found a way to break down the barriers*. I am not joking. Within twenty-four hours that machine near the table will generate waves acting on unrecognized sense-organs that exist in us as atrophied or rudimentary vestiges. Those waves will open up to us many vistas unknown to man, and several unknown to anything we consider organic life. We shall see that at which dogs howl in the dark, and that at which cats prick up their ears after midnight. We shall see these things, and other things which no breathing creature has yet seen. We shall overleap time, space, and dimensions, and without bodily motion peer to the bottom of creation."

When Tillinghast said these things I remonstrated, for I knew him well enough to be frightened rather than amused; but he was a fanatic, and drove me from the house. Now he was no less a fanatic, but his desire to speak had conquered his resentment, and he had written me imperatively in a hand I could scarcely recognize. As I entered the abode of the friend so suddenly metamorphosed to a shivering gargoyle, I became infected with the terror which seemed stalking in all the shadows. The words and beliefs expressed ten weeks before seemed bodied forth in the darkness beyond the small circle of candle light, and I sickened at the hollow, altered voice of my host. I wished the servants were about, and did not like it when he said they had all left three days previously. It seemed strange that old Gregory, at least, should desert his master without telling as tried a friend as I. It was he who had given me all the information I had of Tillinghast after I was repulsed in rage.

Yet I soon subordinated all my fears to my growing curiosity and fascination. Just what Crawford Tillinghast now wished of me I could only guess, but that he had some stupendous secret or discovery to impart, I could not doubt. Before I had protested at his unnatural pryings into the unthinkable; now that he had evidently succeeded to some degree I almost shared his spirit, terrible though the cost of victory appeared. Up through the dark emptiness of the house I followed the bobbing candle in the hand of this shaking parody on man. The electricity seemed to be turned off, and when I asked my guide he said it was for a definite reason.

"It would be too much. . . . I would not dare," he continued to mutter. I especially noted his new habit of muttering, for it was not like him to talk to himself. We entered the laboratory in the attic, and I observed that detestable electrical machine, glowing with a sickly, sinister violet luminosity. It was connected with a powerful chemical battery, but seemed to be receiving no current; for I recalled that in its experimental stage it had sputtered and purred when in action. In reply to my question Tillinghast mumbled that this permanent glow was not electrical in any sense that I could understand.

He now seated me near the machine, so that it was on my right, and turned a switch somewhere below the crowning cluster of glass bulbs. The usual sputtering began, turned to a whine, and terminated in a drone so soft as to suggest a return to silence. Meanwhile the luminosity increased, waned again, then assumed a pale, outré colour or blend of colours which I could neither place nor describe. Tillinghast had been watching me, and noted my puzzled expression.

"Do you know what that is?" he whispered, *"that is ultra-violet."* He chuckled oddly at my surprise. "You thought ultra-violet was invisible, and so it is—but you can see that and many other invisible things *now*.

"Listen to me! The waves from that thing are waking a thousand sleeping senses in us; senses which we inherit from aeons of evolution from the state of detached electrons to the state of organic humanity. I have seen the *truth*, and I intend to show it to you. Do you wonder how it will seem? I will tell you." Here Tillinghast seated himself directly opposite me, blowing out his candle and staring hideously into my eyes. "Your existing sense-organs —ears first, I think—will pick up many of the impressions, for they are closely connected with the dormant organs. Then there will be others. You have heard of the pineal gland? I laugh at the shallow endocrinologist, fellow-dupe and fellow-parvenu of the Freudian. That gland is the great sense organ of organs—I *have found out*. It is like sight in the end, and transmits visual pictures to the brain. If you are normal, that is the way you ought to get most of it . . . I mean get most of the evidence *from beyond.*"

I looked about the immense attic room with the sloping south wall, dimly lit by rays which the every-day eye cannot see. The far corners were all shadows, and the whole place took on a hazy unreality which obscured its nature and invited the imagination to symbolism and phantasm. During the interval that Tillinghast was silent I fancied myself in some vast incredible temple of long-dead gods;

some vague edifice of innumerable black stone columns reaching up from a floor of damp slabs to a cloudy height beyond the range of my vision. The picture was very vivid for a while, but gradually gave way to a more horrible conception; that of utter, absolute solitude in infinite, sightless, soundless space. There seemed to be a void, and nothing more, and I felt a childish fear which prompted me to draw from my hip pocket the revolver I always carried after dark since the night I was held up in East Providence. Then, from the farthermost regions of remoteness, the *sound* softly glided into existence. It was infinitely faint, subtly vibrant, and unmistakably musical, but held a quality of surpassing wildness which made its impact feel like a delicate torture of my whole body. I felt sensations like those one feels when accidentally scratching ground glass. Simultaneously there developed something like a cold draught, which apparently swept past me from the direction of the distant sound. As I waited breathlessly I perceived that both sound and wind were increasing; the effect being to give me an odd notion of myself as tied to a pair of rails in the path of a gigantic approaching locomotive. I began to speak to Tillinghast, and as I did so all the unusual impressions abruptly vanished. I saw only the man, the glowing machines, and the dim apartment. Tillinghast was grinning repulsively at the revolver which I had almost unconsciously drawn, but from his expression I was sure he had seen and heard as much as I, if not a great deal more. I whispered what I had experienced and he bade me to remain as quiet and receptive as possible.

"Don't move," he cautioned, "for in these rays *we are able to be seen as well as to see.* I told you the servants left, but I didn't tell you *how*. It was that thick-witted house-keeper—she turned on the lights downstairs after I had warned her not to, and the wires picked up sympathetic vibrations. It must have been frightful—I could hear the screams up here in spite of all I was seeing and hearing from another direction, and later it was rather awful to find those empty heaps of clothes around the house. Mrs. Updike's clothes were close to the front hall switch—

that's how I know she did it. It got them all. But so long as we don't move we're fairly safe. Remember we're dealing with a hideous world in which we are practically helpless. . . . *Keep still!*"

The combined shock of the revelation and of the abrupt command gave me a kind of paralysis, and in my terror my mind again opened to the impressions coming from what Tillinghast called *"beyond."* I was now in a vortex of sound and motion, with confused pictures before my eyes. I saw the blurred outlines of the room, but from some point in space there seemed to be pouring a seething column of unrecognizable shapes or clouds, penetrating the solid roof at a point ahead and to the right of me. Then I glimpsed the temple-like effect again, but this time the pillars reached up into an aerial ocean of light, which sent down one blinding beam along the path of the cloudy column I had seen before. After that the scene was almost wholly kaleidoscopic, and in the jumble of sights, sounds, and unidentified sense-impressions I felt that I was about to dissolve or in some way lose the solid form. One definite flash I shall always remember. I seemed for an instant to behold a patch of strange night sky filled with shining, revolving spheres, and as it receded I saw that the glowing suns formed a constellation or galaxy of settled shape; this shape being the distorted face of Crawford Tillinghast. At another time I felt the huge animate things brushing past me and occasionally *walking or drifting through my supposedly solid body,* and thought I saw Tillinghast look at them as though his better trained senses could catch them visually. I recalled what he had said of the pineal gland, and wondered what he saw with this preternatural eye.

Suddenly I myself became possessed of a kind of augmented sight. Over and above the luminous and shadowy chaos arose a picture which, though vague, held the elements of consistency and permanence. It was indeed somewhat familiar, for the unusual part was superimposed upon the usual terrestrial scene much as a cinema view may be thrown upon the painted curtain of a theater. I saw the attic laboratory, the electrical machine, and the unsightly form of Tillinghast opposite me; but of all the space unoccupied by familiar objects not one particle was vacant. Indescribable shapes both alive and otherwise were mixed in disgusting disarray, and close to every known thing were whole worlds of alien, unknown entities. It likewise seemed that all the known things entered into the composition of other unknown things, and vice versa. Foremost among the living objects were inky, jellyish monstrosities which flabbily quivered in harmony with the vibrations from the machine. They were present in loathsome profusion, and I saw to my horror that they *overlapped;* that they were semi-fluid and capable of passing through one another and through what we know as solids. These things were never still, but seemed ever floating about with some malignant purpose. Sometimes they appeared to devour one another, the attacker launching itself at its victim and instantaneously obliterating the latter from sight. Shudderingly I felt that I knew what had obliterated the unfortunate servants, and could not exclude the things from my mind as I strove to observe other properties of the newly visible world that lies unseen around us. But Tillinghast had been watching me, and was speaking.

"You see them? You see them? You see the things that float and flop about you and through you every moment of your life? You see the creatures that form what men call the pure air and the blue sky? Have I not succeeded in breaking down the barrier; have I not shown you worlds that no other living men have seen?" I heard his scream through the horrible chaos, and looked at the wild face thrust so offensively close to mine. His eyes were pits of flame, and they glared at me with what I now saw was overwhelming hatred. The machine droned detestably.

"You think those floundering things wiped out the servants? Fool, they are harmless! But the servants *are* gone, aren't they? You tried to stop me; you discouraged me when I needed every drop of encouragement I could get; you were afraid of the cosmic truth, you damned coward, but now I've got you! What swept up the servants? What made them scream so loud? . . . Don't know, eh! You'll know soon enough. Look at me—listen to what I say—do you suppose there are really any such things as time and magnitude? Do you fancy there are such things as form or matter? I tell you, I have struck depths that your little brain can't picture. I have seen beyond the bounds of infinity and drawn down daemons from the stars. . . . I have harnessed the shadows that stride from world to world to sow death and madness. . . . Space belongs to me, do you hear? Things are hunting me now—the things that devour and dissolve—but I know how to elude them. It is you they will get, as they got the servants. . . . Stirring, dear sir? I told you it was dangerous to move, I have saved you so far by telling you to keep still—saved you to see more sights and to listen to me. If you had moved, they would have been at you long ago. Don't worry, they won't *hurt* you. They didn't hurt the servants—it was the *seeing* that made the poor devils scream so. My pets are not pretty, for they come out of places where aesthetic standards are—*very different*. Disintegration is quite painless, I assure you—*but I want you to see them*. I almost saw them, but I knew how to stop. You are curious? I always knew you were no scientist. Trembling, eh. Trembling with anxiety to see the ultimate things I have discovered. Why don't you move, then? Tired? Well, don't worry, my friend, *for they are coming*. . . . Look, look, curse you, look . . . it's just over your left shoulder. . . ."

What remains to be told is very brief, and may be familiar to you from the newspaper accounts. The police heard a shot in the old Tillinghast house and found us there—Tillinghast dead and me unconscious. They arrested me because the revolver was in my hand, but released me in three hours, after they found it was apoplexy which had finished Tillinghast and saw that my shot had been directed at the noxious machine which now lay hopelessly shattered on the laboratory floor. I did not tell very much of what I had seen, for I feared the coroner would be skeptical; but from the evasive outline I did give, the doctor told me that I had undoubtedly been hypnotised by the vindictive and homicidal madman.

I wish I could believe that doctor. It would help my shaky nerves if I could dismiss what I now have to think of the air and the sky about and above me. I never feel alone or comfortable, and a hideous sense of pursuit sometimes comes chillingly on me when I am weary. What prevents me from believing the doctor is this one simple fact —that the police never found the bodies of those servants whom they say Crawford Tillinghast murdered.

THE FESTIVAL

Efficiut Daemones, ut quae non sunt, sic tamen quasi sint, conspicienda hominibus exhibeant.

—LACTANTIUS

I was far from home, and the spell of the eastern sea was upon me. In the twilight I heard it pounding on the rocks, and I knew it lay just over the hill where the twisting willows writhed against the clearing sky and the first stars of evening. And because my fathers had called me to the old town beyond, I pushed on through the shallow, new-fallen snow along the road that soared lonely up to where Aldebaran twinkled among the trees; on toward the very ancient town I had never seen but often dreamed of.

It was the Yuletide, that men call Christmas though they know in their hearts it is older than Bethlehem and Babylon, older than Memphis and mankind. It was the Yuletide, and I had come at last to the ancient sea town where my people had dwelt and kept festival in the elder time when festival was forbidden; where also they had commanded their sons to keep festival once every century, that the memory of primal secrets might not be forgotten. Mine were an old people, and were old even when this land was settled three hundred years before. And they were strange, because they had come as dark furtive folk from opiate southern gardens of orchids, and spoken another tongue before they learnt the tongue of the blue-eyed fishers. And now they were scattered, and shared only the rituals of mysteries that none living could understand. I was the only one who came back that night to the old fishing town as legend bade, for only the poor and the lonely remember.

Then beyond the hill's crest I saw Kingsport outspread frostily in the gloaming; snowy Kingsport with its ancient vanes and steeples, ridgepoles and chimney-pots, wharves and small bridges, willow-trees and graveyards; endless labyrinths of steep, narrow, crooked streets, and dizzy church-crowned central peak that time durst not touch; ceaseless mazes of colonial houses piled and scattered at all angles and levels like a child's disordered blocks; antiquity hovering on grey wings over winter-whitened gables and gambrel roofs; fanlights and small-paned windows one by one gleaming out in the cold dusk to join Orion and the archaic stars. And against the rotting wharves the sea pounded; the secretive, immemorial sea out of which the people had come in the elder time.

Beside the road at its crest a still higher summit rose, bleak and windswept, and I saw that it was a burying-ground where black gravestones stuck ghoulishly through the snow like the decayed fingernails of a gigantic corpse. The printless road was very lonely, and sometimes I thought I heard a distant horrible creaking as of a gibbet in the wind. They had hanged four kinsmen of mine for witchcraft in 1692, but I did not know just where.

As the road wound down the seaward slope I listened for the merry sounds of a village at evening, but did not hear them. Then I thought of the season, and felt that these old Puritan folk might well have Christmas customs strange to me, and full of silent hearthside prayer. So after that I did not listen for merriment or look for wayfarers, kept on down past the hushed lighted farmhouses and shadowy stone walls to where the signs of ancient shops and sea taverns creaked in the salt breeze, and the grotesque knockers of pillared doorways glistened along deserted unpaved lanes in the light of little, curtained windows.

I had seen maps of the town, and knew where to find the home of my people. It was told that I should be known and welcomed, for village legend lives long; so I hastened through Back Street to Circle Court, and across the fresh snow on the one full flagstone pavement in the town, to where Green Lane leads off behind the Market House. The old maps still held good, and I had no trouble; though at Arkham they must have lied when they said the trolleys ran to this place, since I saw not a wire overhead. Snow would have hid the rails in any case. I was glad I had chosen to walk, for the white village had seemed very beautiful from the hill; and now I was eager to knock at the door of my people, the seventh house on the left in Green Lane, with an ancient peaked roof and jutting second story, all built before 1650.

There were lights inside the house when I came upon it, and I saw from the diamond window-panes that it must have been kept very close to its antique state. The upper part overhung the narrow grass-grown street and nearly met the over-hanging part of the house opposite, so that I was almost in a tunnel, with the low stone doorstep wholly free from snow. There was no sidewalk, but many houses had high doors reached by double flights of steps with iron railings. It was an odd scene, and because I was strange to New England I had never known its like before. Though it pleased me, I would have relished it better if there had been footprints in the snow, and people in the streets, and a few windows without drawn curtains.

When I sounded the archaic iron knocker I was half afraid. Some fear had been gathering in me, perhaps because of the strangeness of my heritage, and the bleakness of the evening, and the queerness of the silence in that aged town of curious customs. And when my knock was answered I was fully afraid, because I had not heard any footsteps before the door creaked open. But I was not afraid long, for the gowned, slippered old man in the doorway had a bland face that reassured me; and though he made signs that he was dumb, he wrote a quaint and ancient welcome with the stylus and wax tablet he carried.

He beckoned me into a low, candle-lit room with massive exposed rafters and dark, stiff, sparse furniture of the seventeenth century. The past was vivid there, for not an attribute was missing. There was a cavernous fireplace and a spinning-wheel at which a bent old woman in loose wrapper and deep poke-bonnet sat back toward me, silently spinning despite the festive season. An indefinite dampness seemed upon the place, and I marvelled that no fire should be blazing. The highbacked settle faced the row of curtained windows at the left, and seemed to be occupied, though I was not sure. I did not like everything about what I saw, and felt again the fear I had had. This fear grew stronger from what had before lessened it, for the more I looked at the old man's bland face the more its very blandness terrified me. The eyes never moved and the skin was too much like wax. Finally I was sure it was not a face at all, but a fiendishly cunning mask. But the flabby hands, curiously gloved, wrote genially on the tablet and told me I must wait a while before I could be led to the place of the festival.

Pointing to a chair, table, and pile of books, the old man now left the room; and when I sat down to read I saw that the books were hoary and mouldy, and that they included old Morryster's wild *Marvells of Science,* the terrible *Saducismus Triumphatus* of Joseph Glanvil, published in 1681, the shocking *Daemonolatreia* of Remigius, printed in 1595 at Lyons, and worst of all, the unmentionable *Necronomicon* of the mad Arab Abdul Alhazred, in Olaus Wormius' forbidden Latin translation; a book which I had never seen, but of which I had heard monstrous things whispered. No one spoke to me, but I could hear the creaking of signs in the wind outside, and the whir of the wheel as the bonneted old woman continued her silent spinning, spinning. I thought the room and the books and the people very morbid and disquieting, but because an old tradition of my fathers had summoned me to strange feastings, I resolved to expect queer things. So I tried to read, and soon became tremblingly absorbed by something I found in that accursed *Necronomicon;* a thought and a legend too hideous for sanity or consciousness, but I disliked it when I fancied I heard the closing of one of the windows that the settle faced, as if it had been stealthily opened. It had seemed to follow a whirring that was not of the old woman's spinning-wheel. This was not much, though, for the old woman was spinning very hard, and the aged clock had been striking. After that I lost the feeling that there were persons on the settle, and was reading intently and shudderingly when the old man came back booted and dressed in a loose antique costume, and sat down on that very bench, so that I could not see him. It was certainly nervous waiting, and the blasphemous book in my hands made it doubly so. When eleven struck, however, the old man stood up, glided to a massive carved chest in a corner, and got two hooded cloaks; one of which he donned, and the other of which he draped round the old woman, who was ceasing her monotonous spinning. Then they both started for the outer door; the woman lamely creeping, and the old man, after picking up the very book I had been reading, beckoning me as he drew his hood over that unmoving face or mask.

We went out into the moonless and tortuous network of that incredibly ancient town; went out as the lights in the curtained windows disappeared one by one, and the Dog Star leered at the throng of cowled, cloaked figures that poured silently from every doorway and formed monstrous processions up this street and that, past the creaking signs and antediluvian gables, the thatched roofs and diamond-paned windows; threading precipitous lanes where decaying houses overlapped and crumbled together, gliding across open courts and churchyards where the bobbing lanthorns made eldritch drunken constellations.

Amid these hushed throngs I followed my voiceless guides; jostled by elbows that seemed preternaturally soft, and pressed by chests and stomachs that seemed abnormally pulpy; but seeing never a face and hearing never a word. Up, up, up, the eery columns slithered, and I saw that all the travellers were converging as they flowed near a sort of focus of crazy alleys at the top of a high hill in the centre of the town, where perched a great white church. I had seen it from the road's crest when I looked at Kingsport in the new dusk, and it had made me shiver because Aldebaran had seemed to balance itself a moment on the ghostly spire.

There was an open space around the church; partly a churchyard with spectral shafts, and partly a half-paved square swept nearly bare of snow by the wind, and lined with unwholesomely archaic houses having peaked roofs and overhanging gables. Death-fires danced over the tombs, revealing gruesome vistas, though queerly failing to cast any shadows. Past the churchyard, where there were no houses, I could see over the hill's summit and watch the glimmer of stars on the harbour, though the town was invisible in the dark. Only once in a while a lanthorn bobbed horribly through serpentine alleys on its way to overtake the throng that was now slipping speechlessly into the church. I waited till the crowd had oozed into the black doorway, and till all the stragglers had followed. The old man was pulling at my sleeve, but I was determined to be the last. Crossing the threshold into the swarming temple of unknown darkness, I turned once to look at the outside world as the churchyard phosphorescence cast a sickly glow on the hilltop pavement. And as I did so I shuddered. For though the wind had not left much snow, a few patches did remain on the path near the door; and in that fleeting backward look it seemed to my troubled eyes that they bore no mark of passing feet, not even mine.

The church was scarce lighted by all the lanthorns that had entered it, for most of the throng had already vanished. They had streamed up the aisle between the high pews to the trap-door of the vaults which yawned loathsomely open just before the pulpit, and were now squirming noiselessly in. I followed dumbly down the footworn steps and into the dark, suffocating crypt. The tail of that sinuous line of night-marchers seemed very horrible, and as I saw them wriggling into a venerable tomb they seemed more horrible still. Then I noticed that the tomb's floor had an aperture down which the throng was sliding, and in a moment we were all descending an ominous staircase of rough-hewn stone; a narrow spiral staircase damp and peculiarly odorous, that wound endlessly down into the bowels of the hill past monotonous walls of dripping stone blocks and crumbling mortar. It was a silent, shocking descent, and I observed after a horrible interval that the walls and steps were changing in nature, as if chiselled out of the solid rock. What mainly troubled me was that the myriad footfalls made no sound and set up no echoes. After more aeons of descent I saw some side passages or burrows leading from unknown recesses of blackness to this shaft of nighted mystery. Soon they became excessively numerous, like impious catacombs of nameless menace; and their pungent odour of decay grew quite unbearable. I knew we must have passed down through the mountain and beneath the earth of Kingsport itself, and I shivered that a town should be so aged and maggoty with subterraneous evil.

Then I saw the lurid shimmering of pale light, and heard the insidious lapping of sunless waters. Again I shivered, for I did not like the things that the night had brought, and wished bitterly that no forefather had summoned me to this primal rite. As the steps and the passage grew broader, I heard another sound, the thin, whining mockery of a feeble flute; and suddenly there spread out before me the boundless vista of an inner world—a vast fungous shore litten by a belching column of sick greenish flame and washed by a wide oily river that flowed from abysses frightful and unsuspected to join the blackest gulfs of immemorial ocean.

Fainting and gasping, I looked at that unhallowed Erebus of titan toadstools, leprous fire and slimy water, and saw the cloaked throngs forming a semicircle around the blazing pillar. It was the Yule-rite, older than man and fated to survive him; the primal rite of the solstice and of spring's promise beyond the snows; the rite of fire and evergreen, light and music. And in the stygian grotto I saw them do the rite, and adore the sick pillar of flame, and throw into the water handfuls gouged out of the viscous vegetation which glittered green in the chlorotic glare. I saw this, and I saw something amorphously squatted far away from the light, piping noisomely on a flute; and as the thing piped I thought I heard noxious muffled flutterings in the foetid darkness where I could not see. But what frightened me most was that flaming column; spouting volcanically from depths profound and inconceivable, casting no shadows as healthy flame should, and coating the nitrous stone with a nasty, venomous verdigris. For in all that seething combustion no warmth lay, but only the clamminess of death and corruption.

The man who had brought me now squirmed to a point directly beside the hideous flame, and made stiff ceremonial motions to the semi-circle he faced. At certain stages of the ritual they did grovelling obeisance, especially when he held above his head that abhorrent *Necronomicon* he had taken with him; and I shared all the obeisances because I had been summoned to this festival by the writings of my forefathers. Then the old man made a signal to the half-seen flute-player in the darkness, which player thereupon changed its feeble drone to a scarce louder drone in another key; precipitating as it did so a horror unthinkable and unexpected. At this horror I sank nearly to the lichened earth, transfixed with a dread not of this or any world, but only of the mad spaces between the stars.

Out of the unimaginable blackness beyond the gangrenous glare of that cold flame, out of the tartarean leagues through which that oily river rolled uncanny, unheard, and unsuspected, there flopped rhythmically a horde of tame, trained, hybrid winged things that no sound eye could ever wholly grasp, or sound brain ever wholly remember. They were not altogether crows, nor moles, nor buzzards, nor ants, nor vampire bats, nor decomposed human beings; but something I cannot and must not recall. They flopped limply along, half with their webbed feet and half with their membranous wings; and as they reached the throng of celebrants the cowled figures seized and mounted them, and rode off one by one along the reaches of that unlighted river, into pits and galleries of panic where poison springs feed frightful and undiscoverable cataracts.

The old spinning woman had gone with the throng, and the old man remained only because I had refused when he motioned me to seize an animal and ride like the rest. I saw when I staggered to my feet that the amorphous flute-player had rolled out of sight, but that two of the beasts were patiently standing by. As I hung back, the old man produced his stylus and tablet and wrote that he was the true deputy of my fathers who had founded the Yule worship in this ancient place; that it had been decreed I should come back, and that the most secret mysteries were yet to be performed. He wrote this in a very ancient hand, and when I still hesitated he pulled from his loose robe a seal ring and a watch, both with my family arms, to prove that he was what he said. But it was a hideous proof, because I knew from old papers that that watch had been buried with my great-great-great-great-grandfather in 1698.

Presently the old man drew back his hood and pointed to the family resemblance in his face, but I only shuddered, because I was sure that the face was merely a devilish waxen mask. The flopping animals were now scratching restlessly at the lichens, and I saw that the old man was nearly as restless himself. When one of the things began to waddle and edge away, he turned quickly to stop it; so that the suddenness of his motion dislodged the waxen mask from what should have been his head. And then, because that nightmare's position barred me from the stone staircase down which we had come, I flung myself into the oily underground river that bubbled somewhere to the caves of the sea; flung myself into that putrescent juice of earth's inner horrors before the madness of my screams could bring down upon me all the charnel legions these pest-gulfs might conceal.

At the hospital they told me I had been found half-frozen in Kingsport Harbour at dawn, clinging to the drifting spar that accident sent to save me. They told me I had taken the wrong fork of the hill road the night before, and fallen over the cliffs at Orange Point; a thing they deduced from prints found in the snow. There was nothing I could say, because everything was wrong. Everything was wrong, with the broad windows showing a sea of roofs in which only about one in five was ancient, and the sound of trolleys and motors in the streets below. They insisted that this was Kingsport, and I could not deny it. When I went delirious at hearing that the hospital stood near the old churchyard on Central Hill, they sent me to St. Mary's Hospital in Arkham, where I could have better care. I liked it there, for the doctors were broadminded, and even lent me their influence in obtaining the carefully sheltered copy of Alhazred's objectionable *Necronomicon* from the library of Miskatonic University. They said something about a "psychosis," and agreed I had better get any harassing obsessions off my mind.

So I read that hideous chapter, and shuddered doubly because it was indeed not new to me. I had seen it before, let footprints tell what they might; and where it was I had seen it were best forgotten. There was no one—in waking hours—who could remind me of it; but my dreams are filled with terror, because of phrases I dare not quote. I dare quote only one paragraph, put into such English as I can make from the awkward Low Latin.

"The nethermost caverns," wrote the mad Arab, "are not for the fathoming of eyes that see; for their marvels are strange and terrific. Cursed the ground where dead thoughts live new and oddly bodied, and evil the mind that is held by no head. Wisely did Ibn Schacabao say, that happy is the tomb where no wizard hath lain, and happy the town at night whose wizards are all ashes. For it is of old rumour that the soul of the devil-bought hastes not from his charnel clay, but fats and instructs *the very worm that gnaws;* till out of corruption horrid life springs, and the dull scavengers of earth wax crafty to vex it and swell monstrous to plague it. Great holes secretly are digged where earth's pores ought to suffice, and things have learnt to walk that ought to crawl."

In a letter to Frank Belknap Long, dated January 26, 1921, H.P.L. discussed the next story, "The Nameless City." He wrote:

> At the risk of boring you, I will enclose my latest—just finished and typed—*The Nameless City.* This had its basis in a dream, which in turn was probably caused by contemplation of the peculiar suggestiveness of a phrase in Dunsany's *Book of Wonder*—"the unreverberate blackness of the abyss." The character of the "mad Arab Alhazred" is fictitious. The lines are mine—written especially for this story—and Abdul Alhazred is a pseudonym I took when I was about five years old and crazy about the *Arabian Nights.* I hardly know yet what to think of this story—you are the first to see it—but I certainly put enough work into it. I tore up two beginnings, only hitting the right atmosphere the third time, and destroyed (or rather rearranged) one conclusion. I aim at a cumulative succession of horrors—thrill upon thrill and each one worse! . . .

THE NAMELESS CITY

When I drew nigh the nameless city I knew it was accursed. I was traveling in a parched and terrible valley under the moon, and afar I saw it protruding uncannily above the sands as parts of a corpse may protrude from an ill-made grave. Fear spoke from the age-worn stones of this hoary survivor of the deluge, this great-grandmother of the eldest pyramid; and a viewless aura repelled me and bade me retreat from antique and sinister secrets that no man should see, and no man else had ever dared to see.

Remote in the desert of Araby lies the nameless city, crumbling and inarticulate, its low walls nearly hidden by the sands of uncounted ages. It must have been thus before the first stones of Memphis were laid, and while the bricks of Babylon were yet unbaked. There is no legend so old as to give it a name, or to recall that it was ever alive; but it is told of in whispers around campfires and muttered about by grandams in the tents of sheiks so that all the tribes shun it without wholly knowing why. It was of this place that Abdul Alhazred the mad poet dreamed on the night before he sang his unexplainable couplet:

That is not dead which can eternal lie,
And with strange aeons death may die.

I should have known that the Arabs had good reason for

shunning the nameless city, the city told of in strange tales but seen by no living man, yet I defied them and went into the untrodden waste with my camel. I alone have seen it, and that is why no other face bears such hideous lines of fear as mine; why no other man shivers so horribly when the night wind rattles the windows. When I came upon it in the ghastly stillness of unending sleep it looked at me, chilly from the rays of a cold moon amidst the desert's heat. And as I returned its look I forgot my triumph at finding it, and stopped still with my camel to wait for the dawn.

For hours I waited, till the east grew grey and the stars faded, and the grey turned to roseate light edged with gold. I heard a moaning and saw a storm of sand stirring among the antique stones though the sky was clear and the vast reaches of desert still. Then suddenly above the desert's far rim came the blazing edge of the sun, seen through the tiny sandstorm which was passing away, and in my fevered state I fancied that from some remote depth there came a crash of musical metal to hail the fiery disc as Memnon hails it from the banks of the Nile. My ears rang and my imagination seethed as I led my camel slowly across the sand to that unvocal place; that place which I alone of living men had seen.

In and out amongst the shapeless foundations of houses and places I wandered, finding never a carving or inscription to tell of these men, if men they were, who built this city and dwelt therein so long ago. The antiquity of the spot was unwholesome, and I longed to encounter some sign or device to prove that the city was indeed fashioned by mankind. There were certain *proportions* and *dimensions* in the ruins which I did not like. I had with me many tools, and dug much within the walls of the obliterated edifices; but progress was slow, and nothing significant was revealed. When night and the moon returned I felt a chill wind which brought new fear, so that I did not dare to remain in the city. And as I went outside the antique walls to sleep, a small sighing sandstorm gathered behind me, blowing over the grey stones though the moon was bright and most of the desert still.

I awaked just at dawn from a pageant of horrible dreams, my ears ringing as from some metallic peal. I saw the sun peering redly through the last gusts of a little sandstorm that hovered over the nameless city, and marked the quietness of the rest of the landscape. Once more I ventured within those brooding ruins that swelled beneath the sand like an ogre under a coverlet, and again dug vainly for relics of the forgotten race. At noon I rested, and in the afternoon I spent much time tracing the walls and bygone streets, and the outlines of the nearly vanished buildings. I saw that the city had been mighty indeed, and wondered at the sources of its greatness. To myself I pictured all the splendours of an age so distant that Chaldaea could not recall it, and thought of Sarnath the Doomed, that stood in the land of Mnar when mankind was young, and of Ib, that was carven of grey stone before mankind existed.

All at once I came upon a place where the bed rock rose stark through the sand and formed a low cliff; and here I saw with joy what seemed to promise further traces of the antediluvian people. Hewn rudely on the face of the cliff were the unmistakable façades of several small, squat rock houses or temples; whose interiors might preserve many secrets of ages too remote for calculation, though sandstorms had long since effaced any carvings which may have been outside.

Very low and sand-choked were all the dark apertures near me, but I cleared one with my spade and crawled through it, carrying a torch to reveal whatever mysteries it might hold. When I was inside I saw that the cavern was indeed a temple, and beheld plain signs of the race that had lived and worshipped before the desert was a desert. Primitive altars, pillars, and niches, all curiously low, were not absent; and though I saw no sculptures or frescoes, there were many singular stones clearly shaped into symbols by artificial means. The lowness of the chiselled chamber was very strange, for I could hardly kneel upright; but the area was so great that my torch showed only part of it at a time. I shuddered oddly in some of the far corners; for certain altars and stones suggested forgotten rites of terrible, revolting, and inexplicable nature and made me wonder what manner of men could have made and frequented such a temple. When I had seen all that the place contained, I crawled out again, avid to find what the temples might yield.

Night had now approached, yet the tangible things I had seen made curiosity stronger than fear, so that I did not flee from the long mooncast shadows that had daunted me when first I saw the nameless city. In the twilight I cleared another aperture and with a new torch crawled into it, finding more vague stones and symbols, though nothing more definite than the other temple had contained. The room was just as low, but much less broad, ending in a very narrow passage crowded with obscure and cryptical shrines. About these shrines I was prying when the noise of a wind and my camel outside broke through the stillness and drew me forth to see what could have frightened the beast.

The moon was gleaming vividly over the primitive ruins, lighting a dense cloud of sand that seemed blown by a strong but decreasing wind from some point along the cliff ahead of me. I knew it was this chilly, sandy wind which had disturbed the camel and was about to lead him to a place of better shelter when I chanced to glance up and saw that there was no wind atop the cliff. This astonished me and made me fearful again, but I immediately recalled the sudden local winds that I had seen and heard before at sunrise and sunset, and judged it was a normal thing. I decided it came from some rock fissure leading to a cave, and watched the troubled sand to trace it to its source; soon perceiving that it came from the black orifice of a temple a long distance south of me, almost out of sight. Against the choking sand-cloud I plodded toward this temple, which as I neared it loomed larger than the rest, and shewed a doorway far less clogged with caked sand. I would have entered had not the terrific force of the icy wind almost quenched my torch. It poured madly out of the dark door, sighing uncannily as it ruffled the sand and spread among the weird ruins. Soon it grew fainter and the sand grew more and more still, till finally all was at rest again; but a presence seemed stalking among the spectral stones of the city, and when I glanced at the moon it seemed to quiver as though mirrored in unquiet waters. I was more afraid than I could explain, but not enough to dull my thirst for wonder; so as soon as the wind was quite gone I crossed into the dark chamber from which it had come.

This temple, as I had fancied from the outside, was larger than either of those I had visited before; and was presumably a natural cavern since it bore winds from some region beyond. Here I could stand quite upright, but saw that the stones and altars were as low as those in the other temples. On the walls and roof I beheld for the first time some traces of the pictorial art of the ancient race, curious curling streaks of paint that had almost faded or crumbled away; and on two of the altars I saw with rising excitement a maze of well-fashioned curvilinear carvings. As I held my torch aloft it seemed to me that the shape of the roof was too regular to be natural, and I wondered what the prehistoric cutters of stone had first worked upon. Their engineering skill must have been vast.

Then a brighter flare of the fantastic flame showed that for which I had been seeking, the opening to those remoter abysses whence the sudden wind had blown; and I grew faint when I saw that it was a small and plainly artificial door chiselled in the solid rock. I thrust my torch within, beholding a black tunnel with the roof arching low over a rough flight of very small, numerous and steeply descending steps. I shall always see those steps in my dreams, for I came to learn what they meant. At the time I hardly knew whether to call them steps or mere footholds in a precipitous descent. My mind was whirling with mad thoughts, and the words and warnings of Arab prophets seemed to float across the desert from the lands that men know to the nameless city that men dare not know. Yet I hesitated only for a moment before advancing through the portal and commencing to climb cautiously down the steep passage, feet first, as though on a ladder.

It is only in the terrible phantasms of drugs or delirium that any other man can have such a descent as mine. The narrow passage led infinitely down like some hideous haunted well, and the torch I held above my head could not light the unknown depths toward which I was crawling. I lost track of the hours and forgot to consult my watch, though I was frightened when I thought of the distance I must be traversing. There were changes of direction and of steepness; and once I came to a long, low, level passage where I had to wriggle my feet first along the rocky floor, holding torch at arm's length beyond my head. The place was not high enough for kneeling. After that were more of the steep steps, and I was still scrambling down interminably when my failing torch died out. I do not think I noticed it at the time, for when I did notice it I was still holding it above me as if it were ablaze. I was quite unbalanced with that instinct for the strange and the unknown which had made me a wanderer upon earth and a haunter of far, ancient, and forbidden places.

In the darkness there flashed before my mind fragments of my cherished treasury of daemoniac lore; sentences from Alhazred the mad Arab, paragraphs from the apocryphal nightmares of Damascius, and infamous lines from the delirious *Image du Monde* of Gauthier de Metz. I repeated queer extracts, and muttered of Afrasiab and the daemons that floated with him down the Oxus; later chanting over and over again a phrase from one of Lord Dunsany's tales—"The unreverberate blackness of the abyss." Once when the descent grew amazingly steep I recited something in sing-song from Thomas Moore until I feared to recite more:

A reservoir of darkness, black
As witches' cauldrons are, when fill'd
With moon-drugs in th' eclipse distill'd.
Leaning to look if foot might pass
Down thro' that chasm, I saw, beneath,
As far as vision could explore,
The jetty sides as smooth as glass,

Looking as if just varnish'd o'er
With that dark pitch the Seat of Death
Throws out upon its slimy shore.

Time had quite ceased to exist when my feet again felt a level floor, and I found myself in a place slightly higher than the rooms in the two smaller temples now so incalculably far above my head. I could not quite stand, but could kneel upright, and in the dark I shuffled and crept hither and thither at random. I soon knew that I was in a narrow passage whose walls were lined with cases of wood having glass fronts. As in that Palaeozoic and abysmal place I felt of such things as polished wood and glass I shuddered at the possible implications. The cases were apparently ranged along each side of the passage at regular intervals, and were oblong and horizontal, hideously like coffins in shape and size. When I tried to move two or three for further examination, I found that they were firmly fastened.

I saw that the passage was a long one, so floundered ahead rapidly in a creeping run that would have seemed horrible had any eye watched me in the blackness; crossing from side to side occasionally to feel of my surroundings and be sure the walls and rows of cases still stretched on. Man is so used to thinking visually that I almost forgot the darkness and pictured the endless corridor of wood and glass in its low-studded monotony as though I saw it. And then in a moment of indescribable emotion I did see it.

Just when my fancy merged into real sight I cannot tell; but there came a gradual glow ahead, and all at once I knew that I saw the dim outlines of the corridor and the cases, revealed by some unknown subterranean phosphorescence. For a little while all was exactly as I had imagined it, since the glow was very faint; but as I mechanically kept stumbling ahead into the stronger light I realised that my fancy had been but feeble. This hall was no relic of crudity like the temples in the city above, but a monument of the most magnificent and exotic art. Rich, vivid, and daringly fantastic designs and pictures formed a continuous scheme of mural painting whose lines and colours were beyond description. The cases were of a strange golden wood, with fronts of exquisite glass, and containing the mummified forms of creatures outreaching in grotesqueness the most chaotic dreams of man.

To convey any idea of these monstrosities is impossible. They were of the reptile kind, with body lines suggesting sometimes the crocodile, sometimes the seal, but more often nothing of which either the naturalist or the palaeontologist ever heard. In size they approximated a small man, and their fore-legs bore delicate and evident feet curiously like human hands and fingers. But strangest of all were their heads, which presented a contour violating all known biological principles. To nothing can such things be well compared—in one flash I thought of comparisons as varied as the cat, the bulldog, the mythic Satyr, and the human being. Not Jove himself had had so colossal and protuberant a forehead, yet the horns and the noselessness and the alligator-like jaw placed the things outside all established categories. I debated for a time on the reality of the mummies, half suspecting they were artificial idols; but soon decided they were indeed some palaeogean species which had lived when the nameless city was alive. To crown their grotesqueness, most of them were gorgeously enrobed in the costliest of fabrics, and lavishly laden with ornaments of gold, jewels, and unknown shining metals.

The importance of these crawling creatures must have been vast, for they held first place among the wild designs on the frescoed walls and ceiling. With matchless skill had the artist drawn them in a world of their own, wherein they had cities and gardens fashioned to suit their dimensions; and I could not help but think that their pictured history was allegorical, perhaps shewing the progress of the race that worshipped them. These creatures, I said to myself, were to the men of the nameless city what the she-wolf was to Rome, or some totem-beast is to a tribe of Indians.

Holding this view, I could trace roughly a wonderful epic of the nameless city; the tale of a mighty seacoast metropolis that ruled the world before Africa rose out of the waves, and of its struggles as the sea shrank away, and the desert crept into the fertile valley that held it. I saw its wars and triumphs, its troubles and defeats, and afterward its terrible fight against the desert when thousands of its people—here represented in allegory by the grotesque reptiles—were driven to chisel their way down through the rocks in some marvellous manner to another world whereof their prophets had told them. It was all vividly weird and realistic, and its connection with the awesome descent I had made was unmistakable. I even recognized the passages.

As I crept along the corridor toward the brighter light I saw later stages of the painted epic—the leave-taking of the race that had dwelt in the nameless city and the valley around for ten million years; the race whose souls shrank from quitting scenes their bodies had known so long where they had settled as nomads in the earth's youth, hewing in the virgin rock those primal shrines at which they had never ceased to worship. Now that the light was better I studied the pictures more closely and, remembering that the strange reptiles must represent the unknown men, pondered upon the customs of the nameless city. Many things were peculiar and inexplicable. The civilisation, which included a written alphabet, had seemingly risen to a higher order than those immeasurably later civilisations of Egypt and Chaldaea, yet there were curious omissions. I could, for example, find no pictures to represent deaths or funeral customs, save such as were related to wars, violence, and plagues; and I wondered at the reticence shown concerning natural death. It was as though an ideal of immortality had been fostered as a cheering illusion.

Still nearer the end of the passage were painted scenes of the utmost picturesqueness and extravagance: contrasted views of the nameless city in its desertion and growing ruin, and of the strange new realm of paradise to which the race had hewed its way through the stone. In these views the city and the desert valley were shewn always by moonlight, golden nimbus hovering over the fallen walls and half-revealing the splendid perfection of former times, shown spectrally and elusively by the artist. The paradisal scenes were almost too extravagant to be believed, portraying a hidden world of eternal day filled with glorious cities and ethereal hills and valleys. At the very last I thought I saw signs of an artistic anticlimax. The paintings were less skillful, and much more bizarre than even the wildest of the earlier scenes. They seemed to record a slow decadence of the ancient stock, coupled with a growing ferocity toward the outside world from which it was driven by the desert. The forms of the people—always represented by the sacred reptiles—appeared to be gradually wasting away, though their spirit as shewn hovering above the ruins by moonlight gained in proportion. Emaciated priests, displayed as reptiles in ornate robes, cursed the upper air and all who breathed it; and one terrible final scene shewed a primitive-looking man, perhaps a pioneer of ancient Irem, the City of Pillars, torn to pieces by members of the elder race. I remember how the Arabs fear the nameless city, and was glad that beyond this place the grey walls and ceiling were bare.

As I viewed the pageant of mural history I had approached very closely the end of the low-ceiled hall, and was aware of a gate through which came all of the illuminating phosphorescence. Creeping up to it, I cried aloud in transcendent amazement at what lay beyond; for instead of other and brighter chambers there was only an illimitable void of uniform radiance, such as one might fancy when gazing down from the peak of Mount Everest upon a sea of sunlit mist. Behind me was a passage so cramped that I could not stand upright in it; before me was an infinity of subterranean effulgence.

Reaching down from the passage into the abyss was the head of a steep flight of steps—small numerous steps like those of black passages I had traversed—but after a few feet the glowing vapours concealed everything. Swung back open against the left-hand wall of the passage was a massive door of brass, incredibly thick and decorated with fantastic bas-reliefs, which could if closed shut the whole inner world of light away from the vaults and passages of rock. I looked at the steps, and for the nonce dared not try them. I touched the open brass door, and could not move it. Then I sank prone to the stone floor, my mind aflame with prodigious reflections which not even a death-like exhaustion could banish.

As I lay still with closed eyes, free to ponder, many things I had lightly noted in the frescoes came back to me with new and terrible significance—scenes representing the nameless city in its heyday—the vegetation of the valley around it, and the distant lands with which its merchants traded. The allegory of the crawling creatures puzzled me by its universal prominence, and I wondered that it would be so closely followed in a pictured history of such importance. In the frescoes the nameless city had been shewn in proportions fitted to the reptiles. I wondered what its real proportions and magnificence had been, and reflected a moment on certain oddities I had noticed in the ruins. I thought curiously of the lowness of the primal temples and of the underground corridor, which were doubtless hewn thus out of deference to the reptile deities there honoured; though it perforce reduced the worshippers to crawling. Perhaps the very rites here involved a crawling in imitation of the creatures. No religious theory, however, could easily explain why the level passages in that awesome descent should be as low as the temples—or lower, since one could not even kneel in it. As I thought of the crawling creatures, whose hideous mummified forms were so close to me, I felt a new throb of fear. Mental associations are curious, and I shrank from the idea that except for the poor primitive man torn to pieces in the last painting, mine was the only human form amidst the many relics and symbols of primordial life.

But as always in my strange and roving existence, wonder soon drove out fear; for the luminous abyss and what it might contain presented a problem worthy of the greatest explorer. That a weird world of mystery lay far down that flight of peculiarly small steps I could not doubt, and I hoped to find there those human memorials which the painted corridor had failed to give. The frescoes had pictured unbelieveable cities, and valleys in this lower realm, and my fancy dwelt on the rich and colossal ruins that awaited me.

My fears, indeed, concerned the past rather than the future. Not even the physical horror of my position in that cramped corridor of dead reptiles and antediluvian frescoes, miles below the world I knew and faced by another world of eery light and mist, could match the lethal dread I felt at the abysmal antiquity of the scene and its soul. An ancientness so vast that measurement is feeble seemed to leer down from the primal stones and rock-hewn temples of the nameless city, while the very latest of the astounding maps in the frescoes shewed oceans and continents that man has forgotten, with only here and there some vaguely familiar outline. Of what could have happened in the geological ages since the paintings ceased and the death-hating race resentfully succumbed to decay, no man might say. Life had once teemed in these caverns and in the luminous realm beyond; now I was alone with vivid relics, and I trembled to think of the countless ages through which these relics had kept a silent deserted vigil.

Suddenly there came another burst of that acute fear which had intermittently seized me ever since I first saw the terrible valley and the nameless city under a cold moon, and despite my exhaustion I found myself starting frantically to a sitting posture and gazing back along the black corridor toward the tunnels that rose to the outer world. My sensations were like those which had made me shun the nameless city at night, and were as inexplicable as they were poignant. In another moment, however, I received a still greater shock in the form of a definite sound—the first which had broken the utter silence of these tomb-like depths. It was a deep, low moaning, as of a distant throng of condemned spirits, and came from the direction in which I was staring. Its volume rapidly grew, till it soon reverberated frightfully through the low passage, and at the same time I became conscious of an increasing draught of cold air, likewise flowing from the tunnels and the city above. The touch of this air seemed to restore my balance, for I instantly recalled the sudden gusts which had risen around the mouth of the abyss each sunset and sunrise, one of which had indeed revealed the hidden tunnels to me. I looked at my watch and saw that sunrise was near, so braced myself to resist the gale that was sweeping down to its cavern home as it had swept forth at evening. My fear again waned low, since a natural phenomenon tends to dispel broodings over the unknown.

More and more madly poured the shrieking, moaning night wind into the gulf of the inner earth. I dropped prone again and clutched vainly at the floor for fear of being swept bodily through the open gate into the phosphorescent abyss. Such fury I had not expected, and as I grew aware of an actual slipping of my form toward the abyss I was beset by a thousand new terrors of apprehension and imagination. The malignancy of the blast awakened incredible fancies; once more I compared myself shudderingly to the only human image in that frightful corridor, the man who was torn to pieces by the nameless race, for in the fiendish clawing of the swirling currents there seemed to abide a vindictive rage all the stronger because it was largely impotent. I think I screamed frantically near the last—I was almost mad—but if I did so my cries were lost in the hell-born babel of the howling wind-wraiths. I tried to crawl against the murderous invisible torrent, but I could not even hold my own as I was pushed slowly and inexorably toward the unknown world. Finally reason must have wholly snapped; for I fell to babbling over and over that unexplainable couplet of the mad Arab Alhazred, who dreamed of the nameless city:

> That is not dead which can eternal lie,
> And with strange aeons even death may die.

Only the grim brooding desert gods know what really took place—what indescribable struggles and scrambles in the dark I endured or what Abaddon guided me back to life, where I must always remember and shiver in the night wind till oblivion—or worse—claims me. Monstrous, unnatural, colossal, was the thing—too far beyond all the ideas of man to be believed except in the silent damnable small hours of the morning when one cannot sleep.

I have said that the fury of the rushing blast was infernal—cacodaemoniacal—and that its voices were hideous with the pent-up viciousness of desolate eternities. Presently these voices, while still chaotic before me, seemed to my beating brain to take articulate form behind me; and down there in the grave of unnumbered aeon-dead antiquities, leagues below the dawn-lit world of men, I heard the ghastly cursing and snarling of strange-tongued fiends. Turning, I saw outlined against the luminous aether of the abyss that could not be seen against the dusk of the corridor—a nightmare horde of rushing devils; hate-distorted, grotesquely panoplied, half transparent devils of a race no man might mistake—the crawling reptiles of the nameless city.

And as the wind died away I was plunged into the ghoul-pooled darkness of earth's bowels; for behind the last of the creatures the great brazen door clanged shut with a deafening peal of metallic music whose reverberations swelled out to the distant world to hail the rising sun as Memnon hails it from the banks of the Nile.

To demonstrate how, at this point in his career, Lovecraft could wander back and forth between the two poles of his fiction, producing a proto-Cthulhuoid horror tale one month and a Dunsanian dream-fantasy the next, give witness to the following tale.

Lovecraft wrote "The Nameless City" in January, 1921. "The Quest of Iranon" followed only a couple of months later. On April 23, 1921, he wrote concerning it to his friend Kleiner:

> I am picking up a new style lately—running to pathos as well as horror. The best thing I have yet done is *The Quest of Iranon* whose English Loveman [Samuel Loveman, the poet, an early friend of H.P.L.] calls the most musical and flowing I have yet written, and whose sad plot made one prominent poet actually weep—not at the crudity of the story, but at its sadness. Then I have written another hair-raiser, *The Moon-Bog* . . .

THE QUEST OF IRANON

Into the granite city of Teloth wandered the youth, vine-crowned, his yellow hair glistening with myrrh and his purple robe torn with briers of the mountain Sidrak that lies across the antique bridge of stone. The men of Teloth are dark and stern, and dwell in square houses, and with frowns they asked the stranger whence he had come and what were his name and fortune. So the youth answered:

"I am Iranon, and come from Aira, a far city that I recall only dimly but seek to find again. I am a singer of songs that I learned in the far city, and my calling is to make beauty with the things remembered of childhood. My wealth is in little memories and dreams, and in hopes that I sing in gardens when the moon is tender and the west wind stirs the lotus-buds."

When the men of Teloth heard these things they whispered to one another; for though in the granite city there is no laughter or song, the stern men sometimes look to the Karthian hills in the spring and think of the lutes of distant Oonai whereof travellers have told. And thinking thus, they bade the stranger stay and sing in the square before the Tower of Mlin, though they liked not the colour of his tattered robe, nor the myrrh in his hair, nor his chaplet of vine-leaves, nor the youth in his golden voice. At evening Iranon sang, and while he sang an old man prayed and a blind man said he saw a nimbus over the singer's head. But most of the men of Teloth yawned, and some laughed and some went to sleep; for Iranon told nothing useful, singing only his memories, his dreams, and his hopes.

"I remember the twilight, the moon, and soft songs, and the window where I was rocked to sleep. And through the window was the street where the golden lights came, and where the shadows danced on houses of marble. I remember the square of moonlight on the floor, that was not like any other light, and the visions that danced in the moonbeams when my mother sang to me. And too, I remember the sun of morning bright above the many-coloured hills in summer, and the sweetness of flowers borne on the south wind that made the trees sing.

"O Aira, city of marble and beryl, how many are thy beauties! How I loved the warm and fragrant groves across the hyaline Nithra, and the falls of the tiny Kra that flowed through the verdant valley! In those groves and in that vale the children wove wreaths for one another, and at dusk I dreamed strange dreams under the yath-trees on the mountain as I saw below me the lights of the city, and the curving Nithra reflecting a ribbon of stars.

"And in the city were palaces of veined and tinted marble, with golden domes and painted walls, and green gardens with cerulean pools and crystal fountains. Often I played in the gardens and waded in the pools, and lay and dreamed among the pale flowers under the trees. And sometimes at sunset I would climb the long hilly street to the citadel and the open place, and look down upon Aira, the magic city of marble and beryl, splendid in a robe of golden flame.

"Long have I missed thee, Aira, for I was but young when we went into exile; but my father was thy King and I shall come again to thee, for it is so decreed of Fate. All through seven lands have I sought thee, and some day shall I reign over thy groves and gardens, they streets and palaces, and sing to men who shall know whereof I sing, and laugh not nor turn away. For I am Iranon, who was a Prince in Aira."

That night the men of Teloth lodged the stranger in a stable, and in the morning an archon came to him and told him to go to the shop of Athok the cobbler, and be apprenticed to him.

"But I am Iranon, a singer of songs," he said, "and have no heart for the cobbler's trade."

"All in Teloth must toil," replied the archon, "for that is the law." Then said Iranon:

"Wherefore do ye toil; is it not that ye may live and be happy? And if ye toil only that ye may toil more, when shall happiness find you? Ye toil to live, but is not life made of beauty and song? And if ye suffer no singers among you, where shall be the fruits of your toil? Toil without song is like a weary journey without an end. Were not death more pleasing?" But the archon was sullen and did not understand, and rebuked the stranger.

"Thou art a strange youth, and I like not thy face or thy voice. The words thou speakest are blasphemy, for the gods of Teloth have said that toil is good. Our gods have promised us a haven of light beyond death, where there shall be rest without end, and crystal coldness amidst which none shall vex his mind with thought or his eyes with beauty. Go thou then to Athok the cobbler or be gone out of the city by sunset. All here must serve, and song is folly."

So Iranon went out of the stable and walked over the narrow stone streets between the gloomy square house of granite, seeking something green, for all was of stone. On the faces of men were frowns, but by the stone embankment along the sluggish river Zuro sat a young boy with sad eyes gazing into the waters to spy green budding branches washed down from the hills by the freshets. And the boy said to him:

"Art thou not indeed he of whom the archons tell, who seekest a far city in a fair land? I am Romnod, and born of the blood of Teloth, but am not old in the ways of the granite city, and yearn daily for the warm groves and the distant lands of beauty and song. Beyond the Karthian hills lieth Oonai, the city of lutes and

dancing, which men whisper of and say is both lovely and terrible. Thither would I go were I old enough to find the way, and thither shouldst thou go and thou wouldst sing and have men listen to thee. Let us leave the city of Teloth and fare together among the hills of spring. Thou shalt shew me the ways of travel and I will attend thy songs at evening when the stars one by one bring dreams to the minds of dreamers. And peradventure it may be that Oonai the city of lutes and dancing is even the fair Aira thou seekest, for it is told that thou hast not known Aira since old days, and a name often changeth. Let us go to Oonai, O Iranon of the golden head, where men shall know our longings and welcome us as brothers, nor even laugh or frown at what we say."
And Iranon answered:

"Be it so, small one; if any in this stone place yearn for beauty he must seek the mountains and beyond, and I would not leave thee to pine by the sluggish Zuro. But think not that delight and understanding dwell just across the Karthian hills, or in any spot thou canst find in a day's, or a year's, or a lustrum's journey. Behold, when I was small like thee I dwelt in the valley of Narthos by the frigid Xari, where none would listen to my dreams; and I told myself that when older I would go to Sinara on the southern slope, and sing to smiling dromedary-men in the market place. But when I went to Sinara I found the dromedary-men all drunken and ribald, and saw that their songs were not as mine, so I travelled in a barge down the Xari to onyx-walled Jaren. And the soldiers at Jaren laughed at me and drave me out, so that I wandered to many other cities. I have seen Stethelos that is below the great cataract, and have gazed on the marsh where Sarnath once stood. I have been to Thraa, Ilarnek, and Kadatheron on the winding river Ai, and have dwelt long in Olathoe in the land of Lomar. But though I have had listeners sometimes, they have ever been few, and I know that welcome shall wait me only in Aira, the city of marble and beryl where my father once ruled as King. So for Aira shall we seek, though it were well to visit distant and lute-blessed Oonai across the Karthian hills, which may indeed be Aira, though I think not. Aira's beauty is past imagining, and none can tell of it without rapture, whilst of Oonai the camel-drivers whisper leeringly."

At the sunset Iranon and small Romnod went forth from Teloth, and for long wandered amidst the green hills and cool forests. The way was rough and obscure, and never did they seem nearer to Oonai the city of lutes and dancing; but in the dusk as the stars came out Iranon would sing of Aira and its beauties and Romnod would listen, so that they were both happy after a fashion. They ate plentifully of fruit and red berries, and marked not the passing of time, but many years must have slipped away. Small Romnod was now not so small, and spoke deeply instead of shrilly, though Iranon was always the same, and decked his golden hair with vines and fragrant resins found in the woods. So it came to pass one day that Romnod seemed older than Iranon, though he had been very small when Iranon had found him watching for green budding branches in Teloth beside the sluggish stone-banked Zuro.

Then one night when the moon was full the travellers came to a mountain crest and looked down upon the myriad light of Oonai. Peasants had told them they were near, and Iranon knew that this was not his native city of Aira. The lights of Oonai were not like those of Aira; for they were harsh and glaring, while the lights of Aira shine as softly and magically as shone the moonlight on the floor by the window where Iranon's mother once rocked him to sleep with song. But Oonai was a city of lutes and dancing, so Iranon and Romnod went down the steep slope that they might find men to whom songs and dreams would bring pleasure. And when they were come into the town they found rose-wreathed revellers bound from house to house and leaning from windows and balconies, who listened to the songs of Iranon and tossed him flowers and applauded when he was done. Then for a moment did Iranon believe he had found those who thought and felt even as he, though the town was not an hundredth as fair as Aira.

When dawn came Iranon looked about with dismay, for the domes of Oonai were not golden in the sun, but grey and dismal. And the men of Oonai were pale with revelling, and dull with wine, and unlike the radiant men of Aira. But because the people had thrown him blossoms and acclaimed his songs Iranon stayed on, and with him Romnod, who liked the revelry of the town and wore in his dark hair roses and myrtle. Often at night Iranon sang to the revellers, but he was always as before, crowned only with the vine of the mountains and remembering the marble streets of Aira and the hyaline Nithra. In the frescoed halls of the Monarch did he sing, upon a crystal dais raised over a floor that was a mirror, and as he sang, he brought pictures to his hearers till the floor seemed to reflect old, beautiful, and half-remembered things instead of the wine-reddened feasters who pelted him with roses. And the King bade him put away his tattered purple, and clothed him in satin and cloth-of-gold, with rings of green jade and bracelets of tinted ivory, and lodged him in a gilded and tapestried chamber on a bed of sweet carven wood with canopies and coverlets of flower-embroidered silk. Thus dwelt Iranon in Oonai, the city of lutes and dancing.

It is not known how long Iranon tarried in Oonai, but one day the King brought to the palace some wild whirling dancers from the Liranian desert, and dusky flute-players from Drinen in the East, and after that the revellers threw their roses not so much at Iranon as at the dancers and flute-players. And day by day that Romnod who had been a small boy in granite Teloth grew coarser and redder with wine, till he dreamed less and less, and listened with less delight to the songs of Iranon. But though Iranon was sad he ceased not to sing, and at evening told again his dreams of Aira, the city of marble and beryl. Then one night the reddened and fattened Romnod snorted heavily amidst the poppied silks of his banquet-couch and died writhing, whilst Iranon, pale and slender, sang to himself in a far corner. And when Iranon had wept over the grave of Romnod and strewn it with green budding branches, such as Romnod used to love, he put aside his silks and gauds and went forgotten out of Oonai the city of lutes and dancing clad only in the ragged purple in which he had come, and garlanded with fresh vines from the mountains.

Into the sunset wandered Iranon, seeking still for his native land and for men who would understand and cherish his songs and dreams. In all the cities of Cydathria and in the lands beyond the Bnazie desert gay-faced children laughed at his olden songs and tattered robe of purple; but Iranon stayed ever young, and wore wreaths upon his golden head whilst he sang of Aira, delight of the past and hope of the future.

So came he one night to the squalid cot of an antique shepherd, bent and dirty, who kept flocks on a stony slope above a quicksand marsh. To this man Iranon spoke, as to so many others:

"Canst thou tell me where I may find Aira, the city of marble and beryl, where flows the hyaline Nithra and where the falls of the tiny Kra sing to verdant valleys and hills forested with yath trees?" and the shepherd, hearing, looked long and strangely at Iranon, as if recalling something very far away in time, and noted each line of the stranger's face, and his golden hair, and his crown of vine-leaves. But he was old, and shook his head as he replied:

"O stranger, I have indeed heard the name of Aira, and the other names thou hast spoken, but they come to me from afar down the waste of long years. I heard them in my youth from the lips of a playmate, a beggar's boy given to strange dreams, who would weave long tales about the moon and the flowers and the west wind. We used to laugh at him, for we knew him from his birth though he thought himself a King's son. He was comely, even as thou, but full of folly and strangeness; and he ran away when small to find those who would listen gladly to his songs and dreams. How often hath he sung to me of lands that never were, and things that never can be! Of Aira did he speak much; of Aira and the river Nithra, and the falls of the tiny Kra. There would he ever say he once dwelt as a Prince, though here we knew him from his birth. Nor was there ever a marble city of Aira, or those who could delight in strange songs, save in the dreams of mine old playmate Iranon who is gone."

And in the twilight, as the stars came out one by one and the moon cast on the marsh a radiance like that which a child sees quivering on the floor as he is rocked to sleep at evening, there walked into the lethal quicksands a very old man in tattered purple, crowned with withered vine-leaves and gazing ahead as if upon the golden domes of a fair city where dreams are understood. That night something of youth and beauty died in the elder world.

During this period, not having as yet sold anything to *Weird Tales,* Lovecraft supported himself partly by doing literary revisions for other writers. Some of these were so extensive as to be more collaboration than revision, and were published under a joint authorship such as the tale which follows. Of it he wrote to Frank Belknap Long on June 4, 1921:

> I will send—subject to return—two papers containing collaborated work which you have not seen before. . . . The two tales in question, *The Green Meadow* and *The Crawling Chaos,* were written around ideas of the amateur poet Winifred V. Jackson, who probably possesses the greatest and most singular imagination in amateur journalism, and who will one day be famous in the outside world.* . . . In prose technique she fails, hence can utilise *story* ideas only in collaboration with some technician. [Her ideas are] so curiously like my own conceptions that I can in some cases build upon them—with so little difference that the result shows no sign of dual authorship. Such tales are published under the pseudonyms of "Elizabeth Berkeley" and "Lewis Theobald, Jun."

*Lovecraft was a poor prophet: if Miss Jackson is remembered at all today, it is because she collaborated on "The Crawling Chaos" with the world-famous Mr. Lovecraft!

THE CRAWLING CHAOS*

Of the pleasures and pains of opium much has been written. The ecstasies and horrors of De Quincey and the *paradis artificiels* of Baudelaire are preserved and interpreted with an art which makes them immortal, and the world knows well the beauty, the terror and the mystery of those obscure realms into which the inspired dreamer is transported. But much as has been told, no man has yet dared intimate the *nature* of the phantasms thus unfolded to the mind, or hint at the *direction* of the unheard-of roads along whose ornate and exotic course the partaker of the drug is so irresistibly borne. De Quincey was drawn back into Asia, that teeming land of nebulous shadows whose hideous antiquity is so impressive that "the vast age of the race and name overpowers the sense of youth in the individual," but farther than that he dared not go. Those who *have* gone farther seldom returned, and even when they have, they have been either silent or quite mad. I took opium but once—in the year of the plague, when doctors sought to deaden the agonies they could not cure. There was an overdose—my physician was worn out with horror and exertion—and I travelled very far indeed. In the end I returned and lived, but my nights are filled with strange memories, nor have I ever permitted a doctor to give me opium again.

*with Elizabeth Berkeley.

The pain and pounding in my head had been quite unendurable when the drug was administered. Of the future I had no heed; to escape, whether by cure, unconsciousness, or death, was all that concerned me. I was partly delirious, so that it is hard to place the exact moment of transition, but I think the effect must have begun shortly before the pounding ceased to be painful. As I have said, there was an overdose; so my reactions were probably far from normal. The sensation of falling, curiously dissociated from the idea of gravity or direction, was paramount; though there was a subsidiary impression of unseen throngs in incalculable profusion, throngs of infinitely diverse nature, but all more or less related to me. Sometimes it seemed less as though I were falling, then as though the universe or the ages were falling past me. Suddenly my pain ceased, and I began to associate the pounding with an external rather than internal force. The falling had ceased also, giving place to a sensation of uneasy, temporary rest; and when I listened closely, I fancied the pounding was that of the vast, inscrutable sea as its sinister, colossal breakers lacerated some desolate shore after a storm of titanic magnitude. Then I opened my eyes.

For a moment my surroundings seemed confused, like a projected image hopelessly out of focus, but gradually I realised my solitary presence in a strange and beautiful room lighted by many windows. Of the exact nature of the apartment I could form no idea, for my thoughts were still far from settled, but I noticed vari-coloured rugs and draperies, elaborately fashioned tables, chairs, ottomans, and divans, and delicate vases and ornaments which conveyed a suggestion of the exotic without being actually alien. These things I noticed, yet they were not long uppermost in my mind. Slowly but inexorably crawling upon my consciousness and rising above every other impression, came a dizzying fear of the unknown; a fear all the greater because I could not analyse it, and seeming to concern a stealthily approaching menace; not death, but some nameless, unheard-of thing inexpressibly more ghastly and abhorrent.

Presently I realised that the direct symbol and excitant of my fear was the hideous pounding whose incessant reverberations throbbed maddeningly against my exhausted brain. It seemed to come from a point outside and below the edifice in which I stood, and to associate itself with the most terrifying mental images. I felt that some horrible scene or object lurked beyond the silk-hung walls, and shrank from glancing through the arched, latticed windows that opened so bewilderingly on every hand. Perceiving shutters attached to these windows, I closed them all, averting my eyes from the exterior as I did so. Then, employing a flint and steel which I found on one of the small tables, I lit the many candles reposing about the walls in arabesque sconces. The added sense of security brought by closed shutters and artificial light calmed my nerves to some degree, but I could not shut out the monotonous pounding. Now that I was calmer, the sound became as fascinating as it was fearful, and I felt a contradictory desire to seek out its source despite my still powerful shrinking. Opening a portiere at the side of the room nearest the pounding, I beheld a small and richly draped corridor ending in a carven door and large oriel window. To this window I was irresistibly drawn, though my ill-defined apprehensions seemed almost equally bent on holding me back. As I approached it I could see a chaotic whirl of waters in the distance. Then, as I attained it and glanced out on all sides, the stupendous picture of my surroundings burst upon me with full and devastating force.

I beheld such a sight as I had never beheld before, and which no living person can have seen save in the delirium of fever or the inferno of opium. The building stood on a narrow point of land—or what was *now* a narrow point of land—fully three hundred feet above what must lately have been a seething vortex of mad waters. On either side of the house there fell a newly washed-out precipice of red earth, whilst ahead of me the hideous waves were still rolling in frightfully, eating away the land with ghastly monotony and deliberation. Out a mile or more there rose and fell menacing breakers at least fifty feet in height, and on the far horizon ghoulish black clouds of grotesque contour were resting and brooding like unwholesome vultures. The waves were dark and purplish, almost black, and clutched at the yielding red mud of the bank as if with uncouth, greedy hands. I could not but feel that some noxious marine mind had declared a war of extermination upon all the solid ground, perhaps abetted by the angry sky.

Recovering at length from the stupor into which this unnatural spectacle had thrown me, I realized that my actual physical danger was acute. Even whilst I gazed, the bank had lost many feet, and it could not be long before the house would fall undermined into the awful pit of lashing waves. Accordingly I hastened to the opposite side of the edifice, and finding a door, emerged at once, locking it after me with a curious key which had hung inside. I now beheld more of the strange region about me, and marked a singular division which seemed to exist in the hostile ocean and firmament. On each side of the jutting promontory different conditions held sway. At my left as I faced inland was a gently heaving sea with great green waves rolling peacefully in under a brightly shining sun. Something about that sun's nature and position made me shudder, but I could not then tell, and cannot tell now, what it was. At my right also was the sea, but it was blue, calm, and only gently undulating, while the sky above it was darker and the washed-out bank more nearly white than reddish.

I now turned my attention to the land, and found occasion for fresh surprise; for the vegetation resembled nothing I had ever seen or read about. It was apparently tropical or at least sub-tropical—a conclusion borne out by the intense heat of the air. Sometimes I thought I could trace strange analogies with the flora of my native land, fancying that the well-known plants and shrubs might assume such forms under a radical change of climate; but the gigantic and omnipresent palm trees were plainly foreign. The house I had just left was very small—hardly more than a cottage—but its material was evidently marble, and its architecture was weird and composite, involving a quaint fusion of Western and Eastern forms. At the corners were Corinthian columns, but the red tile roof was like that of a Chinese pagoda. From the door inland there stretched a path of singularly white sand, about four feet wide, and lined on either side with stately palms and unidentifiable flowering shrubs and plants. It lay toward the side of the promontory where the sea was blue and the bank rather whitish. Down this path I felt impelled to flee, as if pursued by some malignant spirit from the pounding ocean. At first it was slightly uphill, then I reached a gentle crest. Behind me I saw the scene I had left; the entire point with the cottage and the black water, with the green sea on one side and the blue sea on the other, and a curse unnamed and unnamable lowering over all. I never saw it again, and often wonder. . . . After this last look I strode ahead and surveyed the inland panorama before me.

The path, as I have intimated, ran along the right-hand shore as one went inland. Ahead and to the left I now viewed a magnificent valley comprising thousands of acres, and covered with a swaying growth of tropical grass higher than my head. Almost at the limit of vision was a colossal palm tree which seemed to fascinate and beckon me. By this time wonder and escape from the imperilled peninsula had largely dissipated my fear, but as I paused and sank fatigued to the path, idly digging with my hands into the warm, whitish-golden sand, a new and acute sense of danger seized me. Some terror in the swishing tall grass seemed added to that of the diabolically pounding sea, and I started up crying aloud and disjointedly, "Tiger? Tiger? Is it Tiger? Beast? Beast? Is it a Beast that I am afraid of?" My mind wandered back to an ancient and classical story of tigers which I had read; I strove to recall the author, but had difficulty. Then in the midst of my fear I remembered that the tale was by Rudyard Kipling; nor did the grotesqueness of deeming him an ancient author occur to me. I wished for the volume containing this story, and had almost started back toward the doomed cottage to procure it when my better sense and the lure of the palm prevented me.

Whether or not I could have resisted the backward beckoning without the counter-fascination of the vast palm tree, I do not know. This attraction was now dominant, and I left the path and crawled on hands and knees down the valley's slope despite my fear of the grass and of the serpents it might contain. I resolved to fight for life and reason as long as possible against all menaces of sea or land, though I sometimes feared defeat as the maddening swish of the uncanny grasses joined the still audible and irritating pounding of the distant breakers. I would frequently pause and put my hands to my ears for relief, but could never quite shut out the detestable sound. It was, as it seemed to me, only after ages that I finally dragged myself to the beckoning palm tree and lay quiet beneath its protecting shade.

There now ensued a series of incidents which transported me to the opposite extremes of ecstasy and horror; incidents which I tremble to recall and dare not seek to interpret. No sooner had I crawled beneath the overhanging foliage of the palm, than there dropped from its branches a young child of such beauty as I never beheld before. Though ragged and dusty, this being bore the features of a faun or demigod, and seemed almost to diffuse a radiance in the dense shadow of the tree. It smiled and extended its hand, but before I could arise and speak I heard in the upper air the exquisite melody of singing; notes high and low blent with a sublime and ethereal harmoniousness. The sun had by this time sunk below the horizon, and in the twilight I saw an aureole of lambent light encircled the child's head. Then in a tone of silver it addressed me: "It is the end. They have come down through the gloaming from the stars. Now all is over, and beyond the Arinurian streams we shall dwell blissfully in Teloe." As the child spoke, I beheld a soft radiance through the leaves of the palm tree, and rising greeted a pair whom I knew to be the chief singers among those I had heard. A god and goddess they must have been, for such beauty is not mortal; and they took my hands, saying, "Come, child, you have heard the voices, and all is well. In Teloe beyond the Milky Way and the

Arinurian streams are cities all of amber and chalcedony. And upon their domes of many facets glisten the images of strange and beautiful stars. Under the ivory bridges of Teloe flow rivers of liquid gold bearing pleasure-barges bound for blossomy Cytharion of the Seven Suns. And in Teloe and Cytharion abide only youth, beauty, and pleasure, nor are any sounds heard, save of laughter, song, and the lute. Only the gods dwell in Teloe of the golden rivers, but among them shalt thou dwell."

As I listened, enchanted, I suddenly became aware of a change in my surroundings. The palm tree, so lately overshadowing my exhausted form, was now some distance to my left and considerably below me. I was obviously floating in the atmosphere; companioned not only by the strange child and the radiant pair, but by a constantly increasing throng of half-luminous, vine-crowned youths and maidens with wind-blown hair and joyful countenance. We slowly ascended together, as if borne on a fragrant breeze which blew not from the earth but from the golden nebulae, and the child whispered in my ear that I must look always upward to the pathways of light, and never backward to the sphere I had just left. The youths and maidens now chanted mellifluous choriambics to the accompaniment of lutes, and I felt enveloped in a peace and happiness more profound than any I had in life imagined, when the intrusion of a single sound altered my destiny and shattered my soul. Through the ravishing strains of the singers and the lutanists, as if in mocking, daemoniac concord, throbbed from gulfs below the damnable, the detestable pounding of that hideous ocean. As those black breakers beat their message into my ears I forgot the words of the child and looked back, down upon the doomed scene from which I thought I had escaped.

Down through the aether I saw the accursed earth slowly turning, ever turning, with angry and tempestuous seas gnawing at wild desolate shores and dashing foam against the tottering towers of deserted cities. And under a ghastly moon there gleamed sights I can never describe, sights I can never forget; deserts of corpselike clay and jungles of ruin and decadence where once stretched the populous plains and villages of my native land, and maelstroms of frothing ocean where once rose the mighty temples of my forefathers. Around the northern pole steamed a morass of noisome growths and miasmal vapours, hissing before the onslaught of the ever-mounting waves that curled and fretted from the shuddering deep. Then a rending report clave the night, and athwart the desert of deserts appeared a smoking rift. Still the black ocean foamed and gnawed, eating away the desert on either side as the rift in the center widened and widened.

There was now no land left but the desert, and still the fuming ocean ate and ate. All at once I thought even the pounding sea seemed afraid of something, afraid of dark gods of the inner earth that are greater than the evil god of waters, but even if it was it could not turn back; and the desert had suffered too much from those nightmare waves to help them now. So the ocean ate the last of the land and poured into the smoking gulf, thereby giving up all it had ever conquered. From the new-flooded lands it flowed again, uncovering death and decay; and from its ancient and immemorial bed it trickled loathsomely, uncovering nighted secrets of the years when Time was young and the gods unborn. Above the waves rose weedy remembered spires. The moon laid pale lilies of light on dead London, and Paris stood up from its damp grave to be sanctified with star-dust. Then rose spires and monoliths that were weedy but not remembered; terrible spires and monoliths of lands that men never knew were lands.

There was not any pounding now, but only the unearthly roaring and hissing of waters tumbling into the rift. The smoke of that rift had changed to steam, and almost hid the world as it grew denser and denser. It seared my face and hands, and when I looked to see how it affected my companions I found they had all disappeared. Then very suddenly it ended, and I knew no more till I awaked upon a bed of convalescence. As the cloud of steam from the Plutonic gulf finally concealed the entire surface from my sight, all the firmament shrieked at a sudden agony of mad reverberations which shook the trembling aether. In one delirious flash and burst it happened; one blinding, deafening holocaust of fire, smoke, and thunder that dissolved the wan moon as it sped outward to the void.

And when the smoke cleared away, and I sought to look upon the earth, I beheld against the background of cold, humorous stars only the dying sun and the pale mournful planets searching for their sister.

Here is a second example of Lovecraft writing in collaboration—his collaborator in this case was a young *Weird Tales* fan named Kenneth Sterling. Sterling is now a mature man, a father, and still occasionally turns up at science fiction conventions and the like; through our mutual acquaintance, Donald A. Wollheim, I have met and talked with Sterling and he and his wife have been guests in my house. Most recently, I ran into Sterling wandering around at the 1970 Lunacon, a yearly science fiction affair held in New York City over the Easter weekend: it was amusing and a trifle sad to see him ignored by the young fans, to whom he was a complete stranger . . . fans who would probably have been struck with awe had they known he had once collaborated with H. P. Lovecraft on a story when he was about their age!

Incidentally, this is Lovecraft's only venture into genuine science fiction, unless you consider stories like "The Shadow out of Time" or "The Colour out of Space," which contain vaguely science-fictional elements, to be the real thing. . . .

IN THE WALLS OF ERYX*

Before I try to rest I will set down these notes in preparation for the report I must make. What I have found is so singular, and so contrary to all past experience and expectations, that it deserves a very careful description.

I reached the main landing on Venus March 18, terrestrial time; VI, 9 of the planet's calendar. Being put in the main group under Miller, I received my equipment—watch tuned to Venus's slightly quicker rotation—and went through the usual mask drill. After two days I was pronounced fit for duty.

Leaving the Crystal Company's post at Terra Nova around dawn, VI, 12, I followed the southerly route which Anderson had mapped out from the air. The going was bad, for these jungles are always half impassable after a rain. It must be the moisture that gives the tangled vines and creepers that leathery toughness; a toughness so great that a knife has to work ten minutes on some of them. By noon it was dryer—the vegetation getting soft and rubbery so that the knife went through it easily—but even then I could not make much speed. These Carter oxygen masks are too heavy—just carrying one half wears an ordinary man out. A Dubois mask with sponge-reservoir instead of tubes would give just as good air at half the weight.

*With Kenneth Sterling.

The crystal-detector seemed to function well, pointing steadily in a direction verifying Anderson's report. It is curious how that principle of affinity works—without any of the fakery of the old "divining rods" back home. There must be a great deposit of crystals within a thousand miles, though I suppose those damnable man-lizards always watch and guard it. Possibly they think we are just as foolish for coming to Venus to hunt the stuff as we think they are for grovelling in the mud whenever they see a piece of it, or for keeping that great mass on a pedestal in their temple. I wish they'd get a new religion, for they have no use for the crystals except to pray to. Barring theology, they would let us take all we want—and even if they learned to tap them for power there'd be more than enough for their planet and the earth besides. I for one am tired of passing up the main deposits and merely seeking separate crystals out of jungle river-beds. Sometime I'll urge the wiping out of these scaly beggars by a good stiff army from home. About twenty ships could bring enough troops across to turn the trick. One can't call the damned things men for all their "cities" and towers. They haven't any skill except building—and using swords and poison darts—and I don't believe their so-called "cities" mean much more than ant-hills or beaver-dams. I doubt if they even have a real language—all the talk about psychological communication through those tentacles down their chests strikes me as bunk. What misleads people is their upright posture; just an accidental physical resemblance to terrestrial man.

I'd like to go through a Venus jungle for once without having to watch out for skulking groups of them or dodge their cursed darts. They may have been all right before we began to take the crystals, but they're certainly a bad enough nuisance now—with their dart-shooting and their cutting of our water pipes. More and more I come to believe that they have a special sense like our crystal-detectors. No one ever knew them to bother a man—apart from long-distance sniping—who didn't have crystals on him.

Around 1 P.M. a dart nearly took my helmet off, and I

thought for a second one of my oxygen tubes was punctured. The sly devils hadn't made a sound, but three of them were closing in on me. I got them all by sweeping in a circle with my flame pistol, for even though their color blended with the jungle, I could spot the moving creepers. One of them was fully eight feet tall, with a snout like a tapir's. The other two were average seven-footers. All that makes them hold their own is sheer numbers—even a single regiment of flame throwers could raise hell with them. It is curious, though, how they've come to be dominant on the planet. Not another living thing higher than the wriggling akmans and skorahs, or the flying tukahs of the other continent—unless of course those holes in the Dionaean Plateau hide something.

About two o'clock my detector veered westward, indicating isolated crystals ahead on the right. This checked up with Anderson, and I turned my course accordingly. It was harder going—not only because the ground was rising, but because the animal life and carnivorous plants were thicker. I was always slashing ugrats and stepping on skorahs, and my leather suit was all speckled from the bursting darohs which struck it from all sides. The sunlight was all the worse because of the mist, and did not seem to dry up the mud in the least. Every time I stepped my feet sank down five or six inches, and there was a sucking sort of *blup* every time I pulled them out. I wish somebody would invent a safe kind of suiting other than leather for this climate. Cloth of course would rot; but some thin metallic tissue that couldn't tear—like the surface of this revolving decay-proof record scroll—ought to be feasible sometime.

I ate about 3:30—if slipping these wretched food tablets through my mask can be called eating. Soon after that I noticed a decided change in the landscape—the bright, poisonous-looking flowers shifting in color and getting wraith-like. The outlines of everything shimmered rhythmically, and bright points of light appeared and danced in the same slow, steady tempo. After that the temperature seemed to fluctuate in unison with a peculiar rhythmic drumming.

The whole universe seemed to be throbbing in deep, regular pulsations that filled every corner of space and flowed through my body and mind alike. I lost all sense of equilibrium and staggered dizzily, nor did it change things in the least when I shut my eyes and covered my ears with my hands. However, my mind was still clear, and in a very few minutes I realized what had happened.

I had encountered at last one of those curious *mirage-plants* about which so many of our men told stories. Anderson had warned me of them, and described their appearance very closely—the shaggy stalk, the spiky leaves, and the mottled blossoms whose gaseous, dream-breeding exhalations penetrate every existing make of mask.

Recalling what happened to Bailey three years ago, I fell into a momentary panic, and began to dash and stagger about in the crazy, chaotic world which the plant's exhalations had woven around me. Then good sense came back, and I realized all I need do was retreat from the dangerous blossoms—heading away from the source of the pulsations, and cutting a path blindly—regardless of what might seem to swirl around me—until safely out of the plant's effective radius.

Although everything was spinning perilously, I tried to start in the right direction and hack my way ahead. My route must have been far from straight, for it seemed hours before I was free of the mirage-plant's pervasive influence. Gradually the dancing lights began to disappear, and the shimmering spectral scenery began to assume the aspect of solidity. When I did get wholly clear I looked at my watch and was astonished to find that the time was only 4:20. Though eternities had seemed to pass, the whole experience could have consumed little more than a half-hour.

Every delay, however, was irksome, and I had lost ground in my retreat from the plant. I now pushed ahead in the uphill direction indicated by the crystal-detector, bending every energy toward making better time. The jungle was still thick, though there was less animal life. Once a carnivorous blossom engulfed my right foot and held it so tightly that I had to hack it free with my knife; reducing the flower to strips before it let go.

In less than an hour I saw that the jungle growths were thinning out, and by five o'clock—after passing through a belt of tree-ferns with very little underbrush—I emerged on a broad mossy plateau. My progress now became rapid, and I saw by the wavering of my detector-needle that I was getting relatively close to the crystal I sought. This was odd, for most of the scattered, egg-like spheroids occurred in jungle streams of a sort not likely to be found on this treeless upland.

The terrain sloped upward, ending in a definite crest. I reached the top about 5:30, and saw ahead of me a very extensive plain with forests in the distance. This, without question, was the plateau mapped by Matsugawa from the air fifty years ago, and called on our maps "Eryx" or the "Erycinian Highland." But what made my heart leap was a smaller detail, whose position could not have been far from the plain's exact center. It was a single point of light, blazing through the mist and seeming to draw a piercing, concentrated luminescence from the yellowish, vapor-dulled sunbeams. This, without doubt, was the crystal I sought—a thing possibly no larger than a hen's egg, yet containing enough power to keep a city warm for a year. I could hardly wonder, as I glimpsed the distant glow, that those miserable man-lizards worship such crystals. And yet they have not the least notion of the powers they contain.

Breaking into a rapid run, I tried to reach the unexpected prize as soon as possible; and was annoyed when the firm moss gave place to a thin, singularly detestable mud studded with occasional patches of weeds and creepers. But I splashed on heedlessly—scarcely thinking to look around for any of the skulking man-lizards. In this open space I was not very likely to be waylaid. As I advanced, the light ahead seemed to grow in size and brilliancy, and I began to notice some peculiarity in its situation. Clearly, this was a crystal of the very finest quality, and my elation grew with every spattering step.

It is now that I must begin to be careful in making my

report, since what I shall henceforward have to say involves unprecedented—though fortunately verifiable—matters. I was racing ahead with mounting eagerness, and had come within a hundred yards or so of the crystal—whose position on a sort of raised place in the omnipresent slime seemed very odd—when a sudden, overpowering force struck my chest and the knuckles of my clenched fists and knocked me over backward into the mud. The splash of my fall was terrific, nor did the softness of the ground and the presence of some slimy weeds and creepers save my head from a bewildering jarring. For a moment I lay supine, too utterly startled to think. Then I half mechanically stumbled to my feet and began to scrape the worst of the mud and scum from my leather suit.

Of what I had encountered I could not form the faintest idea. I had seen nothing which could have caused the shock, and I saw nothing now. Had I, after all, merely slipped in the mud? My sore knuckles and aching chest forbade me to think so. Or was this whole incident an illusion brought on by some hidden mirage-plant? It hardly seemed probable, since I had none of the usual symptoms, and since there was no place nearby where so vivid and typical a growth could lurk unseen. Had I been on the earth, I would have suspected a barrier of N-force laid down by some government to mark a forbidden zone, but in this humanless region such a notion would have been absurd.

Finally pulling myself together, I decided to investigate in a cautious way. Holding my knife as far as possible ahead of me, so that it might be first to feel the strange force, I started once more for the shining crystal—preparing to advance step by step with the greatest deliberation. At the third step I was brought up short by the impact of the knife-point on an apparently solid surface—a solid surface where my eyes saw nothing.

After a moment's recoil I gained boldness. Extending my gloved left hand, I verified the presence of invisible solid matter—or a tactile illusion of solid matter—ahead of me. Upon moving my hand I found that the barrier was of substantial extent, and of an almost glassy smoothness, with no evidence of the joining of separate blocks. Nerving myself for further experiments, I removed a glove and tested the thing with my bare hand. It was indeed hard and glassy, and of a curious coldness as contrasted with the air around. I strained my eyesight to the utmost in an effort to glimpse some trace of the obstructing substance, but could discern nothing whatsoever. There was not even any evidence of refractive power as judged by the aspect of the landscape ahead. Absence of reflective power was proved by the lack of a glowing image of the sun at any point.

Burning curiosity began to displace all other feelings, and I enlarged my investigations as best I could. Exploring with my hands, I found that the barrier extended from the ground to some level higher than I could reach, and that it stretched off indefinitely on both sides. It was, then, a *wall* of some kind—though all guesses as to its materials and its purpose were beyond me. Again I thought of the mirage-plant and the dreams it induced, but a moment's reasoning put this out of my head.

Knocking sharply on the barrier with the hilt of my knife, and kicking at it with my heavy boots, I tried to interpret the sounds thus made. There was something suggestive of cement or concrete in these reverberations, though my hands had found the surface more glassy or metallic in feel. Certainly, I was confronting something strange beyond all previous experience.

The next logical move was to get some idea of the wall's dimensions. The height problem would be hard, if not insoluble, but the length and shape problem could perhaps be sooner dealt with. Stretching out my arms and pressing close to the barrier, I began to edge gradually to the left—keeping very careful track of the way I faced. After several steps I concluded that the wall was not straight, but that I was following part of some vast circle or ellipse. And then my attention was distracted by something wholly different—something connected with the still-distant crystal which had formed the object of my quest.

I have said that even from a greater distance the shining

object's position seemed indefinably queer—on a slight mound rising from the slime. Now—at about a hundred yards—I could see plainly despite the engulfing mist just what that mound was. It was the body of a man in one of the Crystal Company's leather suits, lying on his back, and with his oxygen mask half buried in the mud a few inches away. In his right hand, crushed convulsively against his chest, was the crystal which had led me here —a spheroid of incredible size, so large that the dead fingers could scarcely close over it. Even at the given distance I could see that the body was a recent one. There was little visible decay, and I reflected that in this climate such a thing meant death not more than a day before. Soon the hateful farnoth-flies would begin to cluster about the corpse. I wondered who the man was. Surely no one I had seen on this trip. It must have been one of the old-timers absent on a long roving commission, who had come to this especial region independently of Anderson's survey. There he lay, past all trouble, and with the rays of the great crystal streaming out from between his stiffened fingers.

For fully five minutes I stood there staring in bewilderment and apprehension. A curious dread assailed me, and I had an unreasonable impulse to run away. It could not have been done by those slinking man-lizards, for he still held the crystal he had found. Was there any connexion with the invisible wall? Where had he found the crystal? Anderson's instrument had indicated one in this quarter well before this man could have perished. I now began to regard the unseen barrier as something sinister, and recoiled from it with a shudder. Yet I knew I must probe the mystery all the more quickly and thoroughly because of this recent tragedy.

Suddenly—wrenching my mind back to the problem I faced—I thought of a possible means of testing the wall's height, or at least of finding whether or not it extended indefinitely upward. Seizing a handful of mud, I let it drain until it gained some coherence and then flung it high in the air toward the utterly transparent barrier. At a height of perhaps fourteen feet it struck the invisible surface with a resounding splash, disintegrating at once and oozing downward in disappearing streams with surprising rapidity. Plainly, the wall was a lofty one. A second handful, hurled at an even sharper angle, hit the surface about eighteen feet from the ground and disappeared as quickly as the first.

I now summoned up all my strength and prepared to throw a third handful as high as I possibly could. Letting the mud drain, and squeezing it to maximum dryness, I flung it up so steeply that I feared it might not reach the obstructing surface at all. It did, however, and this time it crossed the barrier and fell in the mud beyond with a violent spattering. At last I had a rough idea of the height of the wall, for the crossing had evidently occurred some twenty or twenty-one feet aloft.

With a nineteen- or twenty-foot vertical wall of glassy flatness, ascent was clearly impossible. I must, then, continue to circle the barrier in the hope of finding a gate, an ending, or some sort of interruption. Did the obstacle form a complete round or other closed figure, or was it merely an arc or semi-circle? Acting on my decision, I resumed my slow leftward circling, moving my hands up and down over the unseen surface on the chance of finding some window or other small aperture. Before starting, I tried to mark my position by kicking a hole in the mud, but found the slime too thin to hold any impression. I did, though, gauge the place approximately by noting a tall cycad in the distant forest which seemed just on a line with the gleaming crystal a hundred yards away. If no gate or break existed I could now tell when I had completely circumnavigated the wall.

I had not progressed far before I decided that the curvature indicated a circular enclosure of about a hundred yards' diameter—provided the outline was regular. This would mean that the dead man lay near the wall at a point almost opposite the region where I had started. Was he just inside or just outside the enclosure? This I would soon ascertain.

As I slowly rounded the barrier without finding any gate, window, or other break, I decided that the body was lying within. On closer view the features of the dead man seemed vaguely disturbing. I found something alarming in his expression, and in the way the glassy eyes stared. By the time I was very near I believed I recognized him as Dwight, a veteran whom I had never known, but who was pointed out to me at the post last year. The crystal he clutched was certainly a prize—the largest single specimen I had ever seen.

I was so near the body that I could—but for the barrier—have touched it, when my exploring left hand encountered a corner in the unseen surface. In a second I had learned that there was an opening about three feet wide, extending from the ground to a height greater than I could reach. There was no door, nor any evidence of hingemarks bespeaking a former door. Without a moment's hesitation I stepped through and advanced two paces to the prostrate body—which lay at right angles to the hallway I had entered, in what seemed to be an intersecting, doorless corridor. It gave me a fresh curiosity to find that the interior of this vast enclosure was divided by partitions.

Bending to examine the corpse, I discovered that it bore no wounds. This scarcely surprised me, since the continued presence of the crystal argued against the pseudo-reptilian natives. Looking about for some possible cause of death, my eyes lit upon the oxygen mask lying close to the body's feet. Here, indeed, was something significant. Without this device no human being could breathe the air of Venus for more than thirty seconds, and Dwight—if it were he—had obviously lost his. Probably it had been carelessly buckled, so that the weight of the tubes worked the straps loose—a thing which could not happen with a Dubois sponge-reservoir mask. The half-minute of grace had been too short to allow the man to stoop and recover his protection—or else the cyanogen content of the atmosphere was abnormally high at the time. Probably he had been busy admiring the crystal—wherever he may have found it. He had, apparently, just taken it from the pouch in his suit, for the flap was unbuttoned.

I now proceeded to extricate the huge crystal from the

dead prospector's fingers—a task which the body's stiffness made very difficult. The spheroid was larger than a man's fist, and glowed as if alive in the reddish rays of the westering sun. As I touched the gleaming surface I shuddered involuntarily—as if by taking this precious object I had transferred to myself the doom which had overtaken its earlier bearer. However, my qualms soon passed, and I carefully buttoned the crystal into the pouch of my leather suit. Superstition has never been one of my failings.

Placing the man's helmet over his dead, staring face, I straightened up and stepped back through the unseen doorway to the entrance hall of the great enclosure. All my curiosity about the strange edifice now returned, and I racked my brain with speculations regarding its material, origin, and purpose. That the hands of men had reared it I could not for a moment believe. Our ships first reached Venus only seventy-two years ago, and the only human beings on the planet have been those at Terra Nova. Nor does human knowledge include any perfectly transparent, non-refractive solid such as the substance of this building. Prehistoric human invasions of Venus can be pretty well ruled out, so that one must turn to the idea of native construction. Did a forgotten race of highly-evolved beings precede the man-lizards as masters of Venus? Despite their elaborately-built cities, it seemed hard to credit the pseudo-reptiles with anything of this kind. There must have been another race aeons ago, of which this is perhaps the last relique. Or will other ruins of kindred origin be found by future expeditions? The *purpose* of such a structure passes all conjecture—but its strange and seemingly non-practical material suggests a religious use.

Realising my inability to solve these problems, I decided that all I could do was to explore the invisible structure itself. That various rooms and corridors extended over the seemingly unbroken plain of mud I felt convinced; and I believed that a knowledge of their plan might lead to something significant. So, feeling my way back through the doorway and edging past the body, I began to advance along the corridor toward those interior regions whence the dead man had presumably come. Later on I would investigate the hallway I had left.

Groping like a blind man despite the misty sunlight, I moved slowly onward. Soon the corridor turned sharply and began to spiral in toward the centre in ever-diminishing curves. Now and then my touch would reveal a doorless intersecting passage, and I several times encountered junctions with two, three, and four diverging avenues. In these latter cases I always followed the inmost route, which seemed to form a continuation of the one I had been traversing. There would be plenty of time to examine the branches after I had reached and returned from the main regions. I can scarcely describe the strangeness of the experience—threading the unseen ways of an invisible structure reared by forgotten hands on an alien planet!

At last, still stumbling and groping, I felt the corridor end in a sizeable open space. Fumbling about, I found I was in a circular chamber about ten feet across; and from the position of the dead man against certain distant forest landmarks I judged that this chamber lay at or near the centre of the edifice. Out of it opened five corridors besides the one through which I had entered, but I kept the latter in mind by sighting very carefully past the body to a particular tree on the horizon as I stood just within the entrance.

There was nothing in this room to distinguish it—merely the floor of thin mud which was everywhere present. Wondering whether this part of the building had any roof, I repeated my experiment with an upward-flung handful of mud, and found at once that no covering existed. If there had ever been one, it must have fallen long ago, for not a trace of debris or scattered blocks ever halted my feet. As I reflected, it struck me as distinctly odd that this apparently primordial structure should be so devoid of tumbling masonry, gaps in the walls, and other common attributes of dilapidation.

What was it? What had it ever been? Of what was it made? Why was there no evidence of separate blocks in the glassy, bafflingly homogeneous walls? Why were there no traces of doors, either interior or exterior? I knew only that I was in a round, roofless, doorless edifice of some hard, smooth, perfectly transparent, non-refractive and non-reflective material, a hundred yards in diameter, with many corridors, and with a small circular room at the centre. More than this I could never learn from a direct investigation.

I now observed that the sun was sinking very low in the west—a golden-ruddy disc floating in a pool of scarlet and orange above the mist-clouded trees of the horizon. Plainly, I would have to hurry if I expected to choose a sleeping-spot on dry ground before dark. I had long before decided to camp for the night on the firm, mossy rim of the plateau near the crest whence I had first spied the shining crystal, trusting to my usual luck to save me from an attack by the man-lizards. It has always been my contention that we ought to travel in parties of two or more, so that someone can be on guard during sleeping hours, but the really small number of night attacks makes the Company careless about such things. Those scaly wretches seem to have difficulty in seeing at night, even with curious glow torches.

Having picked out again the hallway through which I had come, I started to return to the structure's entrance. Additional exploration could wait for another day. Groping a course as best I could through the spiral corridor—with only general sense, memory, and a vague recognition of some of the ill-defined weed patches on the plain as guides—I soon found myself once more in close proximity to the corpse. There were now one or two farnoth flies swooping over the helmet-covered face, and I knew that decay was setting in. With a futile instinctive loathing I raised my hand to brush away this vanguard of the scavengers—when a strange and astonishing thing became manifest. An invisible wall, checking the sweep of my arm, told me that—notwithstanding my careful retracing of the way—I had not indeed returned to the corridor in which the body lay. Instead, I was in a parallel hallway, having no doubt taken some wrong turn or fork among the intricate passages behind.

Hoping to find a doorway to the exit hall ahead, I continued my advance, but presently came to a blank wall. I would, then, have to return to the central chamber and steer my course anew. Exactly where I had made my mistake I could not tell. I glanced at the ground to see if by any miracle guiding footprints had remained, but at once realised that the thin mud held impressions only for a very few moments. There was little difficulty in finding my way to the centre again, and once there I carefully reflected on the proper outward course. I had kept too far to the right before. This time I must take a more leftward fork somewhere—just where, I could decide as I went.

As I groped ahead a second time I felt quite confident of my correctness, and diverged to the left at a junction I was sure I remembered. The spiralling continued, and I was careful not to stray into any intersecting passages. Soon, however, I saw to my disgust that I was passing the body at a considerable distance; this passage evidently reached the outer wall at a point much beyond it. In the hope that another exit might exist in the half of the wall I had not yet explored, I pressed forward for several paces, but eventually came once more to a solid barrier. Clearly, the plan of the building was even more complicated than I had thought.

I now debated whether to return to the centre again or whether to try some of the lateral corridors extending toward the body. If I chose this second alternative, I would run the risk of breaking my mental pattern of where I was; hence I had better not attempt it unless I could think of some way of leaving a visible trail behind me. Just how to leave a trail would be quite a problem, and I ransacked my mind for a solution. There seemed to be nothing about my person which could leave a mark on anything, nor any material which I could scatter—or minutely subdivide and scatter.

My pen had no effect on the invisible wall, and I could not lay a trail of my precious food tablets. Even had I been willing to spare the latter, there would not have been even nearly enough—besides which the small pellets would have instantly sunk from sight in the thin mud. I searched my pockets for an old-fashioned note-book—often used unofficially on Venus despite the quick rotting-rate of paper in the planet's atmosphere—whose pages I could tear up and scatter, but could find none. It was obviously impossible to tear the tough, thin metal of this revolving decay-proof record scroll, nor did my clothing offer any possibilities. In Venus's peculiar atmosphere I could not safely spare my stout leather suit, and underwear had been eliminated because of the climate.

I tried to smear mud on the smooth, invisible walls after squeezing it as dry as possible, but found that it slipped from sight as quickly as did the height-testing handfuls I had previously thrown. Finally I drew out my knife and attempted to scratch a line on the glassy, phantom surface—something I could recognize with my hand, even though I would not have the advantage of seeing it from afar. It was useless, however, for the blade made not the slightest impression on the baffling, unknown material.

Frustrated in all attempts to blaze a trail, I again sought the round central chamber through memory. It seemed easier to get back to this room than to steer a definite, predetermined course away from it, and I had little difficulty in finding it anew. This time I listed on my record scroll every turn I made—drawing a crude hypothetical diagram of my route, and marking all diverging corridors. It was, of course, maddeningly slow work when everything had to be determined by touch, and the possibilities of error were infinite; but I believed it would pay in the long run.

The long twilight of Venus was thick when I reached the central room, but I still had hopes of gaining the outside before dark. Comparing my fresh diagram with previous recollections, I believed I had located my original mistake, so once more set out confidently along the invisible hallways. I veered further to the left than during my previous attempts, and tried to keep track of my turnings on the record scroll in case I was still mistaken. In the gathering dusk I could see the dim line of the corpse, now the centre of a loathsome cloud of farnoth-flies. Before long, no doubt, the mud-dwelling sificlighs would be oozing in from the plain to complete the ghastly work. Approaching the body with some reluctance, I was preparing to step past it when a sudden collision with a wall told me I was again astray.

I now realized plainly that I was lost. The complications of this building were too much for offhand solution, and I would probably have to do some careful checking before I could hope to emerge. Still, I was eager to get to dry ground before total darkness set in; hence I returned once more to the centre and began a rather aimless series of trials and errors—making notes by the light of my electric lamp. When I used this device I noticed with interest that it produced no reflection—not even the faintest glistening—in the transparent walls around me. I was, however, prepared for this; since the sun had at no time formed a gleaming image in the strange material.

I was still groping about when the dusk became total. A heavy mist obscured most of the stars and planets, but the earth was plainly visible as a glowing, bluish-green point in the southeast. It was just past opposition, and would have been a glorious sight in a telescope. I could even make out the moon beside it whenever the vapours momentarily thinned. It was now impossible to see the corpse—my only landmark— so I blundered back to the central chamber after a few false turns. After all, I would have to give up hope of sleeping on dry ground. Nothing could be done till daylight, and I might as well make the best of it here. Lying down in the mud would not be pleasant, but in my leather suit it could be done. On former expeditions I had slept under even worse conditions, and now sheer exhaustion would help to conquer repugnance.

So, here I am, squatting in the slime of the central room and making these notes on my record scroll by the light of the electric lamp. There is something almost humorous in my strange, unprecedented plight. Lost in a building without doors—a building which I cannot see! I shall doubtless get out early in the morning, and ought to be back at Terra Nova with the crystal by late afternoon. It certainly is a beauty—with surprising lustre even in the feeble light of this lamp. I have just had it out examining it. Despite my fatigue, sleep is slow in coming, so I find myself writing at great length. I must stop now. Not much danger of being bothered by those cursed natives in this place. The thing I like least is the corpse—but fortunately my oxygen mask saves me from the worst effects. I am using the chlorate cubes very sparingly. Will take a couple of food tablets now and turn in. More later.

LATER—AFTERNOON, VI, 13

There has been more trouble than I expected. I am still in the building, and will have to work quickly and wisely if I expect to rest on dry ground tonight. It took me a long time to get to sleep, and I did not wake till almost noon today. As it was, I would have slept longer but for the glare of the sun through the haze. The corpse was a rather bad sight—wriggling with sificlighs, and with a cloud of farnoth-flies around it. Something had pushed the helmet away from the face, and it was better not to look at it. I was doubly glad of my oxygen mask when I thought of the situation.

At length I shook and brushed myself dry, took a couple of food tablets, and put a new potassium chlorate cube in the electrolyser of the mask. I am using these cubes slowly, but wish I had a larger supply. I felt much better after my sleep, and expected to get out of the building very shortly.

Consulting the notes and sketches I had jotted down, I was impressed by the complexity of the hallways, and by the possibility that I had made a fundamental error. Of the six openings leading out of the central space, I had chosen a certain one as that by which I had entered—using a sighting-arrangement as a guide. When I stood just within the opening, the corpse fifty yards away was exactly in line with a particular lepidodendron in the far-off forest. Now it occurred to be that this sighting might not have been of sufficient accuracy—the distance of the corpse making its difference of direction in relation to the horizon comparatively slight when viewed from the openings next to that of my first ingress. Moreover, the tree did not differ as distinctly as it might from other lepidodendra on the horizon.

Putting the matter to a test, I found to my chagrin that I could not be sure which of three openings was the right one. Had I traversed a different set of windings at each attempted exit? This time I would be sure. It struck me that despite the impossibility of trail-blazing there was one marker I could leave. Though I could not spare my suit, I could—because of my thick head of hair—spare my helmet; and this was large and light enough to remain visible above the thin mud. Accordingly I removed the roughly hemispherical device and laid it at the entrance of one of the corridors—the right-hand one of the three I must try.

I would follow this corridor on the assumption that it was correct; repeating what I seemed to recall as the proper turns, and constantly consulting and making notes. If I did not get out, I would systematically exhaust all possible variations; and if these failed, I would proceed to cover the avenues extending from the next opening in the same way—continuing to the third opening if necessary. Sooner or later I could not avoid hitting the right path to the exit, but I must use patience. Even at worst, I could scarcely fail to reach the open plain in time for a dry night's sleep.

Immediate results were rather discouraging, though they helped me eliminate the right-hand opening in little more than an hour. Only a succession of blind alleys, each ending at a great distance from the corpse, seemed to branch from this hallway; and I saw very soon that it had not figured at all in the previous afternoon's wanderings. As before, however, I always found it relatively easy to grope back to the central chamber.

About 1 P.M. I shifted my helmet marker to the next

opening and began to explore the hallways beyond it. At first I thought I recognized the turnings, but soon found myself in a wholly unfamiliar set of corridors. I could not get near the corpse, and this time seemed cut off from the central chamber as well, even though I thought I had recorded every move I made. There seemed to be tricky twists and crossings too subtle for me to capture in my crude diagrams, and I began to develop a kind of mixed anger and discouragement. While patience would of course win in the end, I saw that my searching would have to be minute, tireless, and long-continued.

Two o'clock found me still wandering vainly through strange corridors—constantly feeling my way, looking alternately at my helmet and at the corpse, and jotting data on my scroll with decreasing confidence. I cursed the stupidity and idle curiosity which had drawn me into this tangle of unseen walls—reflecting that if I had let the thing alone and headed back as soon as I had taken the crystal from the body, I would even now be safe at Terra Nova.

Suddenly it occurred to me that I might be able to tunnel under the invisible walls with my knife, and thus effect a short cut to the outside—or to some outward-leading corridor. I had no means of knowing how deep the building's foundations were, but the omnipresent mud argued the absence of any floor save the earth. Facing the distant and increasingly horrible corpse, I began a course of feverish digging with the broad, sharp blade.

There was about six inches of semi-liquid mud, below which the density of the soil increased sharply. This lower soil seemed to be of a different colour—a greyish clay rather like the formations near Venus's north pole. As I continued downward close to the unseen barrier I saw that the ground was getting harder and harder. Watery mud rushed into the excavation as fast as I removed the clay, but I reached through it and kept on working. If I could bore any kind of a passage beneath the wall, the mud would not stop my wriggling out.

About three feet down, however, the hardness of the soil halted my digging seriously. Its tenacity was beyond anything I had encountered before, even on this planet, and was linked with an anomalous heaviness. My knife had to split and chip the tightly packed clay, and the fragments I brought up were like solid stones or bits of metal. Finally even this splitting and chipping became impossible, and I had to cease my work with no lower edge of wall in reach.

The hour-long attempt was a wasteful as well as futile one, for it used up great stores of my energy and forced me both to take an extra food tablet, and to put an additional chlorate cube in the oxygen mask. It has also brought a pause in the day's gropings, for I am still much too exhausted to walk. After cleaning my hands and arms of the worst of the mud I sat down to write these notes—leaning against an invisible wall and facing away from the corpse.

That body is simply a writhing mass of vermin now—the odour has begun to draw some of the slimy akmans from the far-off jungle. I notice that many of the efjeh-weeds on the plain are reaching out necrophagous feelers toward the thing; but I doubt if any are long enough to reach it. I wish some really carnivorous organisms like the skorahs would appear, for then they might scent me and wriggle a course through the building toward me. Things like that have an odd sense of direction. I could watch them as they came, and jot down their approximate route if they failed to form a continuous line. Even that would be a great help. When I met any the pistol would make short work of them.

But I can hardly hope for as much as that. Now that these notes are made I shall rest a while longer, and later will do some more groping. As soon as I get back to the central chamber—which ought to be fairly easy—I shall try the extreme left-hand opening. Perhaps I can get outside by dusk after all.

NIGHT—VI, 13

New trouble. My escape will be tremendously difficult, for there are elements I had not suspected. Another night here in the mud, and a fight on my hands tomorrow. I cut my rest short and was up and groping again by four o'clock. After about fifteen minutes I reached the central chamber and moved my helmet to mark the last of the three possible doorways. Starting through this opening, I seemed to find the going more familiar, but was brought up short in less than five minutes by a sight that jolted me more than I can describe.

It was a group of four or five of those detestable man-lizards emerging from the forest far off across the plain. I could not see them distinctly at that distance, but thought they paused and turned toward the trees to gesticulate, after which they were joined by fully a dozen more. The augmented party now began to advance directly toward the invisible building, and as they approached I studied them carefully. I had never before had a close view of the things outside the steamy shadows of the jungle.

The resemblance to reptiles was perceptible, though I knew it was only an apparent one, since these beings have no point of contact with terrestrial life. When they drew nearer they seemed less truly reptilian—only the flat head and the green, slimy, frog-like skin carrying out the idea. They walked erect on their odd, thick stumps, and their suction-discs made curious noises in the mud. These were average specimens, about seven feet in height, and with four long, ropy pectoral tentacles. The motions of those tentacles—if the theories of Fogg, Ekberg, and Janat are right, which I formerly doubted but am now more ready to believe—indicated that the things were in animated conversation.

I drew my flame pistol and was ready for a hard fight. The odds were bad, but the weapon gave me a certain advantage. If the things knew this building they would come through it after me, and in this way would form a key to getting out; just as carnivorous skorahs might have done. That they would attack me seemed certain; for even though they could not see the crystal in my pouch, they could divine its presence through that special sense of theirs.

Yet, surprisingly enough, they did not attack me. Instead they scattered and formed a vast circle around me—at a distance which indicated that they were pressing close to the unseen wall. Standing there in a ring, the beings stared silently and inquisitively at me, waving their tentacles and sometimes nodding their heads and gesturing with their upper limbs. After a while I saw others issue from the forest, and these advanced and joined the curious crowd. Those near the corpse looked briefly at it but made no move to disturb it. It was a horrible sight, yet the man-lizards seemed quite unconcerned. Now and then one of them would brush away the farnoth-flies with its limbs or tentacles, or crush a wriggling sificligh or akman, or an out-reaching efjeh-weed, with the suction discs on its stumps.

Staring back at these grotesque and unexpected intruders, and wondering uneasily why they did not attack me at once, I lost for the time being the will-power and nervous energy to continue my search for the way out. Instead I leaned limply against the invisible wall of the passage where I stood, letting my wonder merge gradually into a chain of the wildest speculations. A hundred mysteries which had previously baffled me seemed all at once to take on a new and sinister significance, and I trembled with an acute fear unlike anything I had experienced before.

I believed I knew why these repulsive beings were hovering expectantly around me. I believed, too, that I had the secret of the transparent structure at last. The alluring crystal which I had seized, the body of the man who had seized it before me—all these things began to acquire a dark and threatening meaning.

It was no common series of mischances which had made me lose my way in this roofless, unseen tangle of corridors. Far from it. Beyond doubt, the place was a genuine maze—a labyrinth deliberately built by these hellish beings whose craft and mentality I had so badly underestimated. Might I not have suspected this before, knowing of their uncanny architectural skill? The purpose was all too plain. It was a trap—a trap set to catch human beings, and with the crystal spheroid as bait. These reptilian things, in their war on the takers of crystals, had turned to strategy and were using our own cupidity against us.

Dwight—if this rotting corpse were indeed he—was a victim. He must have been trapped some time ago, and had failed to find his way out. Lack of water had doubtless maddened him, and perhaps he had run out of chlorate cubes as well. Probably his mask had not slipped accidentally after all. Suicide was a likelier thing. Rather than face a lingering death he had solved the issue by removing the mask deliberately and letting the lethal atmosphere do its work at once. The horrible irony of his fate lay in his position—only a few feet from the saving exit he had failed to find. One minute more of searching and he would have been safe.

And now I was trapped as he had been. Trapped, and with this circling herd of curious starers to mock at my predicament. The thought was maddening, and as it sank in I was seized with a sudden flash of panic which set me running aimlessly through the unseen hallways. For several moments I was essentially a maniac—stumbling, tripping, bruising myself on the invisible walls, and finally collapsing in the mud as a panting, lacerated heap of mindless, bleeding flesh.

The fall sobered me a bit, so that when I slowly struggled to my feet I could notice things and exercise my reason. The circling watchers were swaying their tentacles in an odd, irregular way suggestive of sly, alien laughter, and I shook my fist savagely at them as I rose. My gesture seemed to increase their hideous mirth—a few of them clumsily imitating it with their greenish upper limbs. Shamed into sense, I tried to collect my faculties and take stock of the situation.

After all, I was not as badly off as Dwight had been. Unlike him, I knew what the situation was—and forewarned is forearmed. I had proof that the exit was attainable in the end, and would not repeat his tragic act of impatient despair. The body—or skeleton, as it would soon be—was constantly before me as a guide to the sought-for aperture, and dogged patience would certainly take me to it if I worked long and intelligently enough.

I had, however, the disadvantage of being surrounded by these reptilian devils. Now that I realised the nature of the trap—whose invisible material argued a science and technology beyond anything on earth—I could no longer discount the mentality and resources of my enemies. Even with my flame-pistol I would have a bad time getting away—though boldness and quickness would doubtless see me through in the long run.

But first I must reach the exterior—unless I could lure or provoke some of the creatures to advance toward me. As I prepared my pistol for action and counted over my generous supply of ammunition it occurred to me to try the effect of its blasts on the invisible walls. Had I overlooked a feasible means of escape? There was no clue to the chemical composition of the transparent barrier, and conceivably it might be something which a tongue of fire could cut like cheese. Choosing a section facing the corpse, I carefully discharged the pistol at close range and felt with my knife where the blast had been aimed. Nothing was changed. I had seen the flame spread when it struck the surface, and now I realised that my hope had been vain. Only a long, tedious search for the exit would ever bring me to the outside.

So, swallowing another food tablet and putting another cube in the electrolyser of my mask, I recommenced the long quest; retracing my steps to the central chamber and starting out anew. I constantly consulted my notes and sketches, and made fresh ones—taking one false turn after another, but staggering on in desperation till the afternoon light grew very dim. As I persisted in my quest I looked from time to time at the silent circle of mocking stares, and noticed a gradual replacement in their ranks. Every now and then a few would return to the forest, while others would arrive to take their places. The more I thought of their tactics the less I liked them, for they gave me a hint of the creatures' possible motives. At any time these devils could have advanced and fought me, but they seemed to prefer watching my struggles to escape. I could not but infer that they enjoyed the spectacle—and this made me shrink with double force from the prospect of falling into their hands.

With the dark I ceased my searching, and sat down in the mud to rest. Now I am writing in the light of my lamp, and will soon try to get some sleep. I hope tomorrow will see me out; for my canteen is low, and lacol tablets are a poor substitute for water. I would hardly dare to try the moisture in this slime, for none of the water in the mud-regions is potable except when distilled. That is why we run such long pipe lines to the yellow clay regions—or depend on rain-water when those devils find and cut our pipes. I have none too many chlorate cubes either, and must try to cut down my oxygen consumption as much as I can. My tunnelling attempt of the early afternoon, and my later panic flight, burned up a perilous amount of air. Tomorrow I will reduce physical exertion to the barest minimum until I meet the reptiles and have to deal with them. I must have a good cube supply for the journey back to Terra Nova. My enemies are still on hand; I can see a circle of their feeble glow-torches around me. There is a horror about those lights which will keep me awake.

NIGHT—VI, 14

Another full day of searching and still no way out! I am beginning to be worried about the water problem, for my canteen went dry at noon. In the afternoon there was a burst of rain, and I went back to the central chamber for the helmet which I had left as a marker—using this as a bowl and getting about two cupfuls of water. I drank most of it, but have put the slight remainder in my canteen. Lacol tablets make little headway against real thirst, and I hope there will be more rain in the night. I am leaving my helmet bottom up to catch any that falls. Food tablets are none too plentiful, but not dangerously low. I shall halve my rations from now on. The chlorate cubes are my real worry, for even without violent exercise the day's endless tramping burned a dangerous number. I feel weak from my forced economies in oxygen, and from my constantly mounting thirst. When I reduce my food I suppose I shall feel still weaker.

There is something damnable—something uncanny—about this labyrinth. I could swear that I had eliminated certain turns through charting, and yet each new trial belies some assumption I had thought established. Never before did I realise how lost we are without visual landmarks. A blind man might do better—but for most of us *sight* is the king of the senses. The effect of all these fruitless wanderings is one of profound discouragement. I can understand how poor Dwight must have felt. His corpse is now a skeleton, and the sificlighs and akmans and farnoth-flies are gone. The efjeh-weeds are nipping the leather clothing to pieces, for they were longer and faster growing than I had expected. And all the while those relays of tentacled starers stand gloatingly around the barrier laughing at me and enjoying my misery. Another day and I shall go mad if I do not drop dead from exhaustion.

However, there is nothing to do but persevere. Dwight would have got out if he had kept on a minute longer. It is just possible that somebody from Terra Nova will come looking for me before long, although this is only my third day out. My muscles ache horribly, and I can't seem to rest at all lying down in this loathsome mud. Last night, despite my terrific fatigue, I slept only fitfully, and tonight I fear will be no better. I live in an endless nightmare—poised between waking and sleeping, yet neither truly awake nor truly asleep. My hand shakes, I can write no more for the time being. That circle of feeble glow-torches is hideous.

LATE AFTERNOON—VI, 15

Substantial progress! Looks good. Very weak, and did not sleep much till daylight. Then I dozed till noon, though without being at all rested. No rain, and thirst leaves me very weak. Ate an extra food tablet to keep me going, but without water it didn't help much. I dared to try a little of the slime water just once, but it made me violently sick and left me even thirstier than before. Must save chlorate cubes, so am nearly suffocating for lack of oxygen. Can't walk much of the time, but manage to crawl in the mud. About 2 P.M. I thought I recognized some passages, and got substantially nearer to the corpse—or skeleton—than I had been since the first day's trials. I was sidetracked once in a blind alley, but recovered the main trail with the aid of my chart and notes. The trouble with these jottings is that there are so many of them. They must cover three feet of the record scroll, and I have to stop for long periods to untangle them. My head is weak from thirst, suffocation, and exhaustion, and I cannot understand all I have set down. Those damnable green things keep staring and laughing with their tentacles, and sometimes they gesticulate in a way that makes me think they share some terrible joke just beyond my perception.

It was three o'clock when I really struck my stride. There was a doorway which, according to my notes, I had not traversed before; and when I tried it I found I could crawl circuitously toward the weed-twined skeleton. The route was a sort of spiral, much like that by which I had first reached the central chamber. Whenever I came to a lateral doorway or junction I would keep to the course which seemed best to repeat that original journey. As I circled nearer and nearer to my gruesome landmark, the watchers outside intensified their cryptic gesticulations and sardonic silent laughter. Evidently they saw something grimly amusing in my progress—perceiving no doubt how helpless I would be in any encounter with them. I was content to leave them to their mirth; for although I realised my extreme weakness, I counted on the flame pistol and its numerous extra magazines to get me through the vile reptilian phalanx.

Hope now soared high, but I did not attempt to rise to my feet. Better crawl now, and save my strength for the coming encounter with the man-lizards. My advance was very slow, and the danger of straying into some blind alley very great, but none the less I seemed to curve steadily toward my osseous goal. The prospect gave me new strength, and for the nonce I ceased to worry about my pain, my thirst, and my scant supply of cubes. The creatures were now all massing around the entrance—gesturing, leaping, and laughing with their tentacles. Soon, I reflected, I would have to face the entire horde—and perhaps such reinforcements as they would receive from the forest.

I am now only a few yards from the skeleton, and am pausing to make this entry before emerging and breaking through the noxious band of entities. I feel confident that with my last ounce of strength I can put them to flight despite their numbers, for the range of this pistol is tremendous. Then a camp on the dry moss at the plateau's edge, and in the morning a weary trip through the jungle to Terra Nova. I shall be glad to see living men and the buildings of human beings again. The teeth of that skull gleam and grin horribly.

TOWARD NIGHT—VI, 15

Horror and despair. Baffled again! After making the previous entry I approached still closer to the skeleton, but suddenly encountered an intervening wall. I had been deceived once more, and was apparently back where I had been three days before, on my first futile attempt to leave the labyrinth. Whether I screamed aloud I do not know—perhaps I was too weak to utter a sound. I merely lay dazed in the mud for a long period, while the greenish things outside leaped and laughed and gestured.

After a time I became more fully conscious. My thirst and weakness and suffocation were fast gaining on me, and with my last bit of strength I put a new cube in the electrolyser—recklessly, and without regard for the needs of my journey to Terra Nova. The fresh oxygen revived me slightly, and enabled me to look about more alertly.

It seemed as if I were slightly more distant from poor Dwight than I had been at that first disappointment, and I dully wondered if I could be in some other corridor a trifle more remote. With this faint shadow of hope I laboriously dragged myself forward—but after a few feet encountered a dead end as I had on the former occasion.

This, then, was the end. Three days had taken me nowhere, and my strength was gone. I would soon go mad from thirst, and I could no longer count on cubes enough to get me back. I feebly wondered why the nightmare things had gathered so thickly around the entrance as they mocked me. Probably this was part of the mockery—to make me think I was approaching an egress which they knew did not exist.

I shall not last long, though I am resolved not to hasten matters as Dwight did. His grinning skull has just turned toward me, shifted by the groping of one of the efjeh-weeds that are devouring his leather suit. The ghoulish stare of those empty eye-sockets is worse than the staring of those lizard horrors. It lends a hideous meaning to that dead, white-toothed grin.

I shall lie very still in the mud and save all the strength I can. This record—which I hope may reach and warn those who come after me—will soon be done. After I stop writing I shall rest a long while. Then, when it is too dark for those frightful creatures to see, I shall muster up my last reserves of strength and try to toss the record scroll over the wall and the intervening corridor to the plain outside. I shall take care to send it toward the left, where it will not hit the leaping band of mocking beleaguerers. Perhaps it will be lost forever in the thin mud—but perhaps it will land in some widespread clump of weeds and ultimately reach the hands of men.

If it does survive to be read, I hope it may do more than merely warn men of this trap. I hope it may teach our race to let those shining crystals stay where they are. They belong to Venus alone. Our planet does not truly need them, and I believe we have violated some obscure and mysterious law—some law buried deep in the arcana of the cosmos—in our attempts to take them. Who can tell what dark, potent, and widespread forces spur on these reptilian things who guard their treasure so strangely? Dwight and I had paid, as others have paid and will pay. But it may be that these scattered deaths are only the prelude of greater horrors to come. Let us leave to Venus that which belongs only to Venus.

* * *

I am very near death now, and fear I may not be able to throw the scroll when dusk comes. If I cannot, I suppose the man-lizards will seize it, for they will probably realise what it is. They will not wish anyone to be warned of the labyrinth—and they will not know that my message holds a plea in their own behalf. As the end approaches I feel more kindly toward the things. In the scale of cosmic entity who can say which species stands higher, or more nearly approaches a space-wide organic norm—theirs or mine?

* * *

I have just taken the great crystal out of my pouch to look at in my last moments. It shines fiercely and menacingly in the red rays of the dying day. The leaping horde have noticed it, and their gestures have changed in a way I cannot understand. I wonder why they keep clustered around the entrance instead of concentrating at a still closer point in the transparent wall.

* * *

I am growing numb and cannot write much more. Things whirl around me, yet I do not lose consciousness. Can I throw this over the wall? That crystal glows so, yet the twilight is deepening.

* * *

Dark. Very weak. They are still laughing and leaping around the doorway, and have started those hellish glow-torches.

* * *

Are they going away? I dreamed I heard a sound . . . light in the sky. . . .

REPORT OF WESLEY P. MILLER, SUPT. GROUP A, VENUS CRYSTAL CO.

(TERRA NOVA ON VENUS—VI, 16)

Our Operative A-49, Kenton J. Stanfield of 5317 Marshall Street, Richmond, Va., left Terra Nova early on VI, 12, for a short-term trip indicated by detector. Due back 13th or 14th. Did not appear by evening of 15th, so Scouting Plane FR-58 with five men under my command set out at 8 P.M. to follow route with detector. Needle showed no change from earlier readings.

Followed needle to Erycinian Highland, played strong searchlights all the way. Triple-range flame-guns and D-radiation-cylinders could have dispersed any ordinary hostile force of natives, or any dangerous aggregation of carnivorous skorahs.

When over the open plain on Eryx we saw a group of moving lights which we knew were native glow-torches. As we approached, they scattered into the forest. Probably seventy-five to a hundred in all. Detector indicated crystal on spot where they had been. Sailing low over this spot, our lights picked out objects on the ground. Skeleton tangled in efjeh-weeds, and complete body ten feet from it. Brought plane down near bodies, and corner of wing crashed on unseen obstruction.

Approaching bodies on foot, we came up short against a smooth, invisible barrier which puzzled us enormously. Feeling along it near the skeleton, we struck an opening, beyond which was a space with another opening leading to the skeleton. The latter, though robbed of clothing by weeds, had one of the company's numbered metal helmets beside it. It was Operative B-9, Frederick N. Dwight of Koenig's division, who had been out of Terra Nova for two months on a long commission.

Between this skeleton and the complete body there seemed to be another wall, but we could easily identify the second man as Stanfield. He had a record scroll in his left hand and a pen in his right, and seemed to have been writing when he died. No crystal was visible, but the detector indicated a huge specimen near Stanfield's body.

We had great difficulty in getting at Stanfield, but finally succeeded. The body was still warm, and a great crystal lay beside it, covered by the shallow mud. We at once studied the record scroll in the left hand, and prepared to take certain steps based on its data. The contents of the scroll forms the long narrative prefixed to this report; a narrative whose main descriptions we have verified, and which we append as an explanation of what was found. The later parts of this account show mental decay, but there is no reason to doubt the bulk of it. Stanfield obviously died of a combination of thirst, suffocation, cardiac strain, and psychological depression. His mask was in place, and freely generating oxygen despite an alarmingly low cube supply.

Our plane being damaged, we sent a wireless and called out Anderson with Repair-Plane FG-7, a crew of wreckers, and a set of blasting materials. By morning FH-58 was fixed, and went back under Anderson carrying the two bodies and the crystal. We shall bury Dwight and Stanfield in the company graveyard, and ship the crystal to Chicago on the next earth-bound liner. Later, we shall adopt Stanfield's suggestion—the sound one in the saner, earlier part of his report—and bring across enough troops to wipe out the natives altogether. With a clear field, there can be scarcely any limit to the amount of crystal we can secure.

In the afternoon we studied the invisible building or trap with great care, exploring it with the aid of long guiding cords, and preparing a complete chart for our archives. We were much impressed by the design, and shall keep specimens of the substance for chemical analysis. All such knowledge will be useful when we take over the various cities of the natives. Our type C diamond drills were able to bite into the unseen material, and wreckers are now planting dynamite preparatory to a thorough blasting. Nothing will be left when we are done. The edifice forms a distinct menace to aerial and other possible traffic.

In considering the plan of the labyrinth one is impressed not only with the irony of Dwight's fate, but with that of Stanfield's as well. When trying to reach the second body from the skeleton, we could find no access on the right, but Markheim found a doorway from the first inner space some fifteen feet past Dwight and four or five past Stanfield. Beyond this was a long hall which we did not explore till later, but on the right-hand side of that hall was another doorway leading directly to the body. Stanfield could have reached the outside entrance by walking twenty-two or twenty-three feet if he had found the opening which lay directly *behind* him—an opening which he overlooked in his exhaustion and despair.

This last story is a major piece of ghost-writing, which Lovecraft did in 1924 for the celebrated stage magician and escape artist, Harry Houdini. On February 14 of that year, Lovecraft wrote to Frank Belknap Long:

> Yes, Child, *Weird Tales* is certainly shovin' a lot of work at your aged Grandsire! Entire new job —to rewrite a strange narrative which the magician Houdini related orally to Henneberger [the owner of *Weird Tales*] . . . Henneberger demanded a telegraphed reply as to whether or not I'd accept the job, and promises INSTANT PAY on delivery! I wired him an affirmative . . .

By March 12 the story had been completed. In a letter of that date to James F. Morton, Lovecraft (in great good humor, having just married Sonia H. Greene and moved to Brooklyn) burbled enthusiastically:

> . . . BOY, that Houdini job! It strained me to the limit, and I didn't get it off till after we got back from Philly. I went the limit in descriptive realism in the first part, then when I buckled down to the under-the-pyramid stuff I let myself loose and coughed up some of the most nameless, slithering, unmentionable HORROR that ever stalked cloven-hooved through the tenebrous and necrophagous abysses of elder night.

Lovecraft was always most deeply affected by the mystery and strangeness of antiquity, and this particular story, which wallowed in Ancient Egypt, touched a creative response in him that lifts it from being merely a straight-faced bit of Munchausering into a genuinely exciting work of romance and adventure, unlike anything else in the Lovecraft canon.

IMPRISONED WITH THE PHARAOHS*

Mystery attracts mystery. Ever since the wide appearance of my name as a performer of unexplained feats, I have encountered strange narratives and events which my calling has led people to link with my interests and activities. Some of these have been trivial and irrelevant, some deeply dramatic and absorbing, some productive of weird and perilous experiences and some involving me in extensive scientific and historical research. Many of these matters I have told and shall continue to tell very freely; but there is one of which I speak with great reluctance, and which I am now relating only after a session of grilling persuasion from the publishers of this magazine, who had heard vague rumors of it from other members of my family.

The hitherto guarded subject pertains to my non-professional visit to Egypt fourteen years ago, and has been avoided by me for several reasons. For one thing, I am averse to exploiting certain unmistakably actual facts and conditions obviously unknown to the myriad tourists who throng about the pyramids and apparently secreted with much diligence by the authorities at Cairo, who cannot be wholly ignorant of them. For another thing, I dislike to recount an incident in which my own fantastic imagination must have played so great a part. What I

*With Harry Houdini.

saw—or thought I saw—certainly did not take place; but is rather to be viewed as a result of my then recent readings in Egyptology, and of the speculations anent this theme which my environment naturally prompted. These imaginative stimuli, magnified by the excitement of an actual event terrible enough in itself, undoubtedly gave rise to the culminating horror of that grotesque night so long past.

In January, 1910, I had finished a professional engagement in England and signed a contract for a tour of Australian theatres. A liberal time being allowed for the trip, I determined to make the most of it in the sort of travel which chiefly interests me; so accompanied by my wife I drifted pleasantly down the Continent and embarked at Marseilles on the P. & O. Steamer *Malwa,* bound for Port Said. From that point I proposed to visit the principal historical localities of lower Egypt before leaving finally for Australia.

The voyage was an agreeable one, and enlivened by many of the amusing incidents which befall a magical performer apart from his work. I had intended, for the sake of quiet travel, to keep my name a secret; but was goaded into betraying myself by a fellow-magician whose anxiety to astound the passengers with ordinary tricks tempted me to duplicate and exceed his feats in a manner quite destructive of my incognito. I mention this because of its ultimate effect—an effect I should have foreseen before unmasking to a shipload of tourists about to scatter throughout the Nile valley. What it did was to herald my identity wherever I subsequently went, and deprive my wife and me of all the placid inconspicuousness we had sought. Traveling to seek curiosities, I was often forced to stand inspection as a sort of curiosity myself!

We had come to Egypt in search of the picturesque and the mystically impressive, but found little enough when the ship edged up to Port Said and discharged its passengers in small boats. Low dunes of sand, bobbing buoys in shallow water, and a drearily European small town with nothing of interest save the great De Lesseps statue, made us anxious to get on to something more worth our while.

After some discussion we decided to proceed at once to Cairo and the Pyramids, later going to Alexandria for the Australian boat and for whatever Greco-Roman sights that ancient metropolis might present.

The railway journey was tolerable enough, and consumed only four hours and a half. We saw much of the Suez Canal, whose route we followed as far as Ismailiya and later had a taste of Old Egypt in our glimpse of the restored fresh-water canal of the Middle Empire. Then at last we saw Cairo glimmering through the growing dusk; a winkling constellation which became a blaze as we halted at the great Gare Centrale.

But once more disappointment awaited us, for all that we beheld was European save the costumes and the crowds. A prosaic subway led to a square teeming with carriages, taxicabs, and trolley-cars and gorgeous with electric lights shining on tall buildings; whilst the very theatre where I was vainly requested to play and which I later attended as a spectator, had recently been renamed "American Cosmograph." We stopped at Shepheard's Hotel, reached in a taxi that sped along broad, smartly built-up streets; and amidst the perfect service of its restaurant, elevators and generally Anglo-American luxuries the mysterious East and immemorial past seemed very far away.

The next day, however, precipitated us delightfully into the heart of the *Arabian Nights* atmosphere; and in the winding ways and exotic skyline of Cairo, the Bagdad of Harun-al-Rashid seemed to live again. Guided by our Baedeker, we had struck east past the Ezbekiyeh Gardens along the Mouski in quest of the native quarter, and were soon in the hands of a clamorous cicerone who —notwithstanding later developments—was assuredly a master at his trade.

Not until afterward did I see that I should have applied at the hotel for a licensed guide. This man, a shaven, peculiarly hollow-voiced and relatively cleanly fellow who looked like a Pharaoh and called himself "Abdul Reis el Drogman," appeared to have much power over others of his kind; though subsequently the police professed not to know him, and to suggest that *reis* is merely a name for any person in authority, whilst "Drogman" is obviously no more than a clumsy modification of the word for a leader of tourist parties—*dragoman*.

Abdul led us among such wonders as we had before only read and dreamed of. Old Cairo is itself a story-book and a dream—labyrinths of narrow alleys redolent of aromatic secrets; Arabesque balconies and oriels nearly meeting above the cobbled streets; maelstroms of Oriental traffic with strange cries, cracking whips, rattling carts, jingling money, and braying donkeys; kaleidoscopes of polychrome robes, veils, turbans, and tarbushes; water-carriers and dervishes, dogs and cats, soothsayers and barbers; and over all the whining of blind beggars crouched in alcoves, and the sonorous chanting of muezzins from minarets limned delicately against a sky of deep, unchanging blue.

The roofed, quieter bazaars were hardly less alluring. Spice, perfume, incense beads, rugs, silks, and brass—old Mahmoud Suleiman squats cross-legged amidst his gummy bottles while chattering youths pulverize mustard in the hollowed-out capital of an ancient classic column—a Roman Corinthian, perhaps from neighboring Heliopolis, where Augustus stationed one of his three Egyptian legions. Antiquity begins to mingle with exoticism. And then the mosques and the museum—we saw them all, and tried not to let our Arabian revel succumb to the darker charm of Pharaonic Egypt which the museum's priceless treasures offered. That was to be our climax, and for the present we concentrated on the mediaeval Saracenic glories of the Califs whose magnificent tomb-mosques form a glittering faery necropolis on the dge of the Arabian Desert.

At length Abdul took us along the Sharia Mohammed Ali to the ancient mosque of Sultan Hassan, and the tower-flanked Babel-Azab, beyond which climbs the steep-walled pass to the mighty citadel that Saladin himself built with the stones of forgotten pyramids. It was sunset when we scaled that cliff, circled the modern mosque of Mohammed Ali, and looked down from the dizzy parapet over mystic Cairo—mystic Cairo all golden with its carven domes, its ethereal minarets and its flaming gardens.

Far over the city towered the great Roman dome of the new museum; and beyond it—across the cryptic yellow Nile that is the mother of eons and dynasties—lurked the menacing sands of the Libyan Desert, undulant and iridescent and evil with older arcana.

The red sun sank low, bringing the relentless chill of Egyptian dusk; and as it stood poised on the world's rim like that ancient god of Heliopolis—Re-Harakhte, the Horizon-Sun—we saw silhouetted against its vermeil holocaust the black outlines of the Pyramids of Gizeh—the palaeogean tombs there were hoary with a thousand years when Tut-Ankh-Amen mounted his golden throne in distant Thebes. Then we knew that we were done with Saracen Cairo, and that we must taste the deeper mysteries of primal Egypt—the black Kem of Re and Amen, Isis and Osiris.

The next morning we visited the Pyramids, riding out in a Victoria across the island of Chizereh with its massive lebbakh trees, and the smaller English bridge to the western shore. Down the shore road we drove, between great rows of lebbakhs and past the vast Zoological Gardens to the suburb of Gizeh, where a new bridge to Cairo proper has since been built. Then, turning inland along the Sharia-el-Haram, we crossed a region of glassy canals and shabby native villages till before us loomed the objects of our quest, cleaving the mists of dawn and forming inverted replicas in the roadside pools. Forty centuries, as Napoleon had told his campaigners there, indeed looked down upon us.

The road now rose abruptly, till we finally reached our place of transfer between the trolley station and the Mena House Hotel. Abdul Reis, who capably purchased our Pyramid tickets, seemed to have an understanding with the crowding, yelling and offensive Bedouins who inhabited a squalid mud village some distance away and pestiferously assailed every traveler; for he kept them very decently at bay and secured an excellent pair of camels for us, himself mounting a donkey and assigning the leadership of our animals to a group of men and boys more expensive than useful. The area to be traversed was so small that camels were hardly needed, but we did not regret adding to our experience this troublesome form of desert navigation.

The pyramids stand on a high rock plateau, this group forming next to the northernmost of the series of regal and aristocratic cemeteries built in the neighborhood of the extinct capital Memphis, which lay on the same side of the Nile, somewhat south of Gizeh, and which flourished between 3400 and 2000 B.C. The greatest pyramid, which lies nearest the modern road, was built by King Cheops or Khufu about 2800 B.C., and stands more than 450 feet in perpendicular height. In a line southwest from this are successively the Second Pyramid, built a generation later by King Khephren, and though slightly smaller, looking even larger because set on higher ground, and the radically smaller Third Pyramid of King Mycerinus, built about 2700 B.C. Near the edge of the plateau and due east of the Second Pyramid, with a face probably altered to form a colossal portrait of Khephren, its royal restorer, stands the monstrous Sphinx—mute, sardonic, and wise beyond mankind and memory.

Minor pyramids and the traces of ruined minor pyramids are found in several places, and the whole plateau is pitted with the tombs of dignitaries of less than royal rank. These latter were originally marked by *mastabas*, or stone bench-like structures about the deep burial shafts, as found in other Memphian cemeteries and exemplified by Perneb's Tomb in the Metropolitan Museum of New York. At Gizeh, however, all such visible things have been swept away by time and pillage; and only the rock-hewn shafts, either sand-filled or cleared out by archaeologists, remain to attest their former existence. Connected with each tomb was a chapel in which priests and relatives offered food and prayer to the hovering *ka* or vital principle of the deceased. The small tombs have their chapels contained in their stone *mastabas* or superstructures, but the mortuary chapels of the pyramids, where regal Pharaohs lay, were separate temples, each to the east of its corresponding pyramid, and connected by a causeway to a massive gate-chapel or propylon at the edge of the rock plateau.

The gate-chapel leading to the Second Pyramid, nearly buried in the drifting sands, yawns subterraneously southeast of the Sphinx. Persistent tradition dubs it the "Temple of the Sphinx"; and it may perhaps be rightly called such if the Sphinx indeed represents the Second Pyramid's builder Khephren. There are unpleasant tales of the Sphinx before Khephren—but whatever its elder features were, the monarch replaced them with his own that men might look at the colossus without fear.

It was in the great gateway-temple that the life-size diorite statue of Khephren now in the Cairo museum was found; a statue before which I stood in awe when I beheld it. Whether the whole edifice is now excavated I am not certain, but in 1910 most of it was below ground, with the entrance heavily barred at night. Germans were in charge of the work, and the war or other things may have stopped them. I would give much, in view of my experience and of certain Bedouin whisperings discredited or unknown in Cairo, to know what has developed in connection with a certain well in a transverse gallery where statues of the Pharaoh were found in curious juxtaposition to the statues of baboons.

The road, as we traversed it on our camels that morning, curved sharply past the wooden police quarters, post office, drug store and shops on the left, and plunged south and east in a complete bend that scaled the rock plateau and brought us face to face with the desert under the lee of the Great Pyramid. Past Cyclopean masonry we rode, rounding the eastern face and looking down ahead into a valley of minor pyramids beyond which the eternal Nile glistened to the east, and the eternal desert shimmered to the west. Very close loomed the three major pyramids, the greatest devoid of outer casing and showing its bulk of great stones, but the others retaining here and there the neatly fitted covering which had made them smooth and finished in their day.

Presently we descended toward the Sphinx, and sat silent beneath the spell of those terrible unseeing eyes. On the vast stone breast we faintly discerned the emblem of Re-Harakhte, for whose image the Sphinx was mistaken in a late dynasty; and though sand covered the tablet between the great paws, we recalled what Thutmosis IV inscribed thereon, and the dream he had when a prince. It was then that the smile of the Sphinx vaguely displeased us, and made us wonder about the legends of subterranean passages beneath the monstrous creature, leading down, down, to depths none might dare hint at—depths connected with mysteries older than the dynastic Egypt we excavate, and having a sinister relation to the persistence of abnormal, animal-headed gods in the ancient Nilotic pantheon. Then, too, it was I asked myself an idle question whose hideous significance was not to appear for many an hour.

Other tourists now began to overtake us, and we moved on to the sand-choked Temple of the Sphinx, fifty yards to the southeast, which I have previously mentioned as the great gate of the causeway to the Second Pyramid's mortuary chapel on the plateau. Most of it was still underground, and although we dismounted and descended through a modern passageway to its alabaster corridor and pillared hall, I felt that Adul and the local German attendant had not shown us all there was to see.

After this we made the conventional circuit of the pyramid plateau, examining the Second Pyramid and the peculiar ruins of its mortuary chapel to the east, the Third Pyramid and its miniature southern satellites and ruined eastern chapel, the rock tombs and the honeycombings of the Fourth and Fifth dynasties, and the famous Campbell's Tomb whose shadowy shaft sinks precipitously for fifty-three feet to a sinister sarcophagus which one of our camel drivers divested of the cumbering sand after a vertiginous descent by rope.

Cries now assailed us from the Great Pyramid, where Bedouins were besieging a party of tourists with offers of speed in the performance of solitary trips up and down. Seven minutes is said to be the record for such an ascent and descent, but many lusty sheiks and sons of sheiks assured us they could cut it to five if given the requisite impetus of liberal *baksheesh*. They did not get this impetus, though we did let Abdul take us up, thus obtaining a view of unprecedented magnificence which included not only remote and glittering Cairo with its crowned citadel background of gold-violet hills, but all the pyramids of the Memphian district as well, from Abu Roash on the north to the Dashur on the south. The Sakkara step-pyramid, which marks the evolution of the low *mastaba* into the true pyramid, showed clearly and alluringly in the sandy distance. It is close to this transition-monument that the famed tomb of Perneb was found—more than four hundred miles north of the Theban rock valley where Tut-Ankh-Amen sleeps. Again I was forced to silence through sheer awe. The prospect of such antiquity, and the secrets each hoary monument seemed to hold and brood over, filled me with a reverence and sense of immensity nothing else ever gave me.

Fatigued by our climb, and disgusted with the importunate Bedouins whose actions seemed to defy every rule of taste, we omitted the arduous detail of entering the cramped interior passages of any of the pyramids, though we saw several of the hardiest tourists preparing for the suffocating crawl through Cheops' mightiest memorial. As we dismissed and overpaid our local bodyguard and drove back to Cairo with Abdul Reis under the afternoon sun, we half regretted the omission we had made. Such fascinating things were whispered about lower pyramid passages not in the guide books; passages whose entrances had been hastily blocked up and concealed by certain uncommunicative archaeologists who had found and begun to explore them.

Of course, this whispering was largely baseless on the face of it; but it was curious to reflect how persistently visitors were forbidden to enter the Pyramids at night, or to visit the lowest burrows and crypt of the Great Pyramid. Perhaps in the latter case it was the psychological effect which was feared—the effect on the visitor of feeling himself huddled down beneath a gigantic world of solid masonry; joined to the life he has known by the merest tube, in which he may only crawl, and which any accident or evil design might block. The whole subject seemed so weird and alluring that we resolved to pay the pyramid plateau another visit at the earliest possible opportunity. For me this opportunity came much earlier than I expected.

That evening, the members of our party feeling somewhat tired after the strenuous program of the day, I went alone with Abdul Reis for a walk through the picturesque Arab quarter. Though I had seen it by day, I wished to study the alleys and bazaars in the dusk, when rich shadows and mellow gleams of light would add to their glamor and fantastic illusion. The native crowds were thinning, but were still very noisy and numerous when we came upon a knot of reveling Bedouins in the Suken-Nahhasin, or bazaar of the coppersmiths. Their apparent leader, an insolent youth with heavy features and saucily cocked tarbush, took some notice of us, and evidently recognized with no great friendliness my competent but admittedly supercilious and sneeringly disposed guide.

Perhaps, I thought, he resented that odd reproduction of the Sphinx's half-smile which I had often remarked with amused irritation; or perhaps he did not like the hollow and sepulchral resonance of Abdul's voice. At any rate, the exchange of ancestrally opprobrious language became very brisk; and before long Ali Ziz, as I heard the stranger called when called by no worse name, began to pull violently at Abdul's robe, an action quickly reciprocated and leading to a spirited scuffle in which both combatants lost their sacredly cherished headgear and would have reached an even direr condition had I not intervened and separated them by main force.

My interference, at first seemingly unwelcome on both sides, succeeded at last in effecting a truce. Sullenly each belligerent composed his wrath and his attire, and with an assumption of dignity as profound as it was sudden, the two formed a curious pact of honor which I soon learned is a custom of great antiquity in Cario—a pact for the settlement of their difference by means of a nocturnal fist fight atop the Great Pyramid, long after the departure of the last moonlight sightseer. Each duellist was to assemble a party of seconds, and the affair was to begin at midnight, proceeding by rounds in the most civilized possible fashion.

In all this planning there was much which excited my interest. The fight itself promised to be unique and spectacular, while the thought of the scene on that hoary pile overlooking the antediluvian plateau of Gizeh under the wan moon of the pallid small hours appealed to every fiber of imagination in me. A request found Abdul exceedingly willing to admit me to his party of seconds; so that all the rest of the early evening I accompanied him to various dens in the most lawless regions of the town—mostly northeast of the Ezbekiyeh—where he gathered one by one a select and formidable band of congenial cutthroats as his pugilistic background.

Shortly after nine our party, mounted on donkeys bearing such royal or tourist-reminiscent names as "Rameses," "Mark Twain," "J. P. Morgan," and "Minnehaha," edged through street labyrinths both Oriental and Occidental, crossed the muddy and mast-forested Nile by the bridge of the bronze lions, and cantered philosophically between the lebbakhs on the road to Gizeh. Slightly over two hours were consumed by the trip, toward the end of which we passed the last of the returning tourists, saluted the last inbound trolley-car, and were alone with the night and the past and the spectral moon.

Then we saw the vast pyramids at the end of the avenue, ghoulish with a dim atavistical menace which I had not seemed to notice in the daytime. Even the smallest of them held a hint of the ghastly—for was it not in this that they had buried Queen Nitocris alive in the Sixth Dynasty; subtle Queen Nitocris, who once invited all her enemies to a feast in a temple below the Nile, and drowned them by opening the watergates? I recalled that the Arabs whisper things about Nitocris, and shun the Third Pyramid at certain phases of the moon. It must have been over her that Thomas Moore was brooding when he wrote a thing muttered about by Memphian boatmen:

> The subterranean nymph that dwells
> 'Mid sunless gems and glories hid—
> The lady of the Pyramid!

Early as we were, Ali Ziz and his party were ahead of us; for we saw their donkeys outlined against the desert plateau at Kafrel-Haram; toward which squalid Arab settlement, close to the Sphinx, we had diverged instead of following the regular road to the Mena House, where some of the sleepy, inefficient police might have observed and halted us. Here, where filthy Bedouins stabled camels and donkeys in the rock tombs of Khephren's courtiers, we were led up the rocks and over the sand to the Great Pyramid, up whose time-worn sides the Arabs swarmed eagerly, Abdul Reis offering me the assistance I did not need.

As most travelers know, the actual apex of this structure has long been worn away, leaving a reasonably flat platform twelve yards square. On this eery pinnacle a squared circle was formed, and in a few moments the sardonic desert moon leered down upon a battle which, but for the quality of the ringside cries, might well have occurred at some minor athletic club in America. As I watched it, I felt that some of our less desirable institutions were not lacking; for every blow, feint, and defense bespoke "stalling" to my not inexperienced eye. It was quickly over, and despite my misgivings as to methods I felt a sort of proprietary pride when Abdul Reis was adjudged the winner.

Reconciliation was phenomenally rapid, and amidst the singing, fraternizing and drinking which followed, I found it difficult to realize that a quarrel had ever occurred. Oddly enough, I myself seemed to be more a center of notice than the antagonists; and from my smattering of Arabic I judged that they were discussing my professional performances and escapes from every sort of manacle and confinement, in a manner which indicated not only a surprising knowledge of me, but a distinct hostility and skepticism concerning my feats of escape. It gradually dawned on me that the elder magic of Egypt did not depart without leaving traces, and that fragments of a strange secret lore and priestly cult-practices have survived surreptitiously amongst the fellaheen to such an extent that the prowess of a strange *hahwi* or magician is resented and disputed. I thought of how much my hollow-voiced guide Abdul Reis looked like an old Egyptian priest or Pharaoh or smiling Sphinx . . . and wondered.

Suddenly something happened which in a flash proved the correctness of my reflections and made me curse the denseness whereby I had accepted this night's events as other than the empty and malicious "frameup" they now showed themselves to be. Without warning, and doubtless in answer to some subtle sign from Abdul, the entire band of Bedouins precipitated itself upon me; and having produced heavy ropes, soon had me bound as securely as I was ever bound in the course of my life, either on the stage or off.

I struggled at first, but soon saw that one man could make no headway against a band of over twenty sinewy barbarians. My hands were tied behind my back, my knees bent to their fullest extent, and my wrists and ankles stoutly linked together with unyielding cords. A stifling gag was forced into my mouth, and a blindfold fastened tightly over my eyes. Then, as Arabs bore me aloft on their shoulders and began a jouncing descent of the pyramid, I heard the taunts of my late guide Abdul, who mocked and jeered delightedly in his hollow voice, and assured me that I was soon to have my "magic powers" put to a supreme test which would quickly remove any egotism I might have gained through triumphing over all the tests offered by America and Europe. Egypt, he reminded me, is very old, and full of inner mysteries and antique powers not even conceivable to the experts of today, whose devices had so uniformly failed to entrap me.

How far or in what direction I was carried, I cannot tell; for the circumstances were all against the formation of any accurate judgment. I know, however, that it could not have been a great distance; since my bearers at no point hastened beyond a walk, yet kept me aloft a surprisingly short time. It is this perplexing brevity which makes me feel almost like shuddering whenever I think of Gizeh and its plateau—for one is oppressed by hints of the closeness to everyday tourist routes of what existed then and must exist still.

The evil abnormality I speak of did not become manifest at first. Setting me down on a surface which I recognized as sand rather than rock, my captors passed a rope around my chest and dragged me a few feet to a ragged opening in the ground, into which they presently lowered me with much rough handling. For apparent eons I bumped against the stony irregular sides of a narrow hewn well which I took to be one of the numerous burial-shafts of the plateau until the prodigious, almost incredible depth of it robbed me of all bases of conjecture.

The horror of the experience deepened with every dragging second. That any descent through the sheer solid rock could be so vast without reaching the core of the planet itself, or that any rope made by man could be so long as to dangle me in these unholy and seemingly fathomless profundities of nether earth, were beliefs of such grotesqueness that it was easier to doubt my agitated senses than to accept them. Even now I am uncertain, for I know how deceitful the sense of time becomes when one is removed or distorted. But I am quite sure that I preserved a logical consciousness that far; that at least I did not add any fullgrown phantoms of imagination to a picture hideous enough in its reality, and explicable by a type of cerebral illusion vastly short of actual hallucination.

All this was not the cause of my first bit of fainting. The shocking ordeal was cumulative, and the beginning of the later terrors was a very perceptible increase in my rate of descent. They were paying out that infinitely long rope very swiftly now, and I scraped cruelly against the rough and constricted sides of the shaft as I shot madly downward. My clothing was in tatters, and I felt the trickle of blood all over, even above the mounting and excruciating pain. My nostrils, too, were assailed by a scarcely definable menace: a creeping odor of damp and staleness curiously unlike anything I had ever smelled before, and having faint overtones of spice and incense that lent an element of mockery.

Then the mental cataclysm came. It was horrible—hideous beyond all articulate description because it was all of the soul, with nothing of detail to describe. It was the ecstasy of nightmare and the summation of the fiendish. The suddenness of it was apocalyptic and demoniac—one moment I was plunging agonizingly down that narrow well of million-toothed torture, yet the next moment I was soaring on bat-wings in the gulfs of hell; swinging free and swoopingly through illimitable miles of boundless, musty space; rising dizzily to measureless pinnacles of chilling ether, then diving gaspingly to sucking nadirs of ravenous, nauseous lower vacua. . . . Thank God for the mercy that shut out in oblivion those clawing Furies of consciousness which half unhinged my faculties, and tore harpy-like at my spirit! That one respite, short as it was, gave me the strength and sanity to endure those still greater sublimations of cosmic panic that lurked and gibbered on the road ahead.

II

It was very gradually that I regained my senses after that eldritch flight through stygian space. The process was infinitely painful, and colored by fantastic dreams in which my bound and gagged condition found singular embodiment. The precise nature of these dreams was very clear while I was experiencing them, but became blurred in my recollection almost immediately afterward, and was soon reduced to the merest outline by the terrible events—real or imaginary—which followed. I dreamed that I was in the grasp of a great and horrible paw; a yellow, hairy, five-clawed paw which had reached out of the earth to crush and engulf me. And when I stopped to reflect what the paw was, it seemed to me that it was Egypt. In the dream I looked back at the events of the preceding weeks, and saw myself lured and enmeshed little by little, subtly and insidiously, by some hellish ghoul-spirit of the elder Nile sorcery; some spirit that was in Egypt before ever man was, and that will be when man is no more.

I saw the horror and unwholesome antiquity of Egypt, and the grisly alliance it has always had with the tombs and temples of the dead. I saw phantom processions of priests with the heads of bulls, falcons, cats, and ibises; phantom processions marching interminably through subterraneous labyrinths and avenues of titanic propylaea beside which a man is as a fly, and offering unnameable sacrifice to indescribable gods. Stone colossi marched in endless night and drove herds of grinning androsphinxes down to the shores of illimitable stagnant rivers of pitch. And behind it all I saw the ineffable malignity of primordial necromancy, black and amorphous, and fumbling greedily after me in the darkness to choke out the spirit that had dared to mock it by emulation.

In my sleeping brain there took shape a melodrama of sinister hatred and pursuit, and I saw the black soul of Egypt singling me out and calling me in inaudible whispers; calling and luring me, leading me on with the glitter and glamor of a Saracenic surface, but ever pulling me down to the age-mad catacombs and horrors of its *dead* and abysmal pharaonic heart.

Then the dream faces took on human resemblances, and I saw my guide Abdul Reis in the robes of a king, with the sneer of the Sphinx on his features. And I knew that those features were the features of Khephren the Great, who raised the Second Pyramid, carved over the Sphinx's face in the likeness of his own and built that titanic gateway temple whose myraid corridors the archaeologists think they have dug out of the cryptical sand and the uninformative rock. And I looked at the long, lean, rigid hand of Khephren; the long, lean, rigid hand as I had seen it on the diorite statue in the Cairo Museum—the statue they had found in the terrible gateway temple—and wondered that I had not shrieked when I saw it on Abdul Reis. . . . That hand! It was hideously cold, and it was crushing me; it was the cold and cramping of the sarcophagus . . . the chill and constriction of unrememberable Egypt. . . . It was nighted, necropolitan Egypt itself . . . that yellow paw . . . and they whisper such things of Khephren. . . .

But at this juncture I began to awake—or at least, to assume a condition less completely that of sleep than the one just preceding. I recalled the fight atop the pyramid, the treacherous Bedouins and their attack, my frightful descent by rope through endless rock depths, and my mad swinging and plunging in a chill void redolent of aromatic putrescence. I perceived that I now lay on a damp rock floor, and that my bonds were still biting into me with unloosened force. It was very cold, and I seemed to detect a faint current of noisome air sweeping across me. The cuts and bruises I had received from the jagged sides of the rock shaft were paining me woefully, their soreness enhanced to a stinging or burning acuteness by some pungent quality in the faint draft, and the mere act of rolling over was enough to set my whole frame throbbing with untold agony.

As I turned I felt a tug from above, and concluded that the rope whereby I was lowered still reached to the surface. Whether or not the Arabs still held it, I had no idea; nor had I any idea how far within the earth I was. I knew that the darkness around me was wholly or nearly total, since no ray of moonlight penetrated my blindfold; but I did not trust my senses enough to accept as evidence of extreme depth the sensation of vast duration which had characterized my descent.

Knowing at least that I was in a space of considerable extent reached from the surface directly above by an opening in the rock, I doubtfully conjectured that my prison was perhaps the buried gateway chapel of old Khephren —the Temple of the Sphinx—perhaps some inner corridor which the guides had not shown me during my morning visit, and from which I might easily escape if I could find my way to the barred entrance. It would be a labyrinthine wandering, but no worse than others out of which I had in the past found my way.

The first step was to get free of my bonds, gag, and blindfold; and this I knew would be no great task, since subtler experts than these Arabs had tried every known species of fetter upon me during my long and varied career as an exponent of escape, yet had never succeeded in defeating my methods.

Then it occurred to me that the Arabs might be ready to meet and attack me at the entrance upon any evidence of my probable escape from the binding cords, as would be furnished by any decided agitation of the rope which they probably held. This, of course, was taking for granted that my place of confinement was indeed Khephren's Temple of the Sphinx. The direct opening in the roof, wherever it might lurk, could not be beyond easy reach of the ordinary modern entrance near the Sphinx; if in truth it were any great distance at all on the surface, since the total area known to visitors is not at all enormous. I had not noticed any such opening during my daytime pilgrimage, but knew that these things are easily overlooked amidst the drifting sands.

Thinking these matters over as I lay bent and bound on the rock floor, I nearly forgot the horrors of abysmal descent and cavernous swinging which had so lately reduced me to a coma. My present thought was only to outwit the Arabs, and I accordingly determined to work myself free as quickly as possible, avoiding any tug on the descending line which might betray an effective or even problematical attempt at freedom.

This, however, was more easily determined than effected. A few preliminary trials made it clear that little could be accomplished without considerable motion; and it did not surprise me when, after one especially energetic struggle, I began to feel the coils of falling rope as they piled up about me and upon me. Obviously, I thought, the Bedouins had felt my movements and released their end of the rope; hastening no doubt to the temple's true entrance to lie murderously in wait for me.

The prospect was not pleasing—but I had faced worse in my time without flinching, and would not flinch now. At present I must first of all free myself of bonds, then trust to ingenuity to escape from the temple unharmed. It is curious how implicitly I had come to believe myself in the old temple of Khephren beside the Sphinx, only a short distance below the ground.

That belief was shattered, and every pristine apprehension of preternatural depth and demoniac mystery revived, by a circumstance which grew in horror and significance even as I formulated my philosophical plan. I have said that the falling rope was piling up about and upon me. Now I saw that it was continuing to pile, as no rope of normal length could possibly do. It gained in momentum and became an avalanche of hemp, accumulating mountainously on the floor and half burying me beneath its swiftly multiplying coils. Soon I was completely engulfed and gasping for breath as the increasing convolutions submerged and stifled me.

My senses tottered again, and I vainly tried to fight off a menace desperate and ineluctable. It was not merely that I was tortured beyond human endurance—not merely that life and breath seemed to be crushed slowly out of me—it was the knowledge of what those unnatural lengths of rope implied, and the consciousness of what unknown and incalculable gulfs of inner earth must at this moment be surrounding me. My endless descent and swinging flight through goblin space, then, must have been real, and even now I must be lying helpless in some nameless cavern world toward the core of the planet. Such a sudden confirmation of ultimate horror was insupportable, and a second time I lapsed into merciful oblivion.

When I say oblivion, I do not imply that I was free from dreams. On the contrary, my absence from the conscious world was marked by visions of the most unutterable hideousness. God! . . . If only I had not read so much Egyptology before coming to this land which is the fountain of all darkness and terror! This second spell of 'ainting filled my sleeping mind anew with shivering realization of the country and its archaic secrets, and through some damnable chance my dreams turned to the ancient notions of the dead and their sojournings in soul and body beyond those mysterious tombs which were more houses than graves. I recalled, in dream-shapes which it is well that I do not remember, the peculiar and elaborate construction of Egyptian sepulchers; and the exceedingly singular and terrific doctrines which determined this construction.

All these people thought of was death and the dead. They conceived of a literal resurrection of the body which made them mummify it with desperate care, and preserve all the vital organs in canopic jars near the corpse; whilst besides the body they believed in two other elements, the soul, which after its weighing and approval by Osiris dwelt in the land of the blest, and the obscure and portentous *ka* or life-principle which wandered about the upper and lower worlds in a horrible way, demanding occasional access to the preserved body, consuming the food offerings brought by priests and pious relatives to the mortuary chapel, and sometimes—as men whispered—taking its body or the wooden double always buried beside it and stalking noxiously abroad on errands peculiarly repellent.

For thousands of years those bodies rested gorgeously encased and staring glassily upward when not visited by the *ka,* awaiting the day when Osiris should restore both *ka* and soul, and lead forth the stiff legions of the dead from the sunken houses of sleep. It was to have been a glorious rebirth—but not all souls were approved, nor were all tombs inviolate, so that certain grotesque *mistakes* and fiendish *abnormalities* were to be looked for. Even today the Arabs murmur of unsanctified convocations and unwholesome worship in forgotten nether abysses, which only winged invisible *kas* and soulless mummies may visit and return unscathed.

Perhaps the most leeringly blood-congealing legends are those which relate to certain perverse products of decadent priestcraft—*composite mummies* made by the artificial union of human trunks and limbs with the heads of animals in imitation of the elder gods. At all stages of history the sacred animals were mummified, so that consecrated bulls, cats, ibises, crocodiles and the like might return some day to greater glory. But only in the decadence did they mix the human and animal in the same mummy—only in the decadence, when they did not understand the rights and prerogatives of the *ka* and the soul.

What happened to those composite mummies is not told of—at least publicly—and it is certain that no Egyptologist ever found one. The whispers of Arabs are very wild, and cannot be relied upon. They even hint that old Khephren—he of the Sphinx, the Second Pyramid and the yawning gateway temple—lives far underground wedded to the ghoul-queen Nitocris and ruling over the mummies that are neither of man nor of beast.

It was of these—of Khephren and his consort and his strange armies of the hybrid dead—that I dreamed, and that is why I am glad the exact dream-shapes have faded from my memory. My most horrible vision was connected with an idle question I had asked myself the day before when looking at the great carven riddle of the desert and wondering with what unknown depth the temple close to it might be secretly connected. That question, so innocent and whimsical then, assumed in my dream a meaning of frenetic and hysterical madness . . . *what huge and loathsome abnormality was the Sphinx originally carven to represent?*

My second awakening—if awakening it was—is a memory of stark hideousness which nothing else in my life—save one thing which came after—can parallel; and that life has been full and adventurous beyond most men's. Remember that I had lost consciousness whilst buried beneath a cascade of falling rope whose immensity revealed the cataclysmic depth of my present position. Now, as perception returned, I felt the entire weight gone; and realized upon rolling over that although I was still tied, gagged and blindfolded, *some agency had removed completely the suffocating hempen landslide which had overwhelmed me.* The significance of this condition, of course, came to me only gradually; but even so I think it would have brought unconsciousness again had I not by this time reached such a state of emotional exhaustion that no new horror could make much difference. I was alone . . . *with what?*

Before I could torture myself with any new reflection, or make any fresh effort to escape from my bonds, an additional circumstance became manifest. Pains not formerly felt were racking my arms and legs, and I seemed coated with a profusion of dried blood beyond anything my former cuts and abrasions could furnish. My chest, too, seemed pierced by a hundred wounds, as though some malign, titanic ibis had been pecking at it. Assuredly the agency which had removed the rope was a hostile one, and had begun to wreak terrible injuries upon me when somehow impelled to desist. Yet at the time my sensations were distinctly the reverse of what one might expect. Instead of sinking into a bottomless pit of despair, I was stirred to a new courage and action; for now I felt that the evil forces were physical things which a fearless man might encounter on an even basis.

On the strength of this thought I tugged again at my bonds, and used all the art of a lifetime to free myself as I had so often done amidst the glare of lights and the applause of vast crowds. The familiar details of my escaping process commenced to engross me, and now that the long rope was gone I half regained my belief that the supreme horrors were hallucinations after all, and that there had never been any terrible shaft, measureless abyss or interminable rope. Was I after all in the gateway temple of Khephren beside the Sphinx, and had the sneaking Arabs stolen in to torture me as I lay helpless there? At any rate, I must be free. Let me stand up unbound, ungagged, and with eyes open to catch any glimmer of light which might come trickling from any source, and I could actually delight in the combat against evil and treacherous foes!

How long I took in shaking off my encumbrances I cannot tell. It must have been longer than in my exhibition performances, because I was wounded, exhausted, and enervated by the experiences I had passed through. When I was finally free, and taking deep breaths of a chill, damp evilly spiced air all the more horrible when encountered without the screen of gag and blindfold edges, I found that I was too cramped and fatigued to move at once. There I lay, trying to stretch a frame bent and mangled, for an indefinite period, and straining my eyes to catch a glimpse of some ray of light which would give a hint as to my position.

By degrees my strength and flexibility returned, but my eyes beheld nothing. As I staggered to my feet I peered diligently in every direction, yet met only an ebony blackness as great as that I had known when blindfolded. I tried my legs, blood-encrusted beneath my shredded trousers, and found that I could walk; yet could not decide in what direction to go. Obviously I ought not to walk at random, and perhaps retreat directly from the entrance I sought; so I paused to note the direction of the cold, fetid, natron-scented air-current which I had never ceased to feel. Accepting the point of its source as the possible entrance to the abyss, I strove to keep track of this landmark and to walk consistently toward it.

I had a match-box with me, and even a small electric flashlight; but of course the pockets of my tossed and tattered clothing were long since emptied of all heavy articles. As I walked cautiously in the blackness, the draft grew stronger and more offensive, till at length I could regard it as nothing less than a tangible stream of detestable vapor pouring out of some aperture like the smoke of the genie from the fisherman's jar in the Eastern tale. The East . . . Egypt . . . truly, this dark cradle of civilization was ever the wellspring of horrors and marvels unspeakable!

The more I reflected on the nature of this cavern wind, the greater my sense of disquiet became; for although despite its odor I had sought its source as at least an indirect clue to the outer world, I now saw plainly that this foul emanation could have no admixture or connection whatsoever with the clean air of the Libyan Desert, but must be essentially a thing vomited from sinister gulfs still lower down. I had, then, been walking in the wrong direction!

After a moment's reflection I decided not to retrace my steps. Away from the draft I would have no landmarks, for the roughly level rock floor was devoid of distinctive configurations. If, however, I followed up the strange current, I would undoubtedly arrive at an aperture of some sort, from whose gate I could perhaps work round the walls to the opposite side of this Cyclopean and otherwise unnavigable hall. That I might fail, I well realized. I saw that this was no part of Khephren's gateway temple which tourists know, and it struck me that this particular hall might be unknown even to archaeologists, and merely stumbled upon by the inquisitive and malignant Arabs who had imprisoned me. If so, was there any present gate of escape to the known parts or to the outer air?

What evidence, indeed, did I now possess that this was the gateway temple at all? For a moment all my wildest speculations rushed back upon me, and I thought of that vivid melange of impressions—descent, suspension in space, the rope, my wounds, and the dreams that were frankly dreams. Was this the end of life for me? Or indeed, would it be merciful if this moment *were* the end? I could answer none of my own questions, but merely kept on, till Fate for a third time reduced me to oblivion.

This time there were no dreams, for the suddenness of the incident shocked me out of all thought either conscious or subconscious. Tripping on an unexpected descending step at a point where the offensive draft became strong enough to offer an actual physical resistance, I was precipitated headlong down a black flight of huge stone stairs into a gulf of hideousness unrelieved.

That I ever breathed again is a tribute to the inherent vitality of the healthy human organism. Often I look back to that night and feel a touch of actual humor in those repeated lapses of consciousness; lapses whose succession reminded me at the time of nothing more than the crude cinema melodramas of that period. Of course, it is possible that the repeated lapses never occurred; and that all the features of that underground nightmare were merely the dreams of one long coma which began with the shock of my descent into that abyss and ended with the healing balm of the outer air and of the rising sun which found me stretched on the sands of Gizeh before the sardonic and dawn-flushed face of the Great Sphinx.

I prefer to believe this latter explanation as much as I can, hence was glad when the police told me that the barrier to Khephren's gateway temple had been found unfastened, and that a sizable rift to the surface did actually exist in one corner of the still buried part. I was glad, too, when the doctors pronounced my wounds only those to be expected from my seizure, blindfolding, lowering, struggling with bonds, falling some distance—perhaps into a depression in the temple's inner gallery—dragging myself to the outer barrier and escaping from it, and experiences like that . . . a very soothing diagnosis. And yet I know that there must be more than appears on the surface. That extreme descent is too vivid a memory to be dismissed—and it is odd that no one has ever been able to find a man answering the description of my guide, Abdul Reis el Drogman—the tomb-throated guide who looked and smiled like King Khephren.

I have digressed from my connected narrative—perhaps in the vain hope of evading the telling of that final incident; that incident which of all is most certainly an hallucination. But I promised to relate it, and I do not break promises. When I recovered—or seemed to recover—my senses after that fall down the black stone stairs, I was quite as alone and in darkness as before. The windy stench, bad enough before, was now fiendish; yet I had acquired enough familiarity by this time to bear it stoically. Dazedly I began to crawl away from the place whence the putrid wind came, and with my bleeding hands felt the colossal blocks of a mighty pavement. Once my head struck against a hard object, and when I felt of it I learned that it was the base of a column—a column of unbelievable immensity—whose surface was covered with gigantic chiseled hieroglyphics very perceptible to my touch.

Crawling on, I encountered other titan columns at incomprehensible distances apart; when suddenly my attention was captured by the realization of something which must have been impinging on my subconscious hearing long before the conscious sense was aware of it.

From some still lower chasm in earth's bowels were proceeding certain *sounds,* measured and definite, and like nothing I had ever heard before. That they were very ancient and distinctly ceremonial I felt almost intuitively;

and much reading in Egyptology led me to associate them with the flute, the sambuke, the sistrum, and the tympanum. In their rhythmic piping, droning, rattling and beating I felt an element of terror beyond all the known terrors of earth—a terror peculiarly dissociated from personal fear, and taking the form of a sort of objective pity for our planet, that it should hold within its depths such horrors as must lie beyond these aegipanic cacophonies. The sounds increased in volume, and I felt that they were approaching. Then—and may all the gods of all pantheons unite to keep the like from my ears again —I began to hear, faintly and afar off, the morbid and millennial tramping of the marching things.

It was hideous that footfalls so dissimilar should move in such perfect rhythm. The training of unhallowed thousands of years must lie behind that march of earth's inmost monstrosities . . . padding, clicking, walking, stalking, rumbling, lumbering, crawling . . . and all to the abhorrent discords of those mocking instruments. And then—God keep the memory of those Arab legends out of my head!—the mummies without souls . . . the meeting-place of the wandering *kas* . . . the hordes of the devil-cursed pharaonic dead of forty centuries . . . the *composite mummies* led through the uttermost onyx voids by King Khephren and his ghoul-queen Nitocris. . . .

The tramping drew nearer—Heaven save me from the sound of those feet and paws and hooves and pads and talons as it commenced to acquire detail! Down limitless reaches of sunless pavement a spark of light flickered in the malodorous wind and I drew behind the enormous circumference of a Cyclopic column that I might escape for a while the horror that was stalking million-footed toward me through gigantic hypostyles of inhuman dread and phobic antiquity. The flickers increased, and the tramping and dissonant rhythm grew sickeningly loud. In the quivering orange light there stood faintly forth a scene of such stony awe that I gasped from sheer wonder that conquered even fear and repulsion. Bases of columns whose middles were higher than human sight . . . mere bases of things that must each dwarf the Eiffel Tower to insignificance . . . hieroglyphics carved by unthinkable hands in caverns where daylight can be only a remote legend. . . .

I *would not* look at the marching things. That I desperately resolved as I heard their creaking joints and nitrous wheezing above the dead music and the dead tramping. It was merciful that they did not speak . . . but God! *their crazy torches began to cast shadows on the surface of those stupendous columns. Hippopotami should not have human hands and carry torches . . . men should not have the heads of crocodiles. . . .*

I tried to turn away, but the shadows and the sounds and the stench were everywhere. Then I remembered something I used to do in half-conscious nightmares as a boy, and began to repeat to myself, "This is a dream! This is a dream!" But it was of no use, and I could only shut my eyes and pray . . . at least, that is what I think I did, for one is never sure in visions—and I know this can have been nothing more. I wondered whether I should ever reach the world again, and at times would furtively open my eyes to see if I could discern any feature of the place other than the wind of spiced putrefaction, the topless columns, and the thaumatropically grotesque shadows of abnormal horror. The sputtering glare of multiplying torches now shone, and unless this hellish place were wholly without walls, I could not fail to see some boundary or fixed landmark soon. But I had to shut my eyes again when I realized how many of the things were assembling—and when I glimpsed a certain object walking solemnly and steadily *without any body above the waist.*

A fiendish and ululant corpse-gurgle or death-rattle now split the very atmosphere—the charnel atmosphere poisonous with naftha and bitumen blasts—in one concerted chorus from the ghoulish legion of hybrid blasphemies. My eyes, perversely shaken open, gazed for an instant upon a sight which no human creature could even imagine without panic, fear and physical exhaustion. The things had filed ceremonially in one direction, the direction of the noisome wind, where the light of their torches showed their bended heads—or the bended heads of such as had heads. They were worshipping before a great black fetor-belching aperture which reached up almost out of sight, and which I could see was flanked at right angles by two giant staircases whose ends were far away in shadow. One of these was indubitably the staircase I had fallen down.

The dimensions of the hole were fully in proportion with those of the columns—an ordinary house would have been lost in it, and any average public building could easily have been moved in and out. It was so vast a surface that only by moving the eye could one trace its boundaries . . . so vast, so hideously black, and so aromatically stinking. . . . Directly in front of this yawning Polyphemus-door the things were throwing objects—evidently sacrifices or religious offerings, to judge by their gestures. Khephren was their leader; sneering King Khephren *or the guide Abdul Reis,* crowned with a golden pshent and intoning endless formulae with the hollow voice of the dead. By his side knelt beautiful Queen Nitocris, whom I saw in profile for a moment, noting that the right half of her face was eaten away by rats or other ghouls. And I shut my eyes again when I saw what objects were being thrown as offerings to the fetid aperture or its possible local deity.

It occurred to me that, judging from the elaborateness of this worship, the concealed deity must be one of considerable importance. Was it Osiris or Isis, Horus or Anubis, or some vast unknown God of the Dead still more central and supreme? There is a legend that terrible altars and colossi were reared to an Unknown One before ever the known gods were worshipped. . . .

And now, as I steeled myself to watch the rapt and sepulchral adorations of those nameless things, a thought of escape flashed upon me. The hall was dim, and the columns heavy with shadow. With every creature of that nightmare throng absorbed in shocking raptures, it might be barely possible for me to creep past to the far-away end of one of the staircases and ascend unseen; trusting to Fate and skill to deliver me from the upper reaches. Where I was, I neither knew nor seriously reflected upon

—and for a moment it struck me as amusing to plan a serious escape from that which I knew to be a dream. Was I in some hidden and unsuspected lower realm of Khephren's gateway temple—that temple which generations have persistently called the Temple of the Sphinx? I could not conjecture, but I resolved to ascend to life and consciousness if wit and muscle could carry me.

Wriggling flat on my stomach, I began the anxious journey toward the foot of the left-hand staircase, which seemed the more accessible of the two. I cannot describe the incidents and sensations of that crawl, but they may be guessed when one reflects on what I had to watch steadily in that malign, wind-blown torchlight in order to avoid detection. The bottom of the staircase was, as I have said, far away in shadow, as it had to be to rise without a bend to the dizzy parapeted landing above the titanic aperture. This placed the last stages of my crawl at some distance from the noisome herd, though the spectacle chilled me even when quite remote at my right.

At length I succeeded in reaching the steps and began to climb; keeping close to the wall, on which I observed decorations of the most hideous sort, and relying for safety on the absorbed, ecstatic interest with which the monstrosities watched the foul-breezed aperture and the impious objects of nourishment they had flung on the pavement before it. Though the staircase was huge and steep, fashioned of vast porphyry blocks as if for the feet of a giant, the ascent seemed virtually interminable. Dread of discovery and the pain which renewed exercise had brought to my wounds combined to make that upward crawl a thing of agonizing memory. I had intended, on reaching the landing, to climb immediately onward along whatever upper staircase might mount from there; stopping for no last look at the carrion abominations that pawed and genuflected some seventy or eighty feet below—yet a sudden repetition of that thunderous corpse-gurgle and death-rattle chorus, coming as I had nearly gained the top of the flight and showing by its ceremonial rhythm that it was not an alarm of my discovery, caused me to pause and peer cautiously over the parapet.

The monstrosities were hailing something which had poked itself out of the nauseous aperture to seize the hellish fare proffered it. It was something quite ponderous, even as seen from my height; something yellowish and hairy, and endowed with a sort of nervous motion. It was as large, perhaps, as a good-sized hippopotamus, but very curiously shaped. It seemed to have no neck, but five separate shaggy heads springing in a row from a roughly cylindrical trunk; the first very small, the second good-sized, the third and fourth equal and largest of all, and the fifth rather small, though not so small as the first.

Out of these heads darted curious rigid tentacles which seized ravenously on the excessively great quantities of unmentionable food placed before the aperture. Once in a while the thing would leap up, and occasionally it would retreat into its den in a very odd manner. Its locomotion was so inexplicable that I stared in fascination, wishing it would emerge farther from the cavernous lair beneath me.

Then it *did emerge* . . . it *did* emerge, and at the sight I turned and fled into the darkness up the higher staircase that rose behind me; fled unknowingly up incredible steps and ladders and inclined planes to which no human sight or logic guided me, and which I must ever relegate to the world of dreams for want of any confirmation. It must have been a dream, or the dawn would never have found me breathing on the sands of Gizeh before the sardonic dawn-flushed face of the Great Sphinx.

The Great Sphinx! God!—that idle question I asked myself on that sun-blest morning before . . . *what huge and loathsome abnormality was the Sphinx originally carven to represent?* Accursed is the sight, be it in dream or not, that revealed to me the supreme horror—the unknown God of the Dead, which licks its colossal chops in the unsuspected abyss, fed hideous morsels by soulless absurdities that should not exist. The five-headed monster that emerged . . . that five-headed monster as large as a hippopotamus . . . the five-headed monster—*and that of which it is the merest forepaw . . .*

But I survived, and I know it was only a dream.

A PARTIAL CHRONOLOGY OF LOVECRAFT'S EARLY WORK

NOTE: I have included here the date of all of the Lovecraft items assembled both in this book, *The Doom that Came to Sarnath,* and its predecessor, *The Dream-Quest of Unknown Kadath.*

The dates are those of composition, not of first publication; in some cases the stories did not find their way into print for many years after they were written. It is interesting to note that, with few exceptions, these tales first appeared in amateur journals—the small, privately-circulated periodicals which we would call "fanzines" today. This is true, for example, of "The Cats of Ulthar," "The Quest of Iranon," "The Other Gods," and even of "The Nameless City" and "The Doom that Came to Sarnath" itself.

The source of the chronology which follows is a listing set down by Lovecraft in a letter to one of his friends—a letter whose central matter was not intended for publication and which has not, therefore, been preserved in any of the volumes of Lovecraft's *Selected Letters* which have been published by Arkham House.

The story-sequence, listed in one of Lovecraft's letters, does not include the prose poems "Nyarlathotep," "Ex Oblivione," "What the Moon Brings," and "Memory," or the poem "Nathicana." I have followed the precise order of the stories as given in that letter, interpolating the other items where they seemed to belong, according to the data I could find on them in the relevant correspondence in *Selected Letters* and in various studies of Lovecraft. But there is some uncertainty in my mind that I have inserted these items in their correct places: I include this warning lest it be assumed I have accurate data to warrant my placement of ALL these items.

Most likely, however, the writing of many of the tales overlapped; stories begun were set aside and new stories written before they were taken up again. Hence the entire chronology given above can, at best, be considered only as a good guess, based very largely on Lovecraft's own memory, which may or may not have been strictly accurate. Whatever errors have crept into the chronology, however, are probably only a matter or weeks or of a month or so away from the truth.

—LIN CARTER

PARTIAL LOVECRAFT CHRONOLOGY

The Tomb: 1917
Polaris: 1918
Beyond the Wall of Sleep: 1919
Memory: 1919
The Doom that Came to Sarnath: 1919
The White Ship: 1919
The Cats of Ulthar: 1920
Celephais: 1920
From Beyond: 1920
The Crawling Chaos: 1920
The Tree: 1920
Nyarlathotep: 1920
The Nameless City: 1921
The Other Gods: 1921
Ex Oblivione: 1921

The Quest of Iranon: 1921
Hypnos: 1922
The Festival: 1923
What the Moon Brings: 1923
Imprisoned with the Pharaohs: 1924
The Silver Key: 1926
The Strange High House in the Mist: 1926
The Dream-Quest of Unknown Kadath: 1926
Nathicana: 1927
Through the Gates of the Silver Key: 1932
In the Walls of Eryx: 1935